MR. SWEETCHEEKS IN ALASKA

Published by Evans & Hyde.
c/o robertkinerk@gmail.com
www.robertkinerk.com

This book is a work of fiction. Names, characters, places and incidents either are the product of the author's imagination or are used fictitiously, and any resemblance to actual persons, living or dead, businesses, companies, events or locales is entirely coincidental.

ISBN: 978-1-962931-26-7
LCCN: 2025905003

Printed in the United States of America.

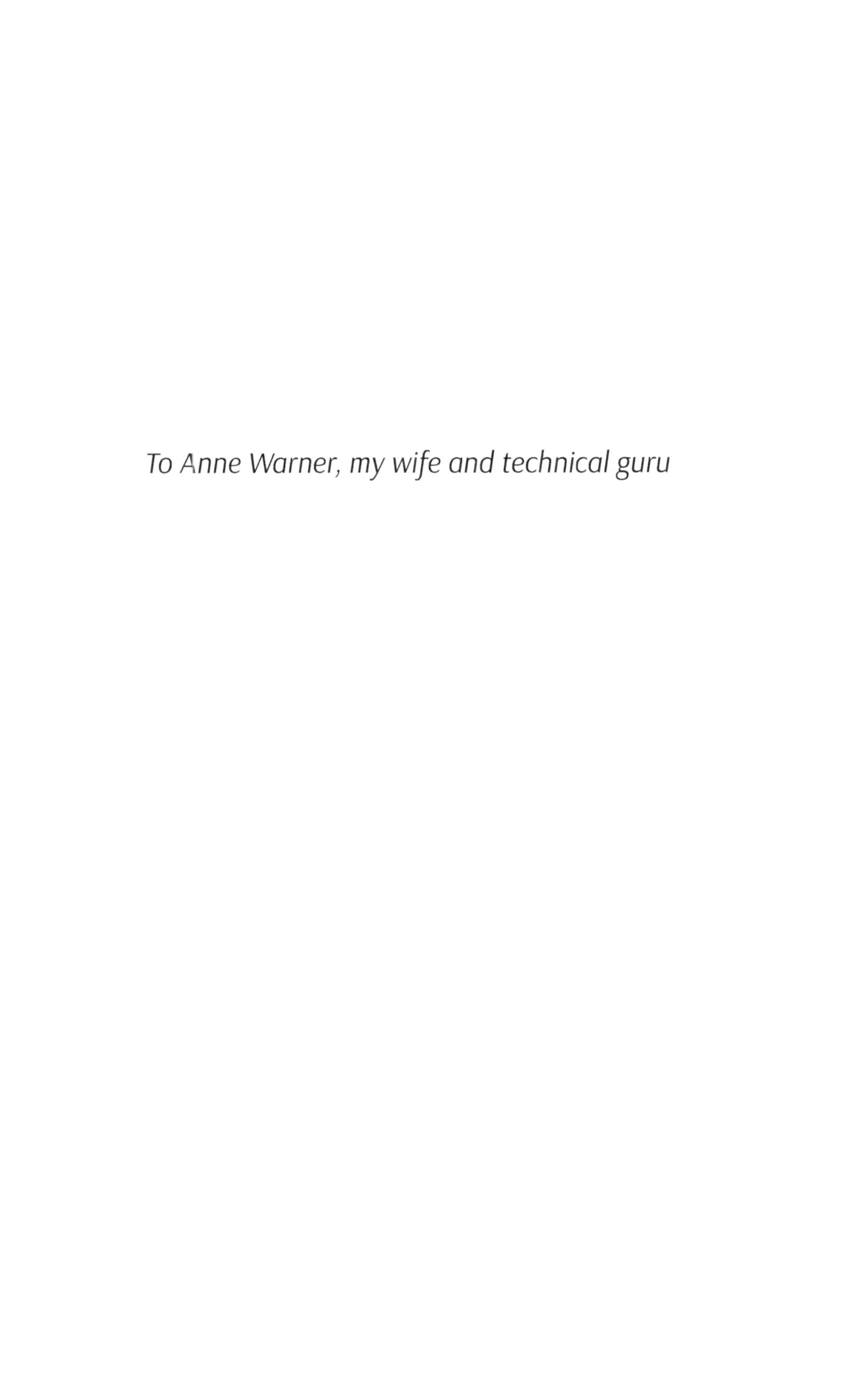

To Anne Warner, my wife and technical guru

ROBERT KINERK

MR. SWEETCHEEKS IN ALASKA

Evans
& Hyde

A stout woman named Celeste commandeered the seat next to mine on a plane going north. On her finger sat a diamond as big as a pea. I tried not to stare. I was a former felon, recently paroled and under contractual obligation not to notice diamond rings. For the slightest misbehavior, any dues-paying member of the nation's vast and benevolent law-enforcement fraternity had the privilege of whipping my sorry ass back in jail.

Celeste tugged her seat belt into obedience around her ample waist. It snapped shut with a metal click, much like the sound handcuffs make when they close around your wrist. The click sobered me. I would be lying if I said the sparkle of her ring had not given me larcenous ideas. I don't think the general public is aware of the plague of larcenous ideas afflicting recent parolees. We suffer in silence. I would no more tell Celeste I coveted her diamond ring than I would have surprised her with the news that she was seated shoulder to shoulder with a convicted killer. She would have jumped out of her seat and made a run for the exit door. I would not have had time to tell her, before she slammed a stewardess against the bulkhead and bolted down the stairs, that I am a very *nice* convicted killer. That is the claim I make on the affections of the world. Yes, I am an admitted killer, but I am also very nice.

"I'm excited to go to Alaska," I told Celeste. "A guy there said he'd help me find work."

"What guy?" Celeste asked.

"Do you know a man named Ellery Tinsel?"

Celeste snorted in a way that registered contempt. She also rolled her eyes. I didn't mind the brush-off. Ladies lovelier than ring-rich Celeste had rolled their eyes at many of my conversational gambits. The impatient world visits its ungenerous and judgmental retributions on parolees left and right. So be it. I would work what little charm I'd so far managed to master in my sorry life to make. And, I would work to master more.

Celeste had carried to her seat aboard the plane a rolled-up copy of the *Saturday Evening Post*, which she held in her fist like a club. After she had snorted at the mention of Mr. Tinsel's unusual name, she unrolled her magazine and pointedly devoted her attention to a Tugboat Annie story.

Scruffy, toughy Tugboat Annie.

Squawly, brawly, kind but canny.

I don't know why I waxed poetical, but perhaps all convicted killers, the first time they are borne aloft, indulge themselves in rhymed and metered rambling.

If so, scholars should investigate that phenomenon. Flight is a form of levitation, after all. Surely studies have been done on what occupies the thoughts, not just of us convicted killers, but of podiatrists, and lumbermen, and housewives, and teachers of algebra wearying the brains of students in high schools all over the country. All human souls may wax poetical. "Somewhere over the rainbow," the song says. I would like to think that 'somewhere' has room for felonious convicts, like me. I did not hope to find that *somewhere* by simply sitting in my padded seat and letting Pan-American convey me to Alaska.

I do think, though, that if I were in the sky, not airborne by big, Boeing engines but under my own power with my arms spread out like wings, I would not know from moment to moment if I were flying or falling. And I don't believe that I'm alone in not knowing what the answer to that question is.

Time will tell me, I suppose.

Time will tell us all.

I had, in the inside breast pocket of the second-hand suit Stateville Prison had tossed my way when it struck off my shackles, a letter from a Mr. Tinsel promising to help me find work. Work sliming fish in a salmon cannery? Chewing on walrus hides to make them soft enough for shoes? What exactly are the entry-level jobs in small Alaska towns? Mr. Tinsel had not been specific.

All I knew for certain, on July 3rd in 1951, was that convicted killer Alan Sweetcheeks, newly set free from Stateville Prison, one of the finest penitentiaries in Joliet, Illinois, sat aboard a Pan-American plane on his first-ever flight, headed toward Alaska, fully prepared to play the role of repentant convicted killer in exchange for whatever gimcrack, slap-dash, jury-rigged benevolence the stingy world could offer in return.

"Is this Boon?" I asked when the plane began its touch-down on an Alaskan runway. What I saw below was a hut and nothing else.

Celeste grimaced. "This? Don't make me laugh. This is just the airport. Boon is on a different island. A little-bitty puddle-jumper comes. You have to get on that."

Peering out the plastic window as our plane rolled to a stop, I could see what I had thought was a mere hut was actually a lodge emblazoned with the name *Pan-Am*. A busy crew of workers had assembled around a metal stairway they soon would wheel to the high door of our plane.

"The puddle-jumper's a seaplane, a Grumman Goose," Celeste said. "You'll land on water. I'm warning you now so you won't wet your pants."

She was equipped with a wiseass mouth, which helped me feel, even at my first glimpse of Alaska, immediately at home.

Our airliner stopped. The helpers on the ground put their shoulders to the job. The tall, impressive staircase slowly rolled, and when its top platform touched the plane a stewardess released the door-lock. She then stood at toothy attention to bid us passengers farewell as we filed down the steel stairs to a plain of scrubby brush. A mile of that stunted brush, pancake-flat, stretched out all around us, just room enough to put an airfield on. Everything else was mountains, or better to say everything else was hills with aspirations. A cap of clouds, gun-metal grey, closed the airport in. I saw a terminal with the same stripped-down-to-the-essentials look of Army installations, and the handlers of baggage in their dust-colored clothes looked very much like conscripts for the second of the world's numbered wars, a war from which our nation had so recently emerged the victor.

Inside Pan-Am's way-station a bandaged man sat in a brooding pose before a fireplace framed in finely worked stone.

"Jesus, Sam," Celeste boomed as soon as she walked in. "A truck hit you?"

Sam's head was wrapped in sterile white. His left arm rested in a sling. Two of the fingers on his right hand were in splints. Both his eyes were so badly bruised the bags below them looked like plums.

He uttered a vulgarity in a hoarse voice.

Celeste, unfazed by his coarse language, felt his forehead and examined his splinted fingers. While she did, the injured Sam looked angrily at me. Perhaps he thought he couldn't speak in private to Celeste as long as I was gawking at his bandages and sling.

No problem. A clerk behind a counter was taking names for the flight aboard the little plane to come. I had been waiting only two minutes in the line to register when Celeste muscled her way to the front. She announced to the clerk in her booming voice that she counted on him to make sure she and all her luggage would be on the earliest plane to Boon. The smile never left the young man's face. "I'll see to it personally," he said in a snappy voice, and he made a point of writing her instructions down in a wonderfully ornate hand.

Satisfied, Celeste tugged my sleeve to tow me away. "Poor Sam," she whispered, and she nodded in the injured man's direction.

Sam had turned his back on the swirl of de-planed passengers. He resolutely faced the stone-framed fireplace.

"Did he tell you what happened, Celeste?"

My new friend hoisted her plump hand and fluttered it like a partridge. She pulled me close and whispered so her words would reach no ears but mine.

"There's people in Boon you don't cross."

She arched her eyebrows and widened her eyes, letting me know she was imparting confidential information, as if the commonplace she'd uttered could be construed as confidential. The pleasant clerk began to call names from his boarding roster exactly at that moment, and if I wished to know more precisely whom in Boon I ought not to cross I was disappointed. Celeste waddled away, leading toward the idling Grumman two airline drudges burdened with her bags.

The rain the clouds had threatened now began to fall, a uniform and plodding kind of rain, not a rain of any drama, a rain with the resigned characteristics of charwomen and baggage handlers, rain with grubby work to do. It puddled up the runway and dripped off the porch marquee. I watched Celeste's bus-sized Grumman taxi to its take-off spot and then roar away into the wet. I soon would follow. I'd go incompletely warned about whom not to cross in Boon. *No matter*, I told myself, *there are probably people in Boon who ought to be warned not to cross convicted killers.*

I had killed a man named Sledge who bought and sold scrap metal. From an age just after teething, I had pedaled through Chicago's streets with scrap to sell. I'd seen a sign: *Scrap Metal*, and underneath it, *Decatur*, which didn't make sense because the scrap merchant's yard was nowhere near Decatur. But you did not ask Sledge questions. You found your way to Scrap Metal Decatur to sell your stolen goods, and just as you did Sledge the courtesy of never asking questions, he did you the same. He never asked you where you got your copper pipes, or your Ford and Chevy bumpers.

I first visited Scrap Metal Decatur in 1939 when I was seventeen. I wobbled up on my bicycle with forty pounds of copper pipe balanced on the handle bars. I came with a revolver. The only thing that changed for me between '39 and '41, when I had my fatal run-in with the metal merchant, was this: instead of a revolver I carried a semi-automatic pistol.

For Sledge, what changed was girlfriends, some of whom helped at the counter. Fran occasionally weighed my copper. As Debbie did. Or Lil. Other girls seemed to be on hand for decoration, and of those the one that caused me trouble was a shapely one named Dot.

I never made a pass at Dot. I am not suicidal. But I told a guy Dot's ass looked like an apple. I said it like a minor joke to a helper at the lot, a man named Cory. Cory was Sledge's intellectual inferior, probably the only person in Illinois who could claim that distinction. He hadn't even asked me what my thoughts about Dot were. He caught me when my eyes had lingered too long on her bottom. He made his glance a question—*"Nice?"* Dot's dress was Winesap red, and I thought it would be funny to make that comparison, speaking in a whispered aside no one but Cory could hear. I never thought of what I'd said as indiscreet until I came back to Scrap Metal Decatur two weeks later with a sack full of ten-penny nails. Sledge came charging toward me, waving an iron pipe. "Want to take a bite?" Even as he yelled it, I pulled out my Smith and Wesson Model 10 and shot.

My first glimpse of Boon, from a Grumman flying at just a little more than treetop level, showed me a town stretched out at the foot of a mountain. Homes and sheds and warehouses lined themselves up along a rain-pocked strait as skinny as a string. Boats lashed to the town's many docks disgorged cargoes. Fishermen unloaded their fish, freighters their freight. A cruise ship with a black hull occupied a queenly tie-up spot near what looked like a downtown business block. Tourist passengers paraded down its gangplank with their cameras worn like necklaces so they could shoot the many sights.

The business district terminated at one end in a lumber mill where a teepee-shaped incinerator about three-stories high belched sooty smoke through its cap of metal mesh. At the small city's other end, the business district didn't terminate so much as peter out. The residential part of town began there. Homes climbed the forested hills in an approximation of the grid-like pattern a more tamed geography allows to cities elsewhere. I say *hills* but what I saw were modest mountains, and if some subterranean hiccup had made the mountains shake, the whole city-on-a-slope would have slid into the sea.

Fanciful thought. Abruptly terminated when the Grumman touched down on the strait and my view of everything was splashed away.

Celeste, although she had preceded me by half an hour, was still packing luggage in a cab as I climbed a covered ramp from the seaplane's floating dock to the taxi line-up on the street. I asked her if she knew where I could find Tinsel's Authentic Alaskan Curio Shop.

She looked at me as if I were an authentic Alaskan curio myself.

"I'm seeing Mr. Tinsel on business," I hastened to remind her. I said it in case she had divined my previous profession and assumed I'd come to Boon to murder and rob. She evidently harbored no such suspicion. She indicated understanding with a nod. She had been directing her cabbie where to stow a suitcase, and she saw that done to her satisfaction before she replied. "Ellery's downtown," was all she said.

We were on the dock side of a two-way street. The terminal and its adjacent hanger crowded the sidewalk. On the curb across the street, a janitor clattered a bar's empty bottles into a sheet-metal tub. In a room above the bar, a woman parted lace curtains long enough to frown at him. She was a blowsy-looking, forty-year-old whom I very nearly saluted by lifting the prison-issue fedora I wore on my recently paroled head.

I'm sure there's a place where it's written: "One ought not to look for love in rented rooms above a bar." Some Ur-text from our forefathers in their beard-and-sandal days. There's a footnote to that warning, too. It says, "Especially do not look for love if someone in the bar below is dropping emptied bottles into a tinny-looking tub."

Romance is candles. It is wine and flowers. I suppose if what I was looking for was not romance but sex I could have done without the greeting-card accessories—the candles, wine and flowers. People fall in love. They do not fall in sex. They yoke themselves together and as a team they pull the cart of trials and tribulations—and of joy and elation as well—along whatever road life sets them on. That fellow-feeling, that sharing of the harness, I can't say it was a constant dream I had, but when we speak of dreams we speak of wisps and vague ephemera. Who knows?

The reason I didn't tip my hat to the woman at the window is because I knew she would have seen me as a very sorry sort of human being and a poor candidate for conjugal entanglements, with extended body parts, and moist, receptive grooves, and ecstatic, frantic couplings as complicated as sonatas or as fugues.

Okay, I *am* a sorry human. I flunk the fundamental American Achievement Test for Sensitive Coupling. I see a buxom woman at a window, and I do not think of showing up on her doorstep with roses and a cheap box of chocolates. What I think of I won't tell. What I think of is too crass and rude and raw.

I had little reason for entertaining any hope concerning conjugal entanglements and the dalliance that implies. My dalliance record, if we can call it that, was pretty spotty for a man of twenty-nine. I hadn't been exactly virginal before I went to jail, but I was just barely post-virginal. A woman who'd organized a neighborhood band had asked me if I played an instrument. I said no to the trumpet and no to the accordion. She finally said, "If I sat you down in front of the drums, Mr. Sweetcheeks, do you think you could learn to play them?" I said if she was willing to teach me, I would be willing to try. It turned out the instrument she had in mind was not the drums per se, but she and I together did go through the motions of instruction. I sat with a snare drum in front of me, and she leaned forward, her ample bosom resting on my neck as she adjusted my grip on the sticks.

She was not a woman anywhere near my age. She was closer to the age my mother would have admitted to, if my mother had ever been sober enough to calculate her age. And my mistress—and isn't that a silly word—conducted a band that played polka fests. If it was not for her mammary appendages, I probably would have gone to jail un-deflowered. The globular appendages did the trick, though, and at times—when she fingered my sparse moustache and cooed endearments—I thought I had been the seducer and she was not exactly an innocent maiden but someone genuinely interested in teaching a seventeen-year-old child of the streets how to bang some spirit into yet another tired rendition of *Roll Out the Barrel.*

My moustache, if it had come in full during the weeks I spent as a snare-drum instructee, would have been of the timid variety, stylish in a way but without the vigor and authority lent an upper lip by moustaches of the bushier breed. Nevertheless, my mentor in snare-drum techniques, when her other duties allowed, liked to stroke those feeble hairs above my upper lip, and I believed I was in love.

I buried my semi-erotic thoughts and asked Celeste the Ample if I could share her cab.

"There's plenty of cabs," she told me. She had finished harassing her driver. He had packed his trunk full of her goods. The glance he shot me was like the secret handshake Masons share, except he and I weren't Masons. We were bums. Bums have a universal language of silent signals. Across the barrier of different tongues and different cultures, we commiserate.

Celeste's parting word to me was, "Walk." Her driver only shrugged. Another secret and commiserative signal. He held the cab door for her. As she waddled off, I raised my middle finger to her smirking back and her expensive hair. She must have caught my homely gesture in a reflection in the window of the cab. She wheeled around and stormed back, her own middle finger raised. "You haven't got the clout to do this to a person you just barely know," she said. "I know *you*, though, and it doesn't take a genius to see that you're a punk. Your dirty hair is a good clue all by itself. You don't smell of cigarettes, at least. You probably can't afford a cigarette. Nor a drink. Nor shoe polish. Nor an undershirt that isn't so ashamed of being frayed it's turned a grimy grey. That's the color of a blush in the underwear world. Whoever gave you that suit shined the knees up very nicely for you. And they almost matched the jacket and the pants. I hate to say your hope to find a job will run into a wall here, but people look at guys like you and want to turn away. You have an air of desperation. You have a look that says, 'I'll mooch. I'll whine. I'll cringe. What I need from you is way, way more than anything I could give you in return.' People steer clear of people like you. You're a liability."

People drag their honesty behind them like a trophy from the hunt, and they fling it in your face when least expected. They score points, and you get gored. Did I need to be told I'm a punk? Did plumpness need to tell me? Or lamb's wool coat? Or somebody who looks like she got her hair poured from a blast furnace and it hardened into iron on her head? Punks know they're punks. The thing is, they don't care. Some people wear their Purple Hearts for Veterans Day. They're proud of being wounded for their country. Punks pin on their punkness the same way. We're proud of being punks. We're wounded like the vets. They don't give us purple h\hearts, though. The hearts we have are real, and they bleed.

Celeste had kept her middle finger raised all the time she harangued, like an invitation for me to impale myself. She folded it back into its holster and storm-trooped to her cab. I was left alone to contemplate the woman at the window above the bar across the street. She, too, had disappeared.

My benefactor, Mr. Tinsel, had been stirred to type his letter—addressed not to me but to a group of patriotic convicts of which I had been one—by news in *Life* magazine of the sacrifice we felons had made during the recently concluded war. We convicts, a select group within the nation's ample supply, had volunteered as guinea pigs in experiments to find a way to yank malaria-infected soldiers off their sick beds and return them to dodging bullets sooner than the standard quinine cure allowed. I had bravely bared my arm to government-issue mosquitoes. I had suffered nausea, headaches, and fatigue in one of America's more progressive dungeons, Stateville Prison in Illinois. I ate my meals in the clamor of that dungeon's mess. I slept on an iron cot. I moved my bowels under scrutiny from guards to whom I snapped, "Yes, sir...no, sir...Whatever you say, sir..." when they directed at my shaved head their snarls and barks and jibes.

Was I patriotic? That's the question the *Life* magazine boys had asked.

"I'm so patriotic, I can shit the stars and stripes. I can sing you *Yankee Doodle* in a dozen different tongues. I could probably fart the national anthem, but it wouldn't be in tune. The land of the free and the home of the brave? I've got that tattooed on my ass. Only the land of the free is in bigger letters because they've had me in this hoosegow for going on five years. If I have to be a patriot before they set me free, I'll be any kind of patriot they want. They can shoot me from a cannon with a flag tied to my dong."

"It was unlike you to say that, Sweetcheeks," my cellmate, Blue, admonished.

Blue functioned as my voice of conscience, his voice very much like the voice of a bug. I could have stomped him out with one heavy step, and turned him into a pool of gunk.

"Of course I shouldn't have, Blue. I should have spoken from the authorized text, the Gospel According to the State of Illinois, Stateville Prison Edition. It has done me so much good to speak from that text before. I have recited the pieties, in my piety voice, with a piety hat on my head. I have lined up for my gruel, like a proper little criminal, and not complained because I didn't get enough. The fact is, as you and I both know, I *did not get enough.* Not get enough money. Not get enough status. Not get enough muscle to prevail over the slick and the sly and the strong who deal from the bottom of the deck in this unfair world of ours. My name, you should notice, is Sweetcheeks. It is not Kissass. It is not Lickbutt. If I really worried about not saying things that offend, I would change my silly name to something meek, like Orange or Yellow or Purple or *Blue.*"

"Be Sweetcheeks, if you like," Blue said. He lay down on his bunk. "Be Alan Prick Wise-Ass Smart-Mouth Sweetcheeks. Don't be Yellow, though. You're too stupid to be yellow. You'll be Sweetcheeks to your grave."

"I'm ignoring your disrespect, Blue,"

"Don't do me any favors, Sweetcheeks."

"I'm ignoring what I heard because I'm grateful to you for the lead on the Alaska job."

I never would have set foot in the territory of Alaska if it hadn't been for Blue. He was a trustee mailman. He had seen Mr. Tinsel's letter and had slipped it to me as a favor, cellmate to cellmate. It was actually addressed to all the cons who'd volunteered for the malaria experiments. "Here's your chance to start your life anew in the tropical part of Alaska," Blue had said.

"What is the tropical part of Alaska?"

"The panhandle part."

"Is it far away, Blue?"

"Not far enough, Sweetcheeks. As far as I'm concerned, not nearly far enough."

I had not suspected Blue—such a mild man—of sarcasm, but I wondered about him and his secrets as I strode down Boon's rain-puddled streets. I strode past the many bars and liquor stores of my new island home, past its sporting-goods stores and its outlets for marine supplies. I made a trek of twenty rain-soaked minutes wondering about a former cellmate's perhaps subtle sarcasm before I arrived in front of a plate-glass window proclaiming in gilt letters *Tinsel's Authentic Alaskan Curios.*

What I saw on display behind the glass were gold-nugget bracelets and totem poles the size of toothbrushes mass produced in the Asian country we had recently defeated in the Second World War. With a fleeting thought that said, 'Sweetcheeks, you have left the hard streets of Chicago. You have left Stateville Penitentiary. You have left the prison infirmary where you coughed and gagged and sweated for your country's victory in the Pacific war. Please don't, after all of that, screw up.'

I opened the door to the rather feeble tinkle of a tiny bell, a lukewarm welcome, I couldn't help but think, to the promise of my new life in Alaska.

No description could exhaust the array of trinkets and gee-gaws displayed on the shelves of the quiet store I entered on this Tuesday, the third day of July, in what the pious would call the year of our Lord 1951. Nor could the condescending description *trinket* and *gee-gaw* be fair, because among the plastic trading beads and keychain fobs shaped like polar bears, I saw carvings from the wild that justified the word *authentic* in the store's gold-painted name. *Tinsel's Authentic Alaska Curios* meant art, both intricately decorative and wildly grotesque. I saw a wooden box painted in a red and black design that looked geometric until I'd rested my eye on it long enough to detect, in its pattern of ovals and squares, the eyes and teeth and claws of beasts, as if the animals were hiding in a forest and the forest was the intricate, painted pattern. More stunning was a carving of a snarling human head. A Native artist had chipped and shaped and smoothed the head out of a knob that had begun its life as part of a cedar root. He'd turned its red lips into a sneer and winked one of its eyes half shut so the knob head had the scrutinizing look of those naturally suspicious.

Any dealer in scrap metal, I couldn't help but note, would have salivated to see the gold bracelets Mr. Tinsel had put so casually on display. I would have made a fortune pedaling treasures of that quality on my bike. That thought occurred to me, of course, and

I didn't entirely dismiss it. I am deft at pocketing valuables left temporarily unguarded. A gold bracelet would be a marked improvement on Zippo lighters. I've light-fingered dozens of Zippos, and foisted them off to strangers for a dollar or even just fifty cents. A guy is glad to get a bargain, like a Zippo for half price. Gold bracelets, though? The guy would probably yell for the police. I had to temper my larcenous instincts, and it's just as well I did, because into his store packed with gee-gaws bustled a white-haired man with the pink face of a healthy toddler. He was, I soon learned, Mr. Tinsel, but while I watched him scamper toward me down an aisle of his store, I didn't know that the man I saw was *my* Mr. Tinsel. I wasn't even sure he was a human sort of creature and not some kind of hybrid grasshopper-and-human, grown-up male. He hopped to the right and dusted the top of a glass case with the sleeve of his jacket. He hopped to the left and adjusted the dangle of earrings on display. Then he ratcheted his head around to throw his glance at me, accoutering that glance with a smile that displayed what I did not doubt were teeth hand-fashioned by the territory's finest dental prosthetist.

Mr. Tinsel fidgeted and fussed. He sat. He stood. He shuffled. He started sentences and abandoned them midway between the subject and the verb. He skittered. He sat again. He stood again. He resumed his seat behind his desk, a battleship-sized thing lodged permanently in a corner of his store. At the so-to-speak helm, he picked up and cradled the sentences he had orphaned earlier. He acknowledged his paternity. He willy-nilly lavished punctuation, welcoming each sentence back to the paternal mansion of language. And when his sentences had moved beyond mere gibberish into the grown-up world of grammar, he awarded each a period, like a graduation cap.

I handed Mr. Tinsel the letter I had carried faithfully across the country. He read it with his glasses on. Then he read it with his glasses off. He twirled his glasses by an arm-stem for almost half a minute while he stared off into space. After he'd accomplished that, he pulled open a drawer in a file cabinet jammed against the wall and plucked out a carbon copy of the letter I'd just handed him.

"Ah!" he exclaimed in a voice of discovery. "Ah! Ah! Ah!"

The carbon copy confirmed my credentials. I wasn't just a con man off the street. I was a genuine felon and one of the volunteer patriot-prisoners who had won, through *Life* magazine, Mr. Tinsel's admiration. From the letter I had handed him and its ditto-copy, he knew I was deserving of his brisk and practical assistance.

"And your name is…?"

"First name Alan."

"And your last name, Alan?"

"Sweetcheeks."

His eyes went blink, blink, blink. They might have betrayed amusement except for the tender sweeping of his lashes.

People who first learn my name sometimes make little jokes. Some have called me Mister Sweetass or Mister Honeybutt. Many of them guffaw. Mr. Tinsel was not a guffawer. He said, "Certainly…certainly," and nodded to add emphasis to his repeated word. "And you're going to need a job." Even as he spoke, he pulled his Rolodex closer. He said he had many friends in Boon's business world. Then he was silent a moment as he flipped through its display of cards. "We'll do this alphabetically," he said.

The Rolodex spun. He lined up the A's. "What's your name again?" he said. He had reached for the phone and put his finger in the dial.

"It's Sweetcheeks," I told him. "Alan."

His dialing finger froze.

"It has no anatomical implications."

"No. No. Of course not. Never thought…" Mr. Tinsel let his semi-sentence drift off. Seconds passed before he spoke again. "German name, is it?"

"I've been told it's Swiss."

"Is it…" He hesitated just a second because the question he was weighing must have seemed indelicate. "Is it your real name?"

"Why would I choose a name like Sweetcheeks if I was going to make a name up, Mr. Tinsel?"

From the way he blinked, as if my question weren't rhetorical and he had to think about his answer, I realized my sarcasm had failed. The failure didn't bother me. I knew I wasn't being graded on the quality of my sneers.

Tinsel said, speaking again in his hesitant, start-and-stop way, "Ah yes. Yes. Of course."

I knew right at that instant I had encountered one of nature's little anomalies—an innocent human being. Innocence is catnip to a punk. Innocence draws punks from all over the neighborhood. Punks stretch out and roll in innocence. On innocence, they exercise their claws.

So I ought to have, instinctively, torn into the tidbit that was mild Mr. Tinsel. Not physically torn into him, of course. I am a punk but I am not demented. I might have sneered and made some sort of verbal slash that would have let him know I enjoyed being snide and supercilious. But the hand of caution stopped me. I was a supplicant. He was—or he had the potential to be—a benefactor. Did I want to alienate him? Did I want him to regret he had written his kind letter to Stateville Prison inviting patriotic convicts to seek his help in finding work? The answer to those questions is, naturally, no.

I made a little joke instead.

"Is Tinsel Swiss?" I asked.

My reward came swifter than a blink. Mr. Tinsel smiled. Not the patented smile his sculpted teeth allowed him. What came and went across his plump, pink face in less than an instant was a boy's smile, as if he and I were ten years old and the possibility existed for a real friendship between a punk and the proprietor of an Alaska curio store.

I only mention this to say the possibility was there. I am not claiming that his smile blossomed into something permanent that would warm my gnarled heart and make it push the little flower head of friendship up above the surface of the earth.

Absolutely nothing changed. Mr. Tinsel continued thumbing his Rolodex in its floppy spin, and I continued manufacturing snide thoughts. Diplomatically keeping them to myself, of course.

Mr. Tinsel tried several shops and enterprises with Alaska in their name. He tried Barton's Plumbing. He waved away *Catherine's Baby Wear.* He couldn't, apparently, picture a convict offering a mommy a choice of bright rompers for her squally tot.

He suggested driving cab. I explained I had no license because I'd never learned to drive.

He suggested painting houses, but then he said that wouldn't do because Boon's rainy weather only let a painter work a half-a-dozen days a month.

He crossed off babysitting and heaved a heartfelt sigh as he forced himself to do so.

Mr. Tinsel, in between his dialing, asked a lot of eager questions about the crew that came from *Life* to Stateville Prison. He wanted to know if the interviewers were as glamorous as reporters are in movies. Were they full of wisecracks? And did they seem fired-up by the adrenaline of deadlines?

I tried to sculpt my answers to preserve the innocence about him I so treasured. It seemed important to him that he be, through me, connected to a smarter, snappier world than his curio world in remote Alaska. What good would I have done by telling him the men from *Life* were business-like and boring? Unreality can be a lot of fun, so to his somewhat breathless questions, I answered with a kindly disregard for dull and stable truth. I figured I owed him that laxness. *Life* had been good to both of us. He got his whiff of glamor, and I got prospects for a job.

Before we at last struck gold, Mr. Tinsel called a number of taverns in hopes of a bartending job. He called a janitorial service. The owner asked for references. He made a long appeal to a contractor extending one of the island's roads, but hiring there was done through unions. Mr. Tinsel sadly shook his head. He and union bosses, he said, did not see eye to eye.

His persistence paid off, though. Pinkham's Dairy, a dairy of which he himself had once been part owner, needed help.

"It's not a real dairy," Mr. Tinsel said while he scribbled the address. "It doesn't have any cows. All the milk in Boon has to be shipped in. But it does make ice cream. In fact, it makes chocolate-dipped ice-cream bars. The kind that come in wrappers on popsicle sticks. Quite a treat, or so I've been told. I don't eat ice cream myself. Cold makes my teeth ache."

He bared his teeth and disproved every unkind thought I'd had about teeth I had guessed must have been provided by a prosthetist. His teeth were firmly anchored in their somewhat purplish gums. He heaved a deep sigh, the sigh of a person who knows he has finished a good job of work, and he asked in his chipper manner, "Where are you staying?"

I said I had come straight from the plane and hadn't found a room yet.

"I can help you," he said, and he jumped to his feet to cup his hands around his mouth. "Santos!" he yelled at the ceiling.

"There's rooms for rent above the store, Mr. Sweetcheeks. Nothing fancy, but..." He interrupted himself to yell *Santos* once more. Then he put on a listener's face, with his head cocked as if the footsteps thudding overhead might be tapping out some sort of coded message.

While he listened, and while his look was vacant, he said, "Of course you'll want to check in with the district attorney, just to dot the i's and cross the t's. Our D.A. is Dick Chambers. Nice guy. I'll call him right away. Let him know you're coming."

I have not known any D.A.s who were nice guys. My expression must have shown the doubts I had.

"It's nothing personal, Mr. Sweetcheeks. But he does have a responsibility. He does enforce the law."

"He doesn't want any funny stuff."

"Exactly. I'm glad you understand." Mr. Tinsel, as he spoke, cast an appraising look on me. It only lasted a moment. It was the kind of look a person wears when he's taking the measure of the man. It seemed to me a perfectly natural pause. Mr. Tinsel, out of kindness, had done a felon a favor. I was the felon and he had pointed me in the direction of a job. The job did not involve chewing walrus hides. For that alone, any felon in the country would have owed the white-haired gentleman his gushing gratitude.

"So, all the way across the continent." Mr. Tinsel started up again, rubbing his hands and letting a smile flicker on and off. "Quite a trip. Quite a journey, I would imagine."

He clearly wished, in his scatter-shot way, to make small talk.

"Did you come straight from…" He backed away from his half sentence before he put his verbal self in forward again. "That is to say…" He paused. His mouth hung open as if the rest of his words would tumble out of their own free will. "I sent my letter, of course, to a…"

This wasn't small talk. I knew what he wanted. He might have stuttered till closing time unless I let him know I understood.

"Your letter came to me in prison, Mr. Tinsel."

"Yes—ah, yes, of course." He was so relieved he dropped down in his chair.

"You probably wonder what I'd done to go to prison."

"No, no. It's none of my business." Mr. Tinsel hesitated for half a second before he fired off his true and real thought. "Of course, it would be good to hear. Not that I'm prying, you understand."

"I killed a man."

"Premeditated?"

"Totally spontaneous."

"Something of a squabble?"

"Sudden, yes, but serious."

"Ah."

"I hope that doesn't preclude me from dipping ice-cream bars in chocolate sauce."

"No. No. Ha ha. Wasn't thinking that. Not at all. Furthest thing from…" He had to pause and blink until a thought came into focus. "The thing is, my wife, Mary Kay…" Another pause, this time for some distracting thought that shot him from his chair and sent him to blow dust off a display case. Mr. Tinsel breathed hard on the glass top and polished a spot with his sleeve. When he'd removed the invisible smudge, he admired the effect of his house-keeping, but for only a second. He abruptly stopped. He turned my way. His mouth opened and closed like a guppy's. "The thing is my wife, Mary Kay, she didn't know I'd sent the letter. Heh heh heh."

The tinny bell above the street door tinkled. Santos, short and dark and maybe Filipino, slouched in carrying a broom. Santos turned out to be a man of all work for Mr. Tinsel's many interests. I was to see him in his coveralls washing the store's show windows. I would see him run errands. I would dodge around him in the upstairs hall when he was vacuuming the carpet. Mr. Tinsel, without the least whisper about me being a convicted killer, cheerfully introduced me as a new arrival in need of a room. Santos nodded understanding and, after I had thanked my bene-factor and shaken his hand, the janitor/handyman led me to an outside door in Mr. Tinsel's building. I followed him up a cramped flight of stairs and down a hallway perfumed by what was to me the familiar smell of dust.

I was grateful for the smell of dust. Dust reminded me of a punk's low standing in the world. So did the hallway's low-watt ceiling lights. Also the wainscoting rail stained dark by the touch of many unsteady hands. The smell, the gloom, the railing reminded me of who I was and of the gratitude I owed the merchant on the floor below. Mr. Tinsel had steered me toward a job. He had done it from the kindness of his heart. The only thing he knew about me was that I'd dispatched a fellow creature, and yet he had devoted a half hour of his busy day to calling acquaintances and friends on my behalf. He had earned my gratitude; and my thought was that if I ever got the chance, I would hang him on my Christmas tree and let him twinkle.

There. I told you that my thoughts were snide. *Let him twinkle.* That was one of them.

We came to the dusty hallway's only open door, Santos stood aside to let me enter.

"Sam's room," he said as I squeezed past. The wink he shot me made me guess he believed he'd shared a joke.

I stood alone in a room almost as Spartan as the cell I'd vacated in Illinois. It held a single bed in a metal frame. It had no closet. A rack nailed to the wall was the only place I could hang up my raggedy clothes. In a greyed-over mirror above a dresser, the veneer chipped on its wearied top, I could see a ghostly image of myself. *Former con*, it said.

Next to the tired dresser stood a slat-back, reed-bottomed chair. A window behind the chair allowed a dreary view of rain-soaked siding on the building next door. If the Sam I knew from the airport was the same Sam Santos meant, the tearful view from the window alone could have driven him to throw himself against the wall until he needed bandaging. But I did not know if Santos's Sam and my Sam were the same. And in my first minutes in my new room, I tried not to draw conclusions that would mar the optimism I'd racked up by meeting Mr. Tinsel. We do not often come across kind strangers on this earth. Yet here on this territorial island, in this wilderness city, a gentleman—only twenty minutes after he had met me—had put me on the path to a paying job. He'd also lodged me right above his own sloped shoulders and white head. By coincidence, I was in the room of somebody named Sam. There are lots of Sams, and my wish was that each of them, going back generations, had been as fortunate as I in finding a patron and a promise of employment, and had been as industrious as I about storing their underwear and hanging up their shirts. And as I explored my options as a non-wiseass human being, I could, thanks to Mr. Tinsel's help, begin by transforming my former-felon self into a dipper of ice cream, and a very handsome dipper, too, I said to my reflection in the clouded mirror. At that exact, self-congratulatory moment, I heard a person clear her throat. A woman standing in the doorway spoke. "You're the one Mr. Tinsel sent his letter to?"

My guess said this was Mrs. Tinsel. She spoke in the way gunfighters in movies fire their revolvers. She aimed to kill. I *was* the one Mr. Tinsel had sent his letter to—I was the prisoner, the convict, the felon. She had just learned of her husband's charitable deed. Though, whatever questions she might have about welcoming a killer underneath her roof shared space in her ample bosom with matters more pertinent. "Did Mr. Tinsel speak to you about the rent?"

I was gawking at a dumpy lady with her hair puffed out in a white halo. She appeared, at first glance, to be made of meringue. She swelled and bulged around the waist and bust. Her pudgy ankles overflowed her black, homely shoes. "The rent is fifteen dollars a week. I am Mrs. Tinsel. If you didn't pay Ellery, you can pay me."

The lady speaking had a flamethrower gaze.

"There are only three days left this week, Mrs. Tinsel."

"Each day is two-fifteen."

I pulled out my wallet. I counted six dollars into her soft palm. She waited with her hand out while I fished two quarters up. I dropped them on the greenbacks, and while she searched her apron pockets for a nickel in change, I asked if she was charging me what she'd charged Sam.

A bit of the old Sweetcheeks had come to the surface. That's what inspired me to make my bold remark. Not exactly the wiseass Sweetcheeks, but the irreverent one, at least.

Whatever Mrs. Tinsel's thoughts may have been, she didn't betray them by changing her stony expression. Her look remained a stern appraisal of the bum her husband had invited to lodge beneath their roof. "Sam made himself useful to Mr. Tinsel," she said. "I'm sure if you made yourself useful, we could negotiate your rent." She dropped a nickel in my palm.

"What line of work was Sam in, may I ask?"

Her gaze stayed level, though it took on a weary tinge. Perhaps she sensed a wise guy with a nickel in his hand. She didn't speak until I'd pocketed my coin. "Sam did his best to do what everybody ought to do. He tried his best to advance the law." Mrs. Tinsel spoke through a veil of wryness. She had none of her husband's fidgety grasshopperiness. She was quieter but she had a core of steel, which Mr. Tinsel, it seemed to me, lacked. They struck me as an odd pair, but what do I know about pairings? I have never been paired myself, either with a female, a male or a duck. Still, I could see already that much of what the future held might require careful tightrope walking between my squirrely benefactor and his hardened wife.

Mrs. Tinsel hurried off. I remembered having seen, many times in my misspent youth, my mother hurry off in exactly the same way. My mother, when sober, did her best with me. She nagged. She cuffed. She cursed. She bellowed. But I am not going to bewail her shortcomings. By the time a boy begins to shave, he has learned the sob-story routine. He knows how to make the teardrops fall. He's learned that people tend to weep over the bruised child who grows up to shoot junk-yard owners. Do not weep for me. I rarely, when sober, weep for myself. That's something I learned from my mother. She may never have shot a junk-yard owner. At least, I hope she didn't. But she did bring to maturity a punk who needed every bandit trick he could acquire to dodge and flee and thwart and skirt his many desperations.

Santos appeared in my doorway with freshly laundered, though somewhat faded, sheets.

"I'll help you make the bed," I told him.

"You'll make it yourself," he replied. His advance across the room took him only two strides. He dropped his armload on the mattress then paused to take in my suitcase, placed to stand obediently at the foot of my bed, and my neat array of hanging shirts and trousers. Then he recited the boarding-house rules. No women visitors. No hot plates. Observe the customary courtesies of cleaning out the communal bathtub after use. No loud music on a radio or phonograph. Prompt payment of the rent each Monday morning. The official list was longer. It didn't seem interminable but it outran the Ten Commandments by probably six volumes.

That thought, I knew, was facetious. I said as much to myself as I plopped my hat on and checked its rakish angle in the mirror. Then I set off to find my way to Pinkham's cow-less dairy. I felt blessed. I had a place to stay. I had the prospect of a job. Rain splattered my hat. But here's the nice thing about the rain in Boon: it's a democratic rain; it doesn't dampen just a former felon's hat; it dampens everyone.

On my way to Pinkham's dairy, I ran through what little I knew about the milk business—cows, pails, stools, rustics. I had never been in the milk business. I had never been *near* the milk business, so what I knew about it was limited to the little I could remember from nursery rhymes.

Mr. Pinkham didn't care. When I showed up at his cow-less dairy the first thing he told me was to take my hat off so he could see my hair. He had arched his eyebrows when he'd heard my name, but he hadn't asked if I was Irish. I'd been prepared to tell him Dutch.

Pinkham admired almost extravagantly what I had always thought of as my average mop of hair, camel-colored and unruly as it was. After he'd expressed his admiration, he pulled off the shapeless cap he wore, an old and blackened thing, and bowed toward me so I could see the knobs on his bald head.

"Notice," he said, "no hair net. Notice why; no hair." He straightened up and slapped his cap back on. "Whereas *you*," he said, pointing to my dirty and disordered hair, "you are in the bloom of youth and blessed with abundant hair. Caution, Alan, caution. Voice of experience speaking here. Sadly, to keep hair out of our various milk products you must contain it with a net. Surprise it with a net before it can escape and do its damage. Vicious things, those strings of hair. They'll get into your ice cream before you can say boo. So here, Mr. Sweetcheeks, is your official hair net. Wear it in good health. I have a lab coat for you, too. I ask all visitors to wear one. We're going to have a look-see at my little milk plant now. You'll like to know what your duties will be, and I'll explain that. If you have questions, ask them, but first the ceremony of the coat and the ceremony of the net. Accept this hairnet, please. And may it bring you luck. The coat is white, and, my, won't you look handsome in it. The very image, I would say, of the scientific purity that is the motto of our plant."

While he watched me put my coat on, he did an odd thing with his legs. He shook them like they had no bones, like they were rubber. It wasn't a spasm. He did it on purpose as an exercise in entertainment. It was Pinkham's nature to be pleasant and entertaining, and over the course of the next half hour, while he toured me through his plant, he did every kind thing he could think of to clasp me to his dairy's stainless-steel heart.

I say stainless steel because, as Mr. Tinsel had explained, no cows were involved in Pinkham's operation. The milk Pinkham's drivers delivered to Boon's grocery stores came off a freighter from Seattle in stainless-steel tanks. Under conditions of optimal refrigeration that milk was tipped into Pinkham's local tank, also stainless steel, positioned above a conveyor belt on which rode an endless supply of bottles, not stainless steel but sanitized glass. The sanitizing machinery itself was all stainless steel. What milk did not go into quart bottles was churned by yet more stainless-steel equipment into ice cream. One of my duties, Pinkham explained, would be adding various flavors to the not-yet frozen cream so the product filling up the freezer cases of Boon's many grocery stores would be chocolate, strawberry, vanilla or a combination of those three flavors, a concoction, Mr. Pinkham announced with a grandiose flourish, popularly known as Neapolitan.

The last stop on our tour, after I'd absorbed instructions on maintaining temperatures and judging consistencies and adhering to the strictest sanitary standards, was the spotless room where ice-cream bars were dipped in a bath of melted chocolate.

The room in which this operation took place was not large. I probably could have spit across it if I practiced long enough.

But of course one does not spit in spotless ice-cream dipping rooms. Not if one is awed, as I was awed, at the operation's ingenious synchronization. Arms of stainless steel plucked the bars up from the bins in which they came. The arms became racks for transporting the bars, ice-cream side down, to where they could be dipped in their chocolate bath. One dip sufficed. The bars emerged covered with melted chocolate congealing so quickly the coating tenaciously clung.

"It makes a shell of chocolate," Mr. Pinkham explained, "delicate enough to fracture at a bite but sturdy enough to keep its shape when fragments break free and drop to one's shirt. Then one has to scoop it up on a finger and shove it in one's mouth."

He demonstrated the scooping process, even licking his finger as if a dab of sweet chocolate were attached.

The same mobile rack carried the coated bars to the wrapper apparatus where they slid into their colorful paper envelopes and were immediately laid into grey, cardboard cartons.

"Of all the gifts engineering has given the world," Mr. Pinkham proudly said, "I think there's none more beneficial than the chocolate-dipping ice-cream-bar machine. Its only purpose is the happiness of all. Millions, on a daily basis, lighten their workload and ease their worries by pausing to enjoy this frozen treat."

He patted my arm in a paternal manner before he went on.

"And you will be in charge of this benevolent machine, Alan. Not to feed the ice-cream treat to millions, naturally, but to make the treat available to hundreds of the residents of Boon—to children on their breaks from sweaty play, to longshoreman with their pallets of potatoes, to firemen idling in front of their stations, to postmen plodding their endless rounds, to piano teachers and to street sweepers and to housewives gathering their strength to cook the evening meal."

"The concept overwhelms me," I told my new employer.

Pinkham responded with his rubber-legs routine. That was something of a habit with him, I would come to understand. But he didn't release me right away. He wanted to know what books I had read, and what movies I had seen, and whether I liked Frankie Laine better than Perry Como. He told me he acted in community plays, including musicals, and he asked me if I played an instrument or sang.

I mentioned with appropriate modesty that I had played drums in a neighborhood band.

"A jazz band?" he asked in an excited shout. His legs went rubbery again.

I did not have time to tell him that the band, on those rare occasions when it got a gig, played for polka parties. I couldn't explain because Pinkham was regaling me with news about a band he and friends had formed.

"We try to play just like Red Nichols," he said. "If you want to sit in as our drummer, you'd be welcome."

I said I hadn't practiced for ten years.

"No problem," he said as he guided me toward the door. "We're none of us professionals. All amateurs. Amateurs all. And amateur means that what you do is done for love. Did you know that, Alan? Amateur means done for love."

I said I was glad to learn that amateur means done for love and that I hoped I'd see him early the next morning.

He grabbed my arm to stop me on my exit to the street. "No! Not tomorrow, Alan. Tomorrow's Independence Day. The dairy will be closed. You have cause to celebrate. Set aside your worries and enjoy." He did his rubber-leg routine again. A goofy man, but in a world often over-calculating, isn't goofiness a welcome trait? In the space of an hour and seventeen minutes I had acquired a goofy employer and an innocent benefactor. I had entered into a bargain with my new boss to spend my days dipping ice-cream bars in baths of chocolate. Those bars would reach the hands of stevedores and firemen and housewives, as Mr. Pinkham had explained. The cold bars would be savored, and thanks would be offered for the process that makes such welcome treats possible. I would be part of that process.

I had stepped out of a Grumman Goose seventy-seven minutes earlier a felon and a punk. I left Mr. Pinkham's ice-cream manufactory an apprentice benefactor of mankind, just like my new landlord, the patron saint of patriotic cons.

A bum approached me with a mumbled plea. "Could you spare a little something?"

Certainly, I could.

I felt like a million bucks.

I gave the man a dime.

"Live it up," I told him.

I found District Attorney Richard Chamber's office on the fifth floor of Boon's bile-green Federal Building. The D.A.'s office, and the offices of both the district and superior courts, occupied the floor directly underneath the city's lock-up. The proximity seemed practical. No sooner could a miscreant be pronounced guilty—stamped and, as it were, authenticated—than he could be whisked upstairs to cavort in cells with concrete walls and iron bars among fellows of his ilk. Though I doubt Boon's criminals did much cavorting. My experience of Illinois prisons tells me cavorting is rarely high on a criminal's to-do list.

I removed my hat when I stepped into Mr. Chambers' quarters. A woman with her back to me chatted at the desk with someone I assumed was Mr. Chambers' receptionist. I didn't mind waiting. I was in no rush to present myself to the district attorney's scrutiny. I have been eyeballed in the gimlet fashion many times before. I've never learned to like the process. It sours me to come under suspicion. I suppose it sours all convicted killers, and I ought not to complain. But I have a soul prone to complaining, so I passed the seconds I stood waiting in sneering at the office's shabby visitor chairs and the American flag on its tilted pole with its somewhat tarnished golden-eagle finial.

I heard the woman ahead of me say, "I've got to run, Darlene." She brushed past me with the swift, apologetic smile almost all attractive women award a youngish, not too unpresentable man. After I had nodded a thanks for her smile, I lifted my eyes to the woman who'd been called Darlene. The name 'Darlene,' I have learned only recently, derives from *darling*. It's safe for mommies to say 'darling' to an importuning child, or for a woman to say to her lover or a man to say to the woman he holds in his heart. It was fashionable and considered smart in the thirties to call everybody 'darling.' In fact, there was a popular song with very nearly that title. *You Call Everybody Darling*. Line two: "And everybody calls you *darling*, too." No need to explain the implications there. That excessive use of *darling* gives any accompanying statement the stamp of insincerity. Probably whoever wrote that song, and whoever sang it, and whoever enjoyed listening to the lyrics never walked into the office of Boon's district attorney and locked eyes with the Darlene who served D.A. Richard Chambers as a combination receptionist and secretary, though.

Darlene had blue eyes that picked you up the moment they alighted on you and waltzed you around for several seconds before they released you to let you stagger back to stability. She had what I would inadequately describe as yellow hair. She wore it braided, and the braids circled her head like a crown. The careful twining of the strands of her hair created its own pattern of shadow and light. Where the shadow held sway, the yellow was honey-colored, or tawny you might say. But where the light fell full, the strands were the color of the sun in pictures little children draw; a crayon-yellow star with a big smiley face telling the whole world how happy the sun is to be shining and sharing its beauty and warmth.

Her gaze was direct. Her eyes communicated what I took to be a wish to assist. They voiced for her what her whole appearance seemed to say: "How can I help you?"

She wore, of course, the blouse and skirt a woman busy in an office would choose, clothes not fussy nor showy nor complicated. They made her trim. They made her efficient. They made her attractive, although the Darlene I was staring at could have dressed in the habit of a Carmelite nun and still have been attractive. Her attractiveness came from inside and poured out all around her like a halo. It wasn't just a physical attractiveness. What she had, by its nature, was grace.

She directed her warm smile at me and spoke with relaxed courtesy. "You must be the gentleman Mr. Tinsel called about. I'm Darlene Sandusky. I'll let Mr. Chambers know you're here."

Miss Sandusky rose quickly to carry out the errand she'd announced. I harbored for about a half a second a hope she hadn't noticed how I had gaped. I knew I was not the gentleman she said she would announce, although I behaved in the interval of her disappearance as if I deserved that honorary appellation. I stood with my hat in my hand in front of Miss Sandusky's temporarily abandoned desk. A Royal typewriter sat on its own wheeled stand next to that mildly cluttered desk. I imagined Miss Sandusky speeding her shapely fingers across the Royal's keys, clattering out on white paper black messages of doom for criminals like me. Miss Sandusky was part of the machinery of the law. I had no need to think of her in any other way.

"The *gentleman*," she had said.

I squared my shoulders just a little. It was as if I had to shrug myself into the invisible garment her description wove for me, as if I had to try on a new role.

Miss Sandusky returned almost at once to say Mr. Chambers would see me soon. "Sit, if you'd like, Mr. Sweetcheeks."

Obedient, I sat.

"Where are you from, Mr. Sweetcheeks?"

"From Illinois, Miss Sandusky."

"I've been in Illinois twice. Both times from what was my home then, in New Hampshire. One trip to Springfield with my folks, because of Lincoln. The second time I was just passing through on my way up here, up to Alaska."

She smiled as if saying 'up to Alaska' was some sort of pleasantry. I smiled back, and was still smiling, trying desperately to think of some pleasantry to prolong our conversation when the occupant of the office behind Miss Sandusky yanked open his door. A man I guessed must be D.A. Richard Chambers barked, "Sweetcheeks?" in a guard-dog's voice. "Is that your real name?"

The district attorney seemed to be about my age, but he was dark-haired and my hair, when it was clean, was the color of wet sand. He had a robust build, heavier than mine. I was probably just robust enough to pedal forty pounds of stolen copper to a scrap yard on my bike. Clearly, though, our biggest difference was in our clothes. His dark suit fit him with a made-to-measure sharpness, whereas my scarecrow garments had been tossed, more or less in my direction, out of a prison closet.

I said Sweetcheeks truly was my name.

"Russian?" he asked, suspicion in his voice.

"Latvian."

He said, "What's the difference," and jerked his head to tell me I should follow him inside.

I did so at once, and meekly took the chair to which his nod directed me. I watched Mr. Chambers put on a pair of dark-rimmed glasses and pick up a scribbled note from his desk. He must have scribbled it himself in a phone conversation with Mr. Tinsel. As he read whatever secrets the message divulged, I distracted my nervous self by studying his cramped office. It had a thrown-to-gether look, as if he dropped one item when another demanded more crucial attention. The many piles of things he'd dropped rose until they teetered. The only window, behind his desk, showed a seamless cloud delivering its freight of steady rain. I found myself ruminating on the significance of that when Mr. Chambers whipped his glasses off and directed a stern look at me.

"How old are you?"

"Twenty-nine."

Before I could add, "Sir," he slid his glasses on again and checked his note, probably in hopes he could catch me in a lie. A second passed. He barked again. "Apparently, Mr. Tinsel didn't know your age."

"I don't know his either, Mr. Chambers."

The district attorney didn't laugh, but he made the kind of snorting noise. The snort did not prevent him from a more serious stretch of reading. Several seconds passed before he set the note to one side, rubbed the space between his eyes, and tilted back in his swivel chair to fix me with a look of appraisal and dislike.

"You killed a junk-yard owner?" He boomed his question as if he were in court and meant to speak it not as if remarking on a fact but as a lawyerly question that might catch a witness in a lie.

"He was a dealer in scrap metal."

"Well, that makes a big difference. We don't have scrap-metal yards in Boon so I guess as far as that goes, we don't have to worry."

My look stayed blank, as one's look must when a person who can cause one harm indulges in sarcasm, and after a second of staring at me Mr. Chambers said, "I'm joking, Sweetcheeks, so lighten up. It doesn't matter if you killed a junk-yard owner or a scrap-metal dealer or the Pope in his gilded palace. The fact is, you killed someone. I wish Mr. Tinsel had consulted me before he invited you to Boon, Sweetcheeks. But I assume he's arranged a job for you already."

"At Pinkham's dairy."

He nodded, then he leaned forward to rest his heavy arms on his desk. "Let me explain how things work here, Alan. We like to keep things quiet. I mean within the normal range of quiet. The guys come in from logging camps and the fishermen come in to blow off a little steam. We tolerate that rowdiness up to a degree. I mean we're not puritans or blue noses or anything like that. But if the rowdiness gets out of hand the police step in. They do not always step lightly. Do you follow my drift? We have a twenty-one-man department in Boon. I don't know all the officers myself but I do know Chief Standard Gallant quite well and I have a great deal of respect for him. If he tells me someone's head had to be conked to preserve the dignity and order of the city, I believe him. I would take his word about how necessary the conking might have been against the word, say, of a Sweetcheeks who had shot a scrap-yard owner in Decatur, Illinois, for example."

"It wasn't Decatur."

He eyed me in an unblinking and unfriendly way as if he had to decide right at that moment if I had a head that needed conking. If so, he restrained himself. He relaxed back in his chair and spoke in an expansive manner.

"Let me tell you something more about our policemen here in Boon. They operate like wolf packs. They cull the weak ones from the herd and they gang up for the kill. Who might be weak is a matter for conjecture, of course, but in the general scheme of things, in the orientation of the way things are, it's probably safe to assume that a pack of police department wolves would naturally think a felon convicted of murder might be the kind of stray it's easy to cull. Not saying that in your case, Mr. Sweetcheeks, culling is a thing they would do. Many of the men on the police force are veterans, and I'm going out on a limb here but I'm willing to say your volunteering as a guinea pig to save the lives of soldiers would stand you in good stead with them. Up to a point. Just up to a point."

He smiled, but his smile wasn't real. It was a smile intended to say he had sufficiently warned me and I could go.

I rose. He offered his hand. I shook it, but even as we shook, he yelled, "Miss Sandusky," and his secretary poked her head in. "Oh," Mr. Chambers said when he saw her. "You're leaving now? Okay."

Miss Sandusky wore a pill-box hat with a net veil.

"What I've got can wait, Darlene. It's not important. The Fourth is almost here. Get out there. Enjoy yourself. Be off."

He waved his hand for emphasis. She gave her smile of composure to her boss and then turned her smile on me. "Elevator, Mr. Sweetcheeks, or stairs?" she asked.

I told her, "Elevator," and in the silence of the fifth-floor hall, while I waited standing next to Miss Sandusky, I felt the natural awkwardness all convicted killers feel when they are unexpectedly alone with an attractive, single woman in a hat with the kind of veil Eleanor Roosevelt wore on her hats. Conversational gambits escape me when I am put in mind of Eleanor Roosevelt. But silence was a burden, too. Perhaps Miss Sandusky felt the awkwardness as much as I. She had the presence of mind, however, to ask the polite kind of question calculated to relieve it. With her kind smile she turned my way. "How did you reach Boon, Mr. Sweetcheeks?"

I told her I hitchhiked across the country and then took my first flight on a plane.

She blinked when she heard me say 'hitchhiked.' Behind the small veil, her eyes lost their focus. A troubled look came, or so it seemed to me.

The elevator reached us. We heard the machinery grumble as the cage settled into place. Then the doors sighed open. I waited for Miss Sandusky to step inside. When I followed her, I remembered to take off my hat. That article of etiquette had been impressed on me many years before by some adult relation whose degree of consanguinity I've now forgotten, but I could still feel that stiff lady's cuffings. They had lodged in my memory. I de-hatted myself hoping that Miss Sandusky would be impressed. Perhaps she was, because even as the doors were sliding shut again she spoke, her voice steady and assured but with a deeper timbre.

"My father had to hitchhike to his mother's funeral. This was in New Hampshire, in January, in the slush and cold. His car broke down when he was halfway to Tilton, where the funeral would be. He couldn't find a phone. A storm was raging, and other drivers, apparently, were showing their good sense by staying off the road. He had to slosh through snow and slush in just his funeral shoes."

She stopped speaking long enough to let her look go blank, as if she were picturing, in an inner vision, her father in his funeral shoes in the bleak New Hampshire cold.

"I had come up from Connecticut, from school. I got to the funeral home, and the person in charge, the mortician, asked if I knew why my father was late. He wondered if he should start my grandmother's service without him. Right away, I told him no. I left the funeral parlor and drove through the storm to look for my dad. I had to guess where he might be, but finally there he was…tramping…soaked. When he was warming his hands at my car's poor heater, he was trying very hard not to let me see him cry."

She finished her recital just as we reached our first-floor destination. She stepped out and turned to watch me follow. She wore her composed smile again. She wished me good luck at the dairy. I said thank you and then I said, "I've never met anyone before whose father had to hitchhike to a funeral."

She touched my hand to tell me thanks. The very moment that we said goodbye, a young man strolled up. He and she locked arms. They moved away, he smiling in goofy delight at her, and she returning his smile, devoid of the goofiness but well supplied with warmth.

A boy friend?

Why had the thought of that not occurred to me before. I had been thinking instead about the well-worn oxfords on my feet. Could they qualify as funeral shoes? They were bulldog shoes, creased and road-weary, the perfect shoes for climbing over fences and sneaking through backyards to pry open windows where an unguarded wallet might await. They were good shoes for alleys. They would have been at home in seedy bars. You could stick them under flop-house beds. You could flee the sound of sirens in them. You could throw them out the window at a yowling cat.

But if I had come upon Darlene Sandusky's father tramping in his funeral shoes through New Hampshire snow, I hope I would have had the grace to trade my shoes for his.

From my shoes I looked down the street where Darlene and Mister America, her handsome boyfriend, were sauntering away. This was the eve of Independence Day, and a festive crowd—as festive as the downpour would allow—churned and stomped and waded and skipped. What I saw in the distance on the sodden street was a billboard-looking couple, suitable for propaganda purposes if displayed above the canyons of a city or along the limitless American road. Arm in arm. Hip to hip. Touching. Not embracing. Projecting, I felt sure, such blissful smiles, they could have been all-American models recruited to advertise something wholesome, like automobile tires, or refrigerators, or suppositories that guarantee relief from piles.

Oh, Sweetcheeks! What is wrong with you? Must someone else's happiness subtract from yours? How like you to look at young lovers and think about suppositories for relief from rectum irritations.

Yes! They made a handsome couple! And yes, you are a convicted killer and a smart-mouthed S.O.B. You cannot, by being snide, be happy. That's a proven, scientific fact. And yet, in the face of bliss, you sour. You are bile, Sweetcheeks. You are stomach acid. Your only function in this entire world is to reduce good meals to excrement. You should be ashamed.

The natal day of liberty in Boon began with a derelict named Tin-Ear Tweet scarecrowing up and down the streets urging residents to wake and celebrate. Tin-Ear was not alone in his heralding duties. Derelicts with similar odd names—Hard-Rock Nelson, Whiskey Pete, and Morris the Pear—staggered and bellowed out of alleys, summoning carousers to their Independence Anniversary duties. The heralds were the tawdry equivalent of angels announcing the resurrection of the Christian God, except the angels at the Easter tomb were sober, and these bums on the Fourth of July had patriotically inebriated themselves.

"Awake! Awake!" the heralds croaked. Ten thousand thirsty souls in Boon heard the bums proclaim that happy news. Roughnecks from the scattered logging camps—choker setters and whistle punks and donkey punchers—had dropped their caulk boots on their bunkhouse floors and rushed to Boon to join the celebration. Salmon in the nearby seas swam in perfect safety, because seiners and trollers and gillnetters—all the varieties of commercial fisherman Southeast Alaska hosts—had moored their vessels at the city's docks to rip and roar through the performance of their Independence Day duties.

And the donkey punchers and whistle punks sharing beds with good-time girls in shabby rooms in cheap hotels fired vulgarities back at Tin-Ear and his brethren, because for those who'd started celebrating on July the Second or July the Third, the festivities on the morning of the Fourth began a bit too early.

Still, even as whistle punks and donkey punchers were pulling the triggers on their vulgarity guns, their good-time girls were leaping out of bed and rolling up the window shades to peer out on plank streets and plank sidewalks at banners and flags and bunting, at booths for games of skill and games of chance, at the platform raised for dignitaries to judge the holiday parade, at early risers storming barrooms freshly stocked not with water turned to wine—though they might have welcomed a miracle that practical—but with Old Grandad and Four Roses, the town's more common ecstasies.

In that extravagantly happy moment, I began to see my new hometown for what it really was—a small American paradise, unselfconscious and unsophisticated, a baby part of the American nation, still a territory, not yet a state, a territory swaddled in its bunting, and singing anthems in its crib. Innocent of dull maturity, but trying hard to act grown-up, eager to shine, eager to please, a place determined to strut and give itself the attractions it would have when it was grown and fully formed and authorized to send a voting representative to the national Congress.

Boon on Independence Day, 1951, was proud and innocent and loud and boisterous and fun.

It boasted, naturally, a parade. I heard the bleat of what sounded like an earnest but not entirely accomplished player of the trumpet. The crowd surged in the direction of the brave attempt. On Hyde Street in front of Bailey's Confectionary Store, a marching band in white shirts and snap-on black bow ties, tootling and blaring and rat-a-tat-tatting, broke into its military stride. I recognized the stirring strain they marched to. It was *The Stars and Stripes Forever*, and right at that moment, stricken like Paul on the road to Damascus, I sank into the sentiment of love for country—love for founding fathers, and pioneers, and God-damned Conestoga wagons. Love for the many veterans following the flag down Boon's cheering streets, as they had followed the same flag into Anzio and Rome and up Iwo Jima's bloody beaches.

I cheered the veterans with their shiny faces. I cheered Miss Boon of 1951 as well. In her ballroom gown and silver tiara, she perched above the back seat of a Cadillac convertible, a bouquet of deep-red roses in her arms. She waved at me—a convicted-killer, former-convict, patriotic barer of my arm to malarial mosquitoes—and energetically, enthusiastically, I waved and smiled back.

I smiled and waved at a fire engine following Miss Boon, some maniac volunteer riding in its cab blasting screeches from its siren every hundred feet. I cheered the noisy engine, and the shriek its siren made. I cheered the Ford Deluxe *Fordor* police car edging forward in its wake. Cheers for the parading Boy and Girl Scouts, for the Boon High School Service Club marching in smart precision. And for the Rotarians, the Eagles, the Ladies Auxiliary of the American Legion and for the Legionnaires themselves.

Members of the Redmen's Club war-whooped into view. All of them disguised as movie-style Indians, their flannel leggings made to look like buckskin, and fake buckskin fringes swaying from their sleeves when they waved their toy tomahawks at squealing little kids.

The dubious authenticity of yarn wigs and flannel buckskins must have been amusing to the many parade spectators who were authentically red themselves. About a quarter of Boon's population was Tlingit or Haida. Natives of the many islands in Alaska's Alexander Archipelago, they had never marauded through the woods, much less down city streets, in costumes of brown flannel, waving plastic tomahawks and scaring little kids.

The Redmen pacified those children with gifts of candy wrapped in cellophane, scattered out of pouches faked-up from the same buckskin-like brown cloth as their shirts and pants.

The patriotic and civic and comic Fourth of July parade wound its way from block to block to finish in the Federal Building's ample parking lot. There, while a panel of dignified judges decided prize winners for floats and marching units, my landlord and benefactor, Ellery Tinsel, the sun turning his white hair into a halo, spoke on inspirational themes.

Not that anyone was paying Mr. Tinsel much attention. The call of the bars, the call of the loggers' rodeo, the revving up of motors for the coming hydroplane race lured away hundreds, but I stayed rooted where I was. I stood nearly at attention while my benefactor, the man who had provided me a life anew in Boon, spoke movingly of small-town values learned in churches and in pious homes. His theme was a new mill the city had been promised. The mill would grind the region's bounty of spruce and hemlock trees to pulp and load that pulp aboard huge freighters to sell it up and down the U.S. coast and across the blue Pacific as far as the island nation of Japan. A whole new industry would blossom. And with that stable industry would come the kind of revenues that cities use to build bigger schools and new civic centers and hospitals with all the latest equipment. Everything clean. Everything bright. Shining proof of American genius and American largesse and America's high principles and standards.

I applauded Mr. Tinsel's fine and noble speech, and off I went to join the crowd cheering the hydroplane races. I added my full-throated din to the noisy celebration given to the victor of each lap. Next, I cheered loggers cross-cut sawing and aiming axes at a target painted on the butt of a sawed tree. I sampled hot dogs steamed to near perfection at the Church of the Nazarene booth. I gambled quarters at the Wheel of Fortune the Elks Club had set up, and I tested my dart-throwing skills at a booth manned by, I believe, the Lions, where the target was inflated balloons.

I cursed the boys who scattered firecrackers at the feet of stumbling drunks. The stumbling drunks, I hope, appreciated the effort I put in on their behalf.

I found space on a crowded dock as the sky began to darken. The highlight of the feast day of Saint Independence was the fireworks display. A barge out on the Narrows held the sacred explosives. Clouds had gathered and the moms and dad and kiddies, the single men and women, the juveniles and grizzled elders, red people and white people, Catholics, Presbyterians, Methodists, Baptists, Lutherans—Boon is a veritable cornucopia of denominations—muttered worries about rain. I imagine the people of faith must have silently prayed. If they did, their prayers were answered. No torrents from the clouds. Not even a sprinkle. That, in Boon on the Fourth of July, counts as an unqualified success and very nearly a miracle.

When the hour was judged dark enough, the first match was put to the first fuse. The whole crowd followed, with its eyes, the flight of the rocket into the clouds. The nearly instant explosion, veiled by vapor, would have disappointed any other crowd on earth. The spectacle was dimmed, its colors no brighter than drips from Popsicles.

And yet undaunted Boon gave those tepid colors a long and rousing cheer. Here is the thing about celebrants in Boon: They know not every effort meets with a textbook success. Clouds dull a firework's explosion. But the fireworks continued, and the oohs and ahhs went up as if every spark of green or red or orange was as perfect as a diamond in the sky.

I saw Darlene Sandusky cheering and oohing and ahhing the slightly sodden spectacle, and my heart—my patriotic heart—hit a speed bump. She was with a male friend. The friend was *not* the Mr. America I had seen her with the day before. Her new friend was possibly the only male on the long stretch of dock, beside Ellery Tinsel himself, who was wearing a suit and tie. He was a well-groomed, prissy looking man who had assumed responsibility, it seemed, for sneering at the sky.

The man I saw close in Darlene's company lacked masculine panache. His gestures all were girlish gestures, and when he spoke his whispered confidences into Darlene's ear, he simpered as he said them.

A boyfriend?

No. Never. Unimaginable.

The fireworks ended. The crowd raised a cheer. A pack of urchins wolfed my way, the same urchins who had tossed firecrackers at the feet of stumbling drunks. I did not give way. I stood like a rock they had to split to flow around. I didn't even know I had struck a pose so heroic. I had been elevated and empowered by a thought. The thought was this: *He*—meaning Mr. Billboard-Ready Handsome—did not *have* to be Darlene's boyfriend. He could be her brother. Had anyone told me contrary? No. Not a whisper. Not a word. I was free to think whatever I wanted. The inside of my head, I realized, belongs entirely to me. This indisputable fact of human existence declares me the king and master—actually the despot of my thoughts. Let my thoughts scurry to do as I bid. They need not conform to any reality but mine. They need not be the platitudes that millions substitute for thought. My thoughts can be frisky. They can be amorous. They can be carnal.

Listen! These ideas came to me on the day of the official celebration of our nation's independence. And didn't I once say I was so patriotic they could fasten the flag to my pecker and shoot me from a cannon? That's the way I felt, thinking about all the things Mr.-Maybe-Darlene's-Boyfriend didn't *have* to be. I felt like they could carry me out to the fireworks barge and set alight my fuse.

I hope I told Blue, in one of my infrequent letters, about the diligence with which we in the Pinkham band approached rehearsals. We huddled over sheets of music. We listened to popular records and tried to duplicate the pop and snap and swing that had won better bands renown. We played at a wedding and won generous applause. At the high school's Sophomore Hop we were begged to play two encores before the dancers let us leave the stage.

Mr. Pinkham rehearsed us in his remodeled garage. My ice-cream boss had transformed the garage's back half into what he called his family room, a space we shared with his children's sleds and other winter toys. On a tile floor, under fluorescent lights, I banged on the drums, Mr. Pinkham plucked the bass. A boy named Richie Gallant exerted himself on the trumpet. Leopold P. Grumbs, in real life a dentist, played the saxophone, and our pianist, a matron named Delilah who had orange-colored hair, sat at a battered upright and complained about the cold. She complained so much that Dr. Grumbs, D.D.S, felt obliged to seat himself beside her and snuggle up to share his body warmth.

It amused Delilah, for reasons I can only guess, to refer to me as *Squirt.*

"My name is Alan," I explained the first time I heard her use that word.

"What's wrong with *Squirt*, Squirt?"

Grumbs butted in. "He's not squirt sized, Delilah."

"You might be surprised, Leopold." Delilah glanced at the dentist; he glanced at her, and both of them broke out in giggles.

What their innuendo might refer to was not that hard to guess. She poked Grumbs in the belly and he spun more giggles out.

Richie was sitting nearby shaking spit out of his mouthpiece. I wandered over. "It's all so wholesome here," I said.

Richie said, "Huh?" A conversation opener if I've ever heard one. I might have lectured the boy a little bit on innuendo, on how, through subtlety and wit, we make known to one another intentions all of us have but few of us are eager to lay on the table. I might have said more, not that I knew a lot about innuendo myself, but right at that moment, Mr. Pinkham, shouted, "Hey! Let's get to work."

What we did was never *work*. Five people individually inept combined their mediocre talents to make good music. That is more or less the epitaph Pinkham's Band deserves. We weren't much good at ballads but with a tune that had to swing we managed pretty well. *Buckle Down Winsocki* was a favorite with the fans. So was *Rag Mop*, which had a solo for Richie he never quite managed to wail on. In place of Richie wailing, I went heavy on the drums. Not with much sophistication but with the energy of youth.

Near the end of October in a talent show before a crowd that packed the high school auditorium, we ended our two-number performance to enthusiastic applause. The crowd had packed the auditorium, partly for us, I liked to think, but also because we shared the stage with eleven other acts, including tap dancers, comedians, and a stout man in a cowboy shirt who sang *Sail Along, Silv'ry Moon* in the style of Gene Autry, accompanied by his wife on the kazoo.

The cowboy singer won first prize, but the Pinkham Band was named first runner-up, and in the bustling hallway after the show, friends and family members crowded up to say, "Well done."

The friend who crowded up to congratulate me—if I can be bold enough to label her a friend—was Darlene Sandusky. She came with the prissy man I had seen at her elbow at the fireworks on the Fourth of July. She introduced him as Warren Arsenault. Warren's superior and somewhat pained expression clearly told me he considered a talent show that featured cowboy singers and their kazoo playing wives beneath him. Miss Sandusky's enthusiasm, though, more than made up for her snobbish escort. Her face glowed with the pleasure only available to those who are by nature kind. When she pressed my hand and said congratulations, I would not have traded that single word for a diamond-studded trophy from the manicured hands of her friend.

My benefactor, Mr. Tinsel, also bustled up, and the pleased look he wore nearly matched Darlene's. He started a sentence. He stopped it. He started another but backed off from that to make another run at the first one. All the while he sputtered, he was squeezing my hand. Whatever he meant to say was lost when Mr. Pinkham did his rubber-leg routine and everybody laughed. Nevertheless, it was clear my benefactor was proud of me. His wife, who stood at his elbow, was not as demonstrative. She was stony, in fact. If some instinct had told her she should offer congratulations, she had taken that instinct out behind the school and strangled it to death before returning to the line of those eager to proclaim how much they'd enjoyed the show. She probably would have taken Mr. Tinsel out behind the school and strangled him as well if he had overcome his sputtering and expressed the pleasure he so obviously felt.

Times come in the lives of convicted killers when they wonder how much respect they ought to show cranky old ladies. What is the margin of return on ignoring sour looks? I wish there was a handbook to answer questions of that sort. It's not that I expected a tit-for-tat exchange for any decency I showed. Even convicted killers have limits to their patience, and Mrs. Tinsel, whom I would call Mrs. Meringue-Hair if I was still the wiseass I had been in my misspent youth, very much tested my limits.

But all of life is not the Mrs. Tinsels of this earth. I had Darlene's congratulations squirreled away in the vault where I keep the paltry treasures of my life. Plus, I was happy dipping ice-cream bars in chocolate and banging on the drums. I ate my fill at breakfast, lunch and dinner. I slept in a warm room. I occupied myself with sanitizing milk bottles and scrubbing stainless-steel tubs. And my off-work hours, which in earlier days I might have devoted to stealing copper pipes and automobile bumpers, were spent instead in making music. Not great music. Runner-up to first-prize music. Runner-up to Gene Autry imitators. But sufficiently runnered-up to bring praise from beaming fans.

Delilah's husband came to offer his large paw and shake my hand. His presence seemed to sober Grumbs, who had family of his own swarming around, his wife and kids ablaze with pride at what he'd helped the band achieve.

The crowd had almost petered out by the time a moose of a man put in his appearance. He threw his arm around the shoulders of our skinny trumpet player, and Mr. Pinkham, turning his legs into rubber, introduced him as Police Chief Standard Gallant.

The chief was Richie's father, though you would not have guessed a relationship when you saw them side by side. Richie was a reed, and Chief Gallant a redwood tree. The chief may have wished he could be offering his son congratulations for an achievement more manly than winning second prize in a hometown talent contest. What the chief would think more manly I can't say. I imagine it involving loud, sustained roars from an arena's crowd—some achievement bringing hundreds to their feet, a cheer over possession of a football, or maybe an event re-quiring boxing gloves, with all the blood and broken noses boxing gloves imply. A trumpet doesn't cut it in comparison, not to a person who has fists the size of sledge hammers and the iron kind of gaze that makes a felon want to shrivel up and slink away.

Chief Gallant, who'd nodded when he heard my name, gave me no other recognition until the cowboy singer and his kazoo-playing mate pasted on grins for a newspaper photographer, and the distraction caused by flashbulbs diverted all the fans still standing in the hall.

I did not stray off to join the flashbulb crowd. Nor did Chief Gallant. In the moment we had in private, he asked, in a low voice, "You keeping your nose clean?"

With a glance, he read what his question had accomplished. He could see that I'd been cowed. "Nice action on the drums," he said, and then he shuffled toward the flashbulb crowd, which parted for him like the fabled Red Sea's waters.

When I went back to my dim room above Mr. Tinsel's trinket store, I studied, in the clouded mirror above my dresser, the broadness of my chest and the bulge of my biceps. Physically speaking, I was a satisfactory specimen of masculine humanity. I was also a proud dipper of ice-cream bars in chocolate sauce, and runner up to the first-prize winner in a small town's talent contest. I had advanced from the solitary, semi-vagabond, light-fingered, petty thief of my early years. I still wore my second-hand suit. I still wore my sloppy fedora. But I boasted in my next letter to Blue that despite my follies and my record and my wise-guy attitude, I had bootstrapped myself up toward some shabby sort of self-respect, and I could allow myself, I hoped, to begin imagining my life *a la* post-punk.

On came November with its winds and rain, much like, I must admit, the winds and rains of October. The second Saturday of the eleventh month brought a snowstorm rated by the weather bureau as of New Hampshire funeral size. It was the evening of the band's third appearance at the Windward Bar, a bar appropriately named, apparently, because gale winds ballooned the tarp Mr. Pinkham had provided to keep the drum set dry. If the wind had been another knot more powerful you would have seen three musicians, their blue tarp a sail, fly across the Narrows and crash into a mountain on the island opposite.

Fortunately, Mr. Pinkham had parked his dairy's van just yards from the back door we had to struggle through to reach the Windward's stage. Grumbs and I carried the drums, and valiant Richie fought to keep the billowing tarp from knocking us over.

"Whew!" Mr. Pinkham said when we finally wormed the drum set safely to the stage. Early patrons at the bar recognized our effort with applause, and Mr. Pinkham did his rubber-leg routine to signal his appreciation.

Gene, the dark-haired man who presided at the Windward, sauntered over from the bar to tell Mr. Pinkham he might close early because of the storm. "You can't count on people coming out in this. Most of them have better sense."

Gene had suffered the loss of two middle fingers from his left hand on a battlefield beach at Okinawa. He hadn't lost them in the actual battle for the beach. Someone he'd accused of cheating in a card game had demonstrated his displeasure with a knife. How Gene drifted from the beach at Okinawa to the Windward Bar in Boon I didn't know, but he brought with him a steely control he probably wished he had exercised at that unfortunate card game. People didn't lightly disagree with what he said, and even Mr. Pinkham, ordinarily so bubbly and optimistic, merely nodded his assent.

"Let us know," he said to Gene, meaning if the bar was going to close, he wouldn't argue.

For the first hour of our tootling and strumming it looked very much as if Gene's forecast had been right. The bar boys stood around and gossiped with each other because hardly anyone was there to order drinks. At the tables crowded up against the tiny dance floor a foursome sat dead center, and at a neighbor table another couple spread their winter garments over empty chairs. The foursome was a party. They had come to have some fun. The women dragged the men out to the floor, and everyone pretended the place was jammed and rocking and they were in the center of a boisterous, happy crowd.

The couple with their winter garments draped on random chairs kept their conversation private and intense. He leaned in toward her and she leaned in toward him. Neither of them smiled when they spoke. A bar boy in his long, white apron who wandered over with an offer to refresh their drinks got waved off in an impatient manner, and moments later the two stood up to put their heavy garments on and go.

Mr. Pinkham called a break right after that. He conferred with Gene, who had watched us from behind the bar with his beefy arms folded on his chest.

"He says to give it one more try," Mr. Pinkham told us when he'd picked his way back through the rows of empty tables to the stage. He had stopped to offer pleasantries to the happy foursome waiting for the band to start its second set. Clearly, if these couples had their way, we would have played all night and on into the dawn. They defied the power of the storm to make them dismal. They were out for a good time, and I'm sure Mr. Pinkham let them know it would be his privilege to provide it. I couldn't hear him from so far away but I saw his legs go rubbery. The two women laughed. One of the men stuck out his paw and Mr. Pinkham shook it. Back on the bandstand, Mr. Pinkham beamed at us. We picked up our instruments again.

Boom! The door flies open. And Boom! In blows a crowd.

That wasn't quite the way it happened, but my impression was the same. The bar's door opened and opened and opened, and in with all the puffs of snow and bitter air came resolutely happy crowds as if all the merrymakers south of Juneau had decided to defy the storm and assemble at the Windward.

Tables filled to overflowing. Bar boys hoisted extra chairs above their heads and wormed their way through walls of flesh to give standees a place to sit. Jitterbuggers with their butts and elbows flying commandeered the floor. Gene and his two helpers shot back and forth behind the bar pouring booze and popping caps off beers. Friends waved and shouted across crowded tables, buying one another drinks and laughing at jokes they couldn't possibly have heard because the din had risen to air-raid-siren level. It boomed. It bounced off walls.

And we—the Pinkham band—we were a good half of all the clamor because the fervor of the crowd and defiance of the howling storm propelled us to perform beyond our powers. Richie's trumpet wailed, and Delilah pounded on the keys so hard the piano positively jumped.

I flailed, and I whopped and bopped and banged. Sweat stung my eyes. When I shook my head, I saw droplets fly off from my hair in a bright cloud.

The floor was like a solid sheet of churning legs and leaping torsos. When we ended a big number—*Open the Door, Richard*, always a crowd pleaser—applause exploded and bravos raised the roof. Mr. Pinkham told me I should stand and take a bow. It was then I saw Darlene Sandusky, seated at a table with the prissy Warren Arsenault and cheerfully applauding. I tapped my drumsticks to my forehead in salute.

Darlene wore her hat, hardly any bigger than a wallet, with its semi-concealing veil. It did not seem the kind of hat that would protect her in a storm. And even I—no connoisseur of women's hats—knew it was old-fashioned. I wondered why she wore it, but I didn't *really* wonder that. My wonder had to do with women's secret nature, with what lies behind their pretty eyes and attractive hair. There is some logic, I'm quite sure, about old-fashioned hats, and because I don't know what that logic might be, because I have no hope of ever knowing, I think and think and think about the mystery. I lock it in my heart, and when my time permits, I tinker with it like a master thief might tinker with a stubborn lock. It isn't that the master thief believes he has the brains to follow all the lock-maker's clever clues. The mystery is what absorbs the master thief. He is lost in tinkering, as I am lost in small, charming, peek-a-boo veils.

I was thinking peek-a-boo thoughts when Mr. Pinkham gave the downbeat, and the band was off once more.

This time, despite the shoe-horned crowd, the bar boys worked an extra table to the dance floor's edge. There wasn't really room for it. People had to pinch themselves up tighter with their knees and elbows squeezed. The bar boys formed a human chain to pass four chairs from hand to hand above the sea of heads, then one of them stood guard to keep trespassers away until a frigid blast came from the door again, and a woman, stiletto-slender and wrapped in fur, cruised in with a snow-speckled claque. The woman had silver hair and from her earlobes to her ankles she was wrapped in red-fox fur. Those in the crowd who didn't make way for what even from the stage seemed clearly to be a well-aged glamor-puss, found themselves muscled aside by her three-man flying wedge. In a bubble of self-assurance, she strolled to the exclusive table at the front. When she let her red-fox coat fall behind her to her chair, she displayed herself, still standing, in a tailored suit of pastel blue. She let her glance around the room establish who was in command. Then she deigned, in a manner reminiscent of some sort of Mongol king, to take the seat a toady henchman held.

No dancers were so frenzied they trespassed near her throne. I could see her sweep her haughty gaze around the room, responding to the shouted greetings of her friends with a slight finger wave. Her stooges tilted close to hear her caustic comments on those whom she'd acknowledged. I only call her comments 'caustic' because I saw her goons all grin. They slid their gaze in the direction of those silver-hair had singled out, then smirked and traded jokes with one another.

Gene, the barman of the missing fingers, squeezed his way up to her table and nearly bowed to give her welcome. After pleasantries had been exchanged, he raised the hand that still had all its fingers and at this signal, by what was clearly pre-arrangement, an ice-bucket with a bottle of Champagne passed from bar-boy one to bar-boy two, and Gene ceremoniously placed it on the favored table.

Many thanks were offered. Bowing and scraping took place. Then, while a goon with a shaved head thumbed up the Champagne's cork, the imperial woman surveyed the raucousness until her superior and sneering gaze reached the companion of Darlene.

Warren Arseneault was doing his best to snidely comment into Darlene's ear. I don't know what the content of his snideness might have been. Each time, before he spoke, his gaze flitted here and there. That was his way of priming himself, I suppose. He simpered as he looked left and right, and when he gestured with his left hand—he guarded some sort of drink concoction with his right—that hand had a tell-tale limpness at the wrist. The hand betrayed him, in other words. It disqualified him from the Manliness Olympics. It retired him before the games of Manly even started, and no one understood disqualification better than the stiletto in her suit of pastel blue. She let her own left hand go limp for just a second. I don't think Warren Arseneault knew. His back was to Silver-Top. But the cruelty of the woman's gesture registered with Darlene. I cannot say she blushed, but her expression dimmed. She forced an artificial smile and pretended that what Warren said amused her.

Here and there, on both sides of Darlene, men and women of discernment suppressed knowing grins. No one wished to be compliant in the silver matron's mockery, but notice must be posted or the knife of vicious notice might plunge down on them.

What I witnessed was a deplorable, understandable weakness. It happened much more quickly than it takes me to describe. It was an instantaneous and souring frippery. The Windward crowd was not in a frippery mood. They wanted music They wanted shouting. They wanted dance, and the Pinkham Band was primed and ready to deliver.

I doubled my earlier efforts. I made the drumsticks fly. Sweat droplets flew off my tossing hair like showers. I felt like I'd discovered a secret language for the drums and could hammer out a message that would say I'd walk through snow in my funeral shoes for you, Darlene, because I admire you and I admire your hat and its veil.

The upshot of my tom-tom message was that when Mr. Pinkham finally called a break, the fox-fur with the thuggish sense of humor sent a bar-boy to the stage with drinks for all five members of the band.

I knew the drinks had come from her because when I looked across the floor to see whom I should thank she raised her Champagne glass in a salute.

I didn't feel like I held a drink. I felt like I held poison. The glass burned my hand, and with my eyes on hers to make sure she would see, I performed an act I hope some recording angel has written down as noble. I turned my gift drink bottoms up and poured the toxic liquid on the floor.

"Richie, who *was* that lady? The one who bought us drinks," I asked.

"She didn't buy *me* a drink."

"She did buy you one, Richie, but you couldn't drink it. You're not twenty-one. If you took a single sip your father would throw you in jail. Imagine all those animals in jail, the guys your father arrested. You'd have to padlock your belt and keep your pants hitched up twenty-four hours a day."

The night was over. The band was breaking up. Snow continued falling and anybody walking home would have to wade through drifts.

"Sometimes I think you exaggerate," Richie told me.

"I always tell the truth, Richie. They made that a requirement before they gave me my parole. So who was that lady? Is she someone you know? I think she had her eye on you. You're catnip to the ladies, aren't you.

Richie answered with a snort.

"I could fix you up. If you tell me her name, I'll see what I can do."

Our thin trumpet player had snapped the clips shut on his instrument case, but he'd volunteered to help me lug the drum set out to Mr. Pinkham's truck. He always helped. He wasn't a chummy person, but he sometimes edged up to the verge of puppyness.

"I'll bet it was your handsome tie that made her eyeball you so much," I said.

He wasn't wearing a tie.

"I'm not wearing a tie," he told me. When I laughed, he grinned. He'd figured out I was kidding.

"Her name is Cal. My father wants to shut her down, but she's got too many crooks that work for her."

"Work for her doing what?" I asked.

"She's a W-H-O-R-E," Richie spelled.

"If you're going to talk dirty, Rich, I'm not going to listen."

"Oh criminy," he said. And then Pinkham came in dusting snow off his arms. He announced, "The truck's outside," which was our signal to carry out the snare drums and the bass drum and the cymbals.

Richie hitched a ride with Pinkham as far as the dairy. Mr. Pinkham said he could try to drive him uphill to his home, but Richie said snow would have made the hill too slippery. From the dairy, he took off on his stork legs to walk.

We'd agreed to leave the drums in the dairy warehouse so we wouldn't have to bang them into the Pinkham garage and maybe wake the family up. My boss and I had maneuvered the set through the doors and put it down, but when I turned toward the door, he placed a hand on my arm. "You shouldn't have done that, Alan," he said.

I didn't have to ask what I shouldn't have done. A lady had bought me a drink and I had poured it on the floor.

"You did it for the lady who came with little Warren." Mr. Pinkham made his voice delicate, and he just grazed the word 'little' with some slight, unsettling suggestion.

"I didn't notice who the lady was with, Mr. Pinkham."

His hand stayed on my arm. He patted the part he held, the part between my elbow and my wrist. His pat was reassuring, like a father's pat on the arm of a son who needs correcting. "Insulting people is not the way a guy survives in this world, Alan. Play tough if you want, but the tough guys almost always cancel one another out."

"You're talking to a guy who's tough himself, Mr. Pinkham. I've got the parole papers that prove it. I've learned a bit about surviving. I survived eleven years in Stateville Prison. You survive by letting people know they can't kick you around."

My boss removed his hand. "I've survived by minding my own business. There's a lesson in that, too, Alan. Although it sounds a little stupid when I say it."

"Words of wisdom, Mr. Pinkham. I'm glad to hear them."

He laughed. He didn't wag his rubber legs, because whatever had amused him wasn't that silly sort of humor. He laughed at what I'd said, which hadn't been something intentionally comic. I don't know what the comic aspect was.

As he was leaving the dairy, he said, "Lock up when you go."

I liked the refrigerated warehouse where we'd stored the drums. Even in the November cold, Mr. Pinkham kept it cool for the new tanks of milk delivered every week. The new tanks came and the old tanks went. In between we bottled milk, we made ice cream, and as long as summer lasted, I reigned over the ice-cream-bar machinery it was my privilege to put into motion. I had other duties, of course. I did all the scrubbing of the emptied milk tanks. I steam-cleaned returned milk bottles. But all of that was labor. What I did for love was conduct the great orchestra of clamps and arms and bars and racks in the synchronized work of making ice-cream treats. By the end of October, demand for bars of vanilla ice cream in solid-chocolate coats had dwindled. It would be the middle of May, Mr. Pinkham had told me, before the music of the chocolate room began to soar again.

I had about a mile to walk to Tinsel's rooming house. The wind had died to just a whisper but snow continued piling up. With the first step I took into a puffy drift I envied Richie and his long, bird legs. They were made for stepping in and out of drifted snow. If I hadn't locked up the dairy, as per Mr. Pinkham's order, I might have gone back inside and found a place to curl up and sleep. Real dairymen must sometimes sleep among their cows—among their Bossies and their Helens and their Daisies. But I'd need hay. I'd need the warmth of farting animals. And bovine creatures, needless to say, were not high on my list of bedding-down-with partners.

When I thought of bedding-down partners, Darlene came to mind. She was the only woman who'd been kind to me in Boon. Churning my way home through drifts of windblown snow, I imagined happiness with her. I mean real happiness. Not just the bedding-down stuff. I imagined coming home from work and finding Darlene waiting for me, some sort of spatula in hand, or a wooden stirring spoon. I could see the very spoon. I could see an apron with a frilly edge tied around her waist. I could smell what she was cooking, something savory. What I couldn't see, in my imagination, was her face, although I knew she would be smiling. I knew her eyes would sparkle. But I couldn't make that smile shine on me. That part of Miss Sandusky stayed blank.

I plunged on through billowy snow. Give the snow a chance to work its magic. That's what I was saying to myself. Let the magic be kindness. Let magic be friendship. Let there be the gradual and natural blossoming of mutual affection.

I was pondering the contours of affection when someone with a baseball bat snuck up from behind and conked me on the head.

The blow left me indisposed for seven weeks. Mr. Pinkham said he'd hold my job for me. Fortunately, it was the slack season in the ice-cream-dipping industry. I paid my rent to Mr. Tinsel in promissory notes. The collector of those notes was Mrs. Tinsel, of course. She handled all the dormitory's financial transactions. On Monday every week she appeared like clockwork in the doorway to my room. I knew that credit had been extended. I had had a conversation with Mr. Tinsel setting up the generous terms. No need to pay till I was back on my feet. Those are the words he employed. Generous words. Kind words. Benevolent words.

And yet I never heard the Monday morning footsteps of his spouse without feeling my heart shrivel, and internal organs panic and begin to palpitate. Thanks to Mrs. Tinsel I had the best palpitated liver, pancreas, and pituitary gland of any former felon on the planet. I always feared that she had come to shoot me straight between the eyes. Nothing she said ever betrayed that ambition. Perhaps she didn't harbor it. My fevered imagination may have created a picture of that plump matron entirely the opposite to what she truly was. She may have been grandmotherly, with candy treats tucked in her apron pockets. If so, I apologize. And yet I never learned to *like* the woman. If she had given me a candy treat, I would have rushed it out for scientific testing. I would have feared she'd made it out of strychnine.

While I reigned as the best internal-organ palpitated person on earth I was also the best peed. In the first five weeks of my recuperation, Santos interpreted any garbled thing I said as a request for bathroom privileges. He'd tug me to my feet, and down the hall we'd totter. Each time he performed his toilet-trotting service he said, "I *told* you to watch out." I don't believe he had told me to watch out, but I'm sure he believed he had. Warning me to watch my step was practically an obligation for those I met in Boon. Celeste had warned me. I dreamt one night of visiting Celeste and telling her in her amplitude that she had been absolutely right:

There *are* people to watch out for in Boon. People one does not lightly cross, not even to the extent of innocently and somewhat merrily pouring a proffered drink out on a dirty bar room floor.

If I could have visited Celeste in my shroud of bandages, she might have apologized for not being more specific. She might have said, 'Oh, I meant you should watch out for an elegant-looking, elderly whore. Cal. She's so accustomed to toadies and hangers-on any sign that you lack deference will result in damage to your skull.' Because what, after all, is the meaning of the pouring out of a proffered drink? It means one does not bow to snottiness and meanness and vile nastiness. It was nasty of the vicious Cal to mock the wimpy gesture of the wrist by Warren Arseneault. Cal deserved to have her drink poured out. What she actually deserved was to have it flung right in her face.

Santos, because I winced at the pain from my ribs each time he helped me out of bed, repeated his admonitory warning. He had the decency, I should also say, to be sorry about my bandaged torso, my wounded head, my blackened eyes, and my split lip. I had plenty of self-pity of my own. I didn't need a lot of auxiliary sympathy. Santos volunteered some bonus information as well: The name of the red-fox woman's sawed-off companion was Mike.

"If he's around, then she's around," the janitor told me. "She's got him on a leash. He's probably the one who banged you on the head."

"He would have had to stand on tiptoe, Santos."

"Ha ha." Santos made no real effort to convince me he was amused. What he aimed to accomplish by saying *Ha ha* was to let me know he recognized I had made an effort at humor, and that in my bandaged condition he appreciated how difficult humor must be.

"I *told* you to watch out," he said again.

Mr. Tinsel never came to help me pee, and in many ways I'm very grateful for that. He appeared in my doorway the day after New Year's, though, in his hands two tangerines the size of apricots.

"Mrs. Tinsel sent these. A belated Christmas present." He baby-stepped his way into my room, and because I had no space on my pill-and-bandage laden bedside table to accommodate his gift, he cleared a place on my dresser top and put the golden globes down there. "We used to call these Japanese oranges, Alan, but with the war and everything they changed the name to tangerines. They're not quite the same as Japanese oranges. I think they come from some place different than Japan. They taste good, though. And Christmas is the only time we get them. Not orange-growing season here. Of course, we're in Alaska so it never is the orange-growing season. What's nice to think of, though, when we're shivering beneath our snow, is that somewhere in the world the sun is shining on green orchards, and people are going out with baskets to collect these oranges."

He dragged my chair from under my window and sat down with his knees nearly touching my bed.

"You sound like a poet, Mr. Tinsel."

"Mrs. Tinsel would laugh to hear you say that."

"How is Mrs. Tinsel? In tip-top shape, I hope."

My landlord eyed me just a second before he spoke. "You know—she didn't really send these tangerines. Bringing them was my idea."

"She doesn't like me, does she, Mr. Tinsel."

I thought that in reply he'd back up to start a sentence and tinker with it before he put it in forward again, but he surprised me. "I should have told her about my letter to the prison before I sent it."

"That letter was much appreciated at the penitentiary, Mr. Tinsel."

I didn't tell him that, with Blue's connivance, his letter hadn't reached any convict except me.

He smiled. He said he'd read the *Life* magazine article about convicts volunteering for malaria experiments to help speed an end to the Second World War. That memory seemed to capture his attention for a moment. He sat with his face turned toward the end of my bed, his expression blank. "I didn't know what to expect." He spoke very quietly, still lost in his thoughts. "Alaska is a long way from Illinois. People there must picture ice and snow. That's their picture of Alaska. All igloos and polar bears. They don't know about this part of it. This part is very pleasant."

"Except for thugs with baseball bats, it's pleasant, Mr. T."

He laughed. "I wish the woman who set her thugs on you could serve a little time in jail herself."

"You are too charitable, Mr. Tinsel. My wish for that woman is that the foxes she stripped nude so she could prance around in a fur coat would devour her alive."

What I said put a fire in his eyes. "I wish the same," he said. "I have put good money into finding foxes who would do that sort of work. Not actual foxes, you understand. I've tried to find people as sly as foxes who could melt into the crowds that pack her bar and observe and record and bring back the kind of evidence a prosecutor, like our good Mr. Chambers, could place before a court. I'd like to see that woman driven out of Boon."

He spoke in a surprisingly straight-forward manner.

"Was Sam the kind of fox you paid for work like that, Mr. Tinsel?"

My landlord's eyes hardened. I had never seen that before. "I was very sorry about Sam, Alan. He tried his best. He hung around her bar. He listened. He watched. He reported back to me all the conversations he'd had with those who knew Cal's doings. She's got her fingers in a lot of dirty deals, and people who have crossed her have come off worse than Sam."

He scratched his chair closer and spoke more confidentially. "Boon has tolerated Cal for a long time. Those times are over now. We aren't a frontier town anymore. For years and years we had our loggers and we had our fishermen come in off their boats and from their camps, flush with money and eager for a good time. Boon was a good-time town. That's what it *used to be*, is what I should say. Now that's begun to change. They're going to build a pulp mill, Alan. Steady jobs. Steady incomes. No more coming to town on weekends to blow your earnings in a fling. Boon won't be a fling place. It will be a place of daytime jobs and homes for families. We'll have better schools. We'll have more churches. People here will live the same life as people in other parts of the United States. No more brothels. No more gambling dens. No more thugs lurking in alleys with clubs."

"You'll need your foxes first, though, Mr. Tinsel."

"Foxes?"

"Your Sams. Your undercover agents. Spies."

"In wartime, spies are necessary, Alan."

"And Cal is war."

My statement made him straighten up. He had been sitting bent in my direction. He didn't answer what I'd said. He kept his poker face on, not giving anything away. I tried again. "Are you recruiting, Mr. Tinsel?"

"Are you interested, Alan?"

"I wouldn't take part in a clean-up campaign as a good citizen, Mr. Tinsel. I might do it for vengeance, though."

"Vengeance is good, too, Alan. Shall we talk?"

"I'm not going anywhere," I said.

He laughed, stood up, put my chair back where it belonged, and even lined up my two tangerines in a more artistic manner. He seemed pleased with himself, and before he left he bestowed on me a smile I had never seen him show before. His smile sealed an unsavory pact, if there is such a smile in the repertoire of ordinary people. His smile signaled understanding, and if the understanding said we would be partners in snooping, and spying, and ratting people out, then fine. OK. The work was necessary work, and someone had to do it.

Plus, I thought as the door closed behind him, there might be cash involved for doing my unsavory good deed. Tinsel surely had paid Sam.

I only had a quarter hour to contemplate how much a snoop could ask in terms of pay. While I still juggled payday figures in my head, Mrs. Tinsel burst into my room. "What on earth are you thinking? What is Mr. Tinsel thinking? Both of you are perfect fools."

She brandished a white envelope as if it were an axe. Her eyes threw flames. I might have been incinerated. So might have been my shirts on their rickety rack, and my socks in their closed drawer, and my stockpiled bandages, and the two tangerines that sat faintly fragrant on my shabby dresser.

The tangerines captured Mrs. Tinsel's attention. She balled her fist up like a hammer and advanced on them. I believe she contemplated smashing the globes and scooping up their pulp to fling in my face, but something about the tangerines—perhaps their connection with Christmas—prevented her from striking. She yelled, "Do you think that awful woman won't know who you are? You, with your brass and your swagger, can you walk into her bar without suspicion? You poured out the drink she sent you. Did you stand on a chair to do it? Did you make yourself a public spectacle? You probably sent a notice to the newspaper—'I'm the guy who dumped the drink Cal sent.' Oh, bravo, Mr. Sweetcheeks. How exemplary of you. You commanded her attention. She's got you in her book of sassy punks. If you have any doubt, just count your stitches. Count your scars. Each scar's a little mouth that says what an idiot you are."

She pointed the white envelope at me and sputtered. Her sputtering was purposeful, like machine-gun fire. "Don't you dare speak. You and your smart mouth! Everything belittled. Nothing honored. Nothing good. I wish I'd been around when you were still a boy. I would have battered all that nonsense out of you."

The thought of battering nonsense out of me must have exhausted Mrs. Tinsel. She stomped to my chair and lifted it by its ladder back. Some new thought gave her pause. She released the chair. It dropped back into place. I couldn't help but think it was relieved. For all the chair knew, Mrs. Tinsel hadn't planned to sit in it. She could have ripped one of its legs off and pounded me to death.

"The vileness of the world, Mr. Sweetcheeks, can you observe all the world's meanness and the selfishness and remain indifferent? Does suffering leave you unbothered? Young women exploited. Has that ever made you blush? Has it fanned some sort of anger? The cheapness. The degradation. Alienation from loved ones. Loss of self-respect. A gutter life. A life of ruin. And you, who displayed a little, tiny glimmer of a conscience but displayed it much too late, you've got a label pinned right to your shirt. It says, 'I'm a wise guy. I won't help. Let the drunks get drunker. Let fools gamble all their grocery money down the drain.' Yes, Mr. Sweetcheeks, let innocent girls sink deeper into shame. Let night win and disgrace win. Atrocity will win because you are such a *mouthy* person, Mr. Sweetcheeks. You have a mouth on you like nobody's business. And people don't trust a mouthy person. It makes them ill at ease to be around that sort of man."

Mrs. Tinsel made herself step back, as if the urge to throttle me in bed would have overwhelmed her if she stayed too close. "You have struck *no* deal with Mr. Tinsel," she thundered. "You have no agreement to strut into that dreadful woman's bar and pull out your little notebook and write down suspicions. What a pair of idiots—both you and Ellery. I've told him he should be ashamed to deal with a man like you. The deal you have is with me, Mr. Sweetcheeks. Inside this envelope I've put a hundred dollars. Take it to the Pan-Am office and buy a ticket out of town."

She flung the envelope on my lap. The door slammed, and she was gone. The door stayed slammed for barely a minute. Santos, while I still reeled, grinned his way into my room, in his hand a folded piece of paper.

"*She* sent this," he whispered.

"Mrs. Tinsel, Santos?"

My thought was that my landlady might be issuing a challenge to a duel. The improbability of that, which occurred to me at once, did not extinguish my alarm about pistols and seconds and measured steps in some forest dell at dawn. Mrs. Tinsel had just flung a hundred dollars in my lap. She was paying to get rid of me. Did she want her hundred dollars back? Had she a cheaper plan for running me out of her wet, island town?

Santos disabused me of the mistake I'd made. He placed his hands to his chest and cupped them in the unmistakable sign that indicated tits.

"Darlene?" I asked.

He handed me the page he carried.

Miss Sandusky had written only two sentences. She said she had learned, over the recently celebrated holiday, that she was in my debt. Then she said, if I could come and see her, would I please suggest a date and time. She had signed her name in full and under that she'd written the address of her home.

CHAPTER

VI

Nothing disqualifies a punk from making social calls. Convicted killers can engage in small talk as blithely as anyone else. They can be as presentable as anybody, providing they shave their sick-bed stubble, and comb their ratty hair, and do their best to chip caked mud off their clod-hopper boots. I had access to a laundromat where I could clean a shirt. I am habitually careful about brushing and flossing. I have made myself familiar with the green and blue and yellow mouthwashes that guarantee to sweeten breath. I have a clipper with a blade that lets me scrape away the grunge from underneath my fingernails. Given my habits of personal hygiene, I felt like I could swain it with the best.

But was swaining what I wished to call on Miss Sandusky for? Would a gallon and a half of Listerine, systematically gargled, make me an eligible suitor? And was making myself eligible a reasonable goal?

What is swaining anyway? Is it polite conversations with delicate tea cups in hand? Does it involve amorous glances? Do participants stroll past babbling brooks conducting airy conversations? Why plight a troth? I have no idea what a troth might be, but on the sliding scale of engagement it might be anywhere in between simply bedding down, then pulling your pants back on and hiking away; or, possibly, shelling out for an engagement ring and standing up in front of friends uncomfortably overdressed to repeat, at the prompting of a pompous clergyman, familiar, formulaic words?

I knew it was silly to think of these things in regard to what essentially could be described as a simple social call, but I was a young male and Miss Sandusky a young female. In addition, she was, as far as I knew, a young female with some sort of attachment to a young male. What I had not yet worked out was what *sort* that 'some sort' was. It was affectionate, certainly. I had seen them lock arms. About that observation, I have no wish to entertain conjectures. Let conjectures entertain themselves. I will stick with the known facts. A young woman named Darlene had invited a young man named Alan to visit. We would meet at her house. Thanks would be proffered for what Miss Sandusky considered a service I had performed. We could have held a meeting of that formality in front of a notary public, for all the intimacy the words 'social visit' implied.

Two other facts deserve consideration: I was a bum, and Miss Sandusky was the secretary-receptionist to the senior law-enforcement official in the town of Boon. Whatever hopes I harbored, and I will tell no one what they might have been, were tissue-paper hopes, were cobweb hopes, were hopes as fragile as the skin of bubbles made of soap.

Nevertheless, a kind invitation had been proffered. I would have been rude to ignore it.

I wrote to Darlene—not immediately but soon—saying I'd be honored to visit and suggesting a date. When acknowledgement came a few days later, I studied my visage in the bathroom mirror. The scars barely showed and the bruises underneath the eyes had mostly disappeared, but to make myself presentable I'd still need a barber's help.

In the search I made for a barber shop, I fell in step behind a man who looked much like a pear. He was walking a cat on a long, dirty string, and the mincing pace the cat set matched almost perfectly the pace I could manage without flare-ups from my wounds. The pear-shape I followed looked like someone who had failed the derelict entrance-exam. He was sufficiently filthy and shabby, but he lacked that desperate cutting edge and display of inner turmoil trained derelicts cultivate. He looked serene, in fact, a person gifted by the gods with the talent it takes for patiently walking cats.

When the pear-shaped man stopped to greet a friend, I dodged first left and then right to try to swing around them. Pear-shape was large enough to block my view of the man he spoke to. His friend, I discovered when I limped my way around the pear impediment, wasn't any taller than a parking meter. I knew at once I'd seen him before. He had been in Cal the Ogre's party at the Windward Bar. He was the one who'd had to stand and crane to appreciate the full effect of the ogre's cruel joke. And Santos had surmised the little man could well have been among the gang that set upon me in the snow.

Sawed-off must have recognized me as well. He froze as if in guilty terror. Even the cat seemed to know who I was. She mewed in my direction with a cat's pronounced disdain, then she minced off on her charcoal-colored feet. Pear-Shape followed. So did the human fence post, whose name, I recollected, was Mike. Mike the Minion. Mike the Moron. Mike the Miniature Mugger. I entertained myself with alliterative nomenclature until the cat-walker and his height-deficient friend disappeared around a corner.

I discovered, as soon as they were out of sight, my trudging had brought me to a place admirably suited to my tonsorial needs. I faced a shop that bore, in gilt letters on its plate-glass window, a legend in script that said, "André—Hairdresser to the Stars."

I turned down my jacket collar, which I'd hiked up against the rain, and stepped into the shop. To the tinkle of a little bell I entered a room rich with tall mirrors in gilt, rococo frames.

The lighting, recessed, brought out purple tints in the velvet-embossed wallpaper. On the walls hung plaster cupids with bellies the size of cantaloupes. An orchestra of strings played on hidden speakers, and from shampoos and pomades exquisitely lined up on glass shelves a scent of secret gardens drifted.

A middle-aged man in a barber's smock stepped out of an alcove at the sound of the bell, but he stopped and said, "Ah," when he saw me.

I had entered wet. I had entered wearing my second-hand prison hat. Perhaps he thought I'd come to rob his place. The *ah* he uttered expressed surprise and probably shock.

"Haircut?" I hastened to say.

He hesitated just a second before he said, "Of course." He waved me to a chair and when I sat, after I had shucked my jacket and hat, I was surprised to find the chair tilting back. When I fought to sit up straight. The man, who'd introduced himself as André, eased me back. "Shampoo?" he spoke in such a kind voice I gave up resisting. Warm water flowed, and a ceremony much like baptism was performed on my scalp. André's soft hands worked up suds that smelled of roses. The suds washed away my grime much like, I'm told, baptismal waters wash away our sins. If the metaphor were accurate, I would have risen from the tilted chair reborn, but the sacrament was interrupted when André stopped massaging. "You've got a scar here," he said.

The truth is, I hadn't thought about my head wound when I'd made my haircut plans. Since my encounter with the baseball bat, fuzz had grown enough to hide the stitches. It was only when I did my combing that I remembered scars were there. "An accident," I said to André.

Discretion or some other professional virtue kept André from asking if the accident involved an iron safe dropping from a fourth-story window and bouncing off my head, the way safes do in comic books. He rinsed my sudsed-up head in silence, and when he'd turbaned me with a towel and was guiding me to his padded barber chair I asked what stars he had been hairdresser to.

"Just José Ferrer. It was before *Cyrano*, though. Before Mr. Ferrer was famous. I was never the kind of hairdresser who worked on the set or anything like that. I mean, I think I could have done it if I had known the right people. You have to sell yourself to make it when you work in Hollywood."

He didn't speak like he was bitter. He seemed pretty much incapable of harboring hard feelings. He busied himself with the towel, manipulating it with the dainty touch a little man might have, although he wasn't particularly little. He was of average height and of a paunchy, middle-aged weight. He kept himself well shaved and his cheeks were scented, but even with the careful shave, his blue whiskers showed. What hair he had was dark and oiled and trained to lie across the bare spot on his scalp.

"Do people normally ask about the stars? Your sign says *stars* in plural. I'm just wondering," I said.

He answered very nonchalantly. "I lie." When I chuckled, he said, "You're the only *man* who's ever asked. The ladies like to hear a little gossip. They like to hear about Lana Turner and Myrna Loy."

"Big tips, I'll bet."

"Tips are funny," André told me. "The people you think cannot afford it often give you more than you expect. The ones who've got it keep it. They tend to be a little more close-fisted."

He sheared the sides of my head in silence. While my hair in its brass-colored strands snowed across my shoulders I fell into the kind of reverie a sight like that can cause. André would send me off looking much better, and I would call on Miss Sandusky confident of my appearance. Confident enough to act maturely, and to converse the way adults converse—about the weather and what's in the news and how much it costs to heat a house these days. A discourse you could print in Sunday-school pamphlets. Subjects civilized and safe, and paving the way, I would think, to calm discussions about being ordered out of town.

My low-life credentials had come up for review. Everything despicable about me had been found in order. The gavel had pounded on the judge's table, and a hundred dollars had been tossed into my lap. There's a lot of material for adult conversation in that. I would be taking my floral-scented self to Miss Sandusky's house. There was a little sadness in my heart when 'floral-scented self' occurred to me. I knew what stinks I hoped the barber's scent would cover.

"I probably shouldn't tell you this because it's speaking out of turn." André had begun his scissors work on top. "I won't mention any names, and I don't think you'd know her even if I did. The woman who tips worst is the one who's got the most. And I do wonders on her hair. She likes it at exactly the right length. A boyish length is what I call it. She probably wouldn't like to hear me say that. She calls it feathered. She wants it feathered along the sides and almost crew-cut short on top. She comes in twice a month. That's how particular she is. And on each second visit I do highlights. She wants the same shade as a snow fox. That's how she describes it. Silver but not too silvery. A kind of non-color, if you see what I mean, except with the way she dresses it's exactly right."

"I'm picturing a Mrs. Santa Claus, André."

André clipped more on my scalp before he answered. "Not exactly. If she slides down chimneys it's only to bring coal. She isn't poor. That's one thing I can say for sure. She's got a lot of dough, but also a tight fist."

André sighed and perhaps would have said more but the little bell above the door went ting-a-ling. I heard a man ask, "You busy?" and André answer, "Take a seat." When I could steal a glance at the newcomer, I saw a man who could have been a pharmacist. He looked undistinguished by choice, and when he meekly did what he'd been told—when he took a seat against the purple wall—he picked up a copy of *Look* magazine and began to read in such a civilized and patient way I couldn't help but weigh what his calm behavior said about the world in which he lived.

The soul of civilization, I told myself, is barbershop decorum. It's being told to take a seat, and it's obeying that instruction. It's waiting your turn. My father, whoever he might have been, walked into barber shops and was told to take a seat. If I'd had brothers, they would have done the same. Should I have sons, the chain will be unbroken—into barber shops they'll go, and they'll pick up *Look* to pass the time of waiting.

That's what I was thinking when André interrupted his patient clipping and spoke to the seated man. "We were just talking about you-know-who, Sid. Miss Got-Rocks. Miss Snooty. You can tell from her gold DeSoto and her fancy pastel suits she's got more dough than anybody needs."

I knew whom he meant by 'she.' The silver hair. The snootiness. The fancy pastel suits. I did not have to search my mind a lot to picture someone seated in the Windward Bar sipping complimentary Champagne.

"What do you think she does with all that money, Sid?" André only asked his question to keep the conversation going. He may have hoped that Sid would make some witticism in reply.

But Sid spoke soberly: "She hides it from the IRS."

Andre laughed. He said, "Al Capone made that same mistake. What it got him was eleven years."

"He had a dumb lawyer." Sid spoke without lifting his eyes from *Look*.

Andre clipped a few stray hairs, then he said, "Capone played banjo in the Alcatraz band."

From Sid, his eyes on *Look*: "He had syphilis so bad Johns Hopkins wouldn't treat him."

"He could have been saved with penicillin, Sid."

"Saved for what?"

Sid spoke so sourly what he said was not a contribution to the conversation. It was a means for killing it.

André, silent, brought his hand mirror into exactly the position needed for me to admire the back of my head. How rarely one gets that opportunity. How sad the back of the head must feel to be so frequently ignored. I can't remember ever hearing the beauty of it praised. And yet it does its humble work day after day, covering the brain and growing hair. Providing a rear platform for the hat. Getting combed and brushed in a mostly cursory manner. I'm sure it feels neglected. Perhaps it feels wronged. The day may come—I'm only mentioning this as a remote possibility—when all the backs-of-heads in the whole world revolt. I can imagine them popping off like nutshells. Running up and down the streets, and arming themselves. Overthrowing governments. Dissolving legislatures. Hanging tyrants. Establishing the universal brotherhood of the backs-of-heads and proclaiming liberty to all, including former felons off to call on female beauties, and as shy as boys about it, shy and nervous, feeling woefully inadequate, even though they've gone to the expense of laying out two-fifty to a barber for a trim.

I had been tonsorially splendified, and André, sweeping off the barber's bib that had covered my chest and lap, released me from the adjustable throne and sent me forth into the world, suitable for swaining.

I stood at the bottom of the Seward Street hill counting the stairs I'd have to climb to Miss Sandusky's house. Her street had been carved out between two bluffs, and stairs climbed each side of it like wooden brackets corralling the stream of concrete pavement. The stairs and their railings had been fashioned from spruce. The wet wood gleamed, and the stairs climbed into a veil of mist. Staring up, I thought I could surely be forgiven for imagining I was climbing to a castle in the clouds. Not a magic castle with cupids drawing golden bows and shooting silver arrows. Arrows piercing my prison-suit-wrapped flesh at the top of Miss Sandusky's stairs would have been the arrows of self-doubt. How reliable was my underarm deodorant? Was my pocket hanky clean? Were my pants appropriately zipped?

I hate confessing to the weakness of these thoughts. I'd rather report I shot up Miss Sandusky's stairs like the hero in a romantic movie. I'd like to say I boldly hammered on her door. I did not face the task ahead of me with heart-pounding dread, but I faced it with uncertainty. I knew my knock on Miss Sandusky's door would be tepid. Tepid is the bland face of fear.

I doggedly climbed the stairs, and before I knocked, I turned to see the view Miss Sandusky's hilltop gave me. Through the mist, I saw cloud tatters clinging to the mountains across the Narrows. Not mountains, actually, but, on the larger island facing

Boon, hills ambitious to have mountain status. Another smaller island in between had no hills big enough to give it ambition privileges. That island lay lumpy, like a fallen, twisted branch. Along its rocky shore, lights had started showing in windows of cabins or shacks, and smoke rose pencil-thin from cockeyed chimneys made of steel pipe.

I turned from the landscape. I summoned my nerve. I knocked. A large man answered. He thrust a paw in my direction. "Hi," he said. "I'm Chip. You must be the knight in shining armor."

"Don't let Chip scare you, Alan," Miss Sandusky called from somewhere out of sight. "I've got his collar and his leash. If he gets frisky, I can take him for a walk."

She came in view with a frilly apron on, an apron the size of a tea towel. She grinned at the man who was, I already knew, the one I had seen her stroll away with on the first day we had met. He seemed to appreciate what she had said in jest about a collar and a leash. Not only his face, but his whole body lit up with a smile. His smile had a lot of work to do, because his body wasn't small. It was big and awkward-looking, like something put together out of spare parts commandeered from body junk yards. He had more knobs than it seemed necessary for a human being to lay claim to. He protruded, but he didn't bulge. There was nothing fat about him. Except in his puppy friendliness, he didn't seem one bit like the dog Miss Sandusky's joke had implied. He seemed like a young colt, with a young colt's bumpkin wholesomeness. He looked like he had not yet gotten his limbs under his supervision and control. If he had stepped sideways unexpectedly, I imagine he would have fallen over. He even had ruddy, reddish hair that slid in one great slab across his forehead, like the forelock of a colt. It fell so far it almost needed brushing back so he could peer out of his warm, friendly eyes and take in all the things that delighted and amused him. Such as convicted killers spruced-up and made presentable enough to call on attractive employees of the D.A.'s office, like Darlene, who offered me her hand and while I held it lightly in my own did something totally surprising. She kissed my perfumed cheek.

"Whoa!" Chip roared. He seemed to have no way of talking except to roar. "I didn't get a kiss when I came in."

Both he and Miss Sandusky laughed about his comical complaint.

"He doesn't bite, Mr. Sweetcheeks." Darlene still held my hand. She led me from her entry hall into her living room.

Lumbering behind me came the very friendly Chip. "She's got crab-salad sandwiches." He roared that news in what I had already come to recognize was his standard bellow. "And guess who cut the crusts off each slice of sandwich bread. Go ahead and guess who volunteered for that hard work."

"Chip would win the crust-cutting prize, if there was such a thing." As Miss Sandusky spoke, she turned to leave the room. At the door, she paused and looked back over her shoulder. "He's in the Coast Guard, Mr. Sweetcheeks. Ask him what he does."

She disappeared at the same time her other guest let out a whoop. Whooping, I would come to learn, was the way Chip greeted every new idea that came into his head. Before he spoke in words, when his whoop still lingered fog-horn sized in the calm air of the living room, he took my arms, both of them, standing at my back, and guided me to where he wanted me to sit. When I was on a floral-patterned couch, facing a low coffee table, he stepped back and sucked in so much air his chest seemed to expand to dirigible proportions.

"I am the Coast Guard's dental hygienist," Chip announced. "I shouldn't say 'the' because I'm not the only dental hygienist in the entire Coast Guard. Good Lord, what a job that would be. I'd have to flit all over the country, wouldn't I. I couldn't stand still for a moment. Hawaii one day. Pensacola, Florida, the next. No. I am 'a' Coast Guard dental hygienist, and my range of endeavors—is that what I should say? should I say 'range of endeavors'—is the southeast portion of Alaska. All the towns along the coast, and the villages scattered here and there among the islands. In fact, almost entirely villages, because the towns have their own dental hygienists, don't they. The towns of southeast Alaska are well served, dental hygienist-wise, but the villagers are not. The villagers appreciate occasional visits by hygienists the Coast Guard sends to teach dental hygiene ABCs. I don't know if there actually are dental hygiene ABCCs. What I teach them—what I teach the children mostly—is the proper way to brush. You surely know the proper way yourself, Mr. Sweetcheeks. It's up on the down teeth and down on the up teeth."

As Chip spoke, he demonstrated what he meant. He parted his big lips to expose as many of his teeth as he could. He held his hand close to his mouth, demonstrating, roughly, how he'd hold it if he had a toothbrush to maneuver. When he'd established what his pantomime would be, he vigorously demonstrated what he taught, saying "Up on the down teeth," as he pretend-brushed his inferior dental arch, and 'Down on the up teeth," as he did the same, with equal energetic spirit, to his superior dental arch.

He was still in full pretend-brushing mode when Darlene returned from the kitchen, or wherever it was she had gone, minus her dainty apron. She was carrying a platter about the same size as a hub-cap heaped with crab-salad treats.

"Gosh, I could have brought that, Darlene," Chip said. "I'll go get the tea pot, though." In two steps, he had left the room. He left it the way I imagine a giraffe would have left it, with a certain clownish grace, almost freakishly displayed.

What Miss Sandusky wore was a dress I'd say was purple, because that's all my limited color-vocabulary permits me to say. It was about the same color as a plum. But it caught the light dramatically, the way something silken would. Light shimmered at her hips and at her bosom. I was glad I'd gotten my hair tended. I was glad I'd cleaned the mud off my shoes.

She sat beside me after she had set down her laden tray. "I owe you thanks," she said.

"Crab sandwiches are thanks enough," I told her. "More than I deserve. I want you to know that."

She smiled and gave the platter a quarter turn. Perhaps she thought the new alignment placed within my easy reach the sandwiches she considered most delectable.

"I hope we have the opportunity sometime to go out crabbing, Mr. Sweetcheeks. We can't do that in winter, but when summer comes it's wonderful for friends to whip out on a boat and place a few crab pots. On shore, we'll build a roaring fire out of driftwood. We'll fill a pan with water so it's boiling when crabs have been dropped into the pots. What a feast we'll have. We should make plans right now. We should pick a summer date."

"If I am here this summer, Miss Sandusky."

What I'd said gave Darlene pause. She had to weigh what her reply should be, so a silence of several seconds passed before she spoke again. "Boon has not been kind to you."

"I don't claim I suffered excessively. Someone bopped me on the head. A glancing blow. Only twelve stitches. Maybe they were being nice."

Miss Sandusky and I both smiled, like co-conspirators in a plot to elevate weak jokes.

"I'm sorry you haven't found Boon more to your liking, Mr. Sweetcheeks. Getting knocked on the head and left in the snow would sour almost anyone's opinion. Are your plans definite? When would you be leaving? Do you have a date in mind?"

She reached for a crab-salad sandwich. I reached for one myself.

"I have not entirely made up my mind, Miss Sandusky. The conking on the head goes into the *leave* part of the scale. Crab-salad sandwiches, I must admit, go into the part that tells me *stay*."

She smiled. "There's lots of crab salad."

We said no more, because right at that moment, Chip, with all the subtlety of a mine-shaft explosion, burst out of the kitchen with tea things on a tray. He had no more to say about techniques for brushing teeth, but he filled us in on the Louisiana home he'd left when he'd signed up for the Coast Guard. He said he had a cousin who yodeled on a lot of records country-western artists made. First, Chip yodeled a little bit himself, apologizing immediately after for his lack of skill. Then he named a lot of country-western artists, many more than my slim acquaintance with that branch of the music industry allowed me to recognize. The best I could manage by way of reply was a wan smile and frequent nods.

Chip was half-way through another story about a dog he used to own who could tell fortunes. Before he could completely explain the animal's unusual talent, he held up a finger, the way a person does to give a warning. "Uh-oh, folks," he said. "Flatulence."

He rose at once, wiping crab-salad remnants off his lips with a paper napkin, and tiptoed from the room, as if tiptoeing could ward off the wind he had to break.

When he was gone, Miss Sandusky, who had maintained a somewhat rigidly straight face while he was still in hearing range, explained, "He's spoken to his doctor about his colon health. His doctor thinks it's too much fiber in his diet."

Darlene and I then sat in silence, because once you've explained the cause for flatulence, what else is there to say?

"I'm back," Chip boomed with the same explosive power a typhoon or an earthquake would have used to announce it had returned. We three sat in conversation then, touching on topics of movies, and popular bars, and favorite ways to fry chicken—safe, dull, ordinary topics having nothing to do with proper tooth-brushing techniques or fortune-telling dogs, until the time seemed right for me to rise and say how much I had enjoyed seeing both of them. I heard them say—sincerely, I believed—they hoped they'd see me again.

Darlene, when my hat was in my hand and I was at the door, said she hoped I'd let her know about my plans to stay or leave.

"You'll be the first person I tell," I answered

She smiled in reply. She kissed me on the lips. Her puppy friend then did exactly the same thing. He applied his soft, warm, slightly soggy lips to mine and then we parted, as if what we'd done had been as normal as shaking someone's hand.

I was shown out to the porch, already drenched in early-evening dark, and the door to Miss Sandusky's closed behind me with a click that sounded as soft as a sigh, as if the door was glad to see the last of a convicted killer.

January is a cruel time to convince yourself you should remain on a rain-slicked island in the southeast part of Alaska. I returned, all wet, to my sparsely furnished rented room. I stretched out on my skinny mattress and applied my meager powers of analysis to the question: Should I go or stay? I thought about crab-salad sandwiches. I thought about a Coast Guard dental hygienist preaching to a congregation of six-year-olds the gospel of approved tooth-brushing techniques. *Up on the down teeth. Down on the up teeth.* I knew that little jingle-admonition would stay with me until I died. Staring in the bathroom mirror, I would repeat it every morning. Also, I would know, for the rest of my natural life, that an excess of fiber in the diet can cause flatulence. I would carry that nugget of practical knowledge around with me in my worn-out, shabby gladstone bag of understanding, which I would also fill with unexpected kisses, and *Open the Door, Richard* played well enough to win second-place trophies in small-town talent contests.

I wished I was smarter. I wished I was wiser. I wished I had answers to the big questions of my life. The big question currently grinding away like a Rototiller at my greasy, grey insides was whether or not I should stay in Boon or pack up and try my luck elsewhere. I had a hundred dollars. I was single. I was male. I could try my fortune somewhere nicer. Oregon, perhaps, Or I could hitchhike further south and sprawl on California's sunny beaches.

I fell asleep imagining the grittiness of sand clinging to my swimming trunks, and the cleansing power of big, Pacific Ocean waves. When I blinked awake, I had to hustle off to reach my favorite fine-dining establishment before it kicked its last bum out the door and locked up for the night.

The establishment to which I gave most of my dining trade stood on shaky piling half a block from the waterfront, beneath a faded sign that said 'Frontier Café.' The café sold, among other questionable offerings, chili from a steel tub for a dollar and a quarter a bowl. With one's chili, one got a cup of coffee and a slice of bread. One also had the pleasure of observing the cook, called Skid, stand on a stool to dump salt in his stovetop tub. Skid needed the stool because he couldn't do his pouring without a little height embellishment, and he emptied an entire, one-pound box of Morton's at a time. It may be that he washed his pot occasionally, but I had never seen him do it. As far as I could tell, beans went in, hamburger went in, sauce went in, and with adequate stirring chili con carne could be ladled out. The pot perpetually bubbled atop the burner. I didn't think of the process as cooking. I looked on it as a religious ceremony, or that's the way I would have thought of it if Skid, the tattooed cook, did not perform his pouring of the salt so obscenely. While he poured, he demonized politicians, bureaucrats, inspectors from the health department, and one of Boon's most prominent pest exterminators whose work, Skid insisted, was so inept cockroaches told jokes about him and rats knit him sweaters for Christmas.

Among those enjoying Skid's running commentary on the evening after my hilltop teté-a-teté, was the sawed-off dope who worked for Cal, the moron named Mike. He sat at the counter with the kind of grin a primate might display. With a bowl of the famous chili in front of him, he fingered his oyster crackers. He sipped his coffee, and he chuckled at the non-stop obscenities streaming out of Skid. I sat as far from Mike as I could get. If he recognized me from last November's blood-letting he gave no sign.

I had entered the Frontier in time to hear Skid holding forth on the iniquities of optometrists. I don't know why he was mad at optometrists. He then turned his wrath on certified public accountants. On he went, even while he took my order, to excoriate radio announcers. He declared all disc jockeys fairies. That blanket condemnation prompted laughs from Feeble-Minded Mike, in between his bites of steaming chili.

I had heard a bit more than I cared to about the sexual proclivities of D.J.s, when a fragrant bum beside me, having survived his bowl of chili, slid off his chrome-edged stool to slouch toward the door. I recognized the emaciated boy who slunk into his place. He was the child vagrant on whom I'd lavished a dime on the day Mr. Pinkham hired me. My first day in Boon, a day so full of promise—or so it seemed to me—I could squander a whole dime on a charitable extravagance.

Skid settled his furious gaze on the raggedy youngster. He halted his anti-D.J. tirade. The unexpected quiet put even Mike on edge. Up and down the counter, customers sat poised in suspense.

"Where's my god-damned money?" When Skid spoke, he pointed a scrawny finger at the skeleton child. The newcomer wore a jacket ripped under one armpit, and blue jeans with peek-a-boo knee holes. His lank hair hid his eyes, and from what I saw of his jaw and hands I would have guessed what he washed in was pond scum. His scabby hands disappeared as soon as Skid mentioned money. The young man plunged them into his jacket pockets and then the pockets of his pants. He dredged up quarters and dimes and nickels. Seventy cents. Seventy-five. Ninety. A counting of pennies. Ten of them. More searching of fathomless pockets. Another nickel. Another dime. At last, a dollar and a quarter, which Skid slid into his palm, counting each coin and announcing the total. He clamped the money in his fist but before he turned to his cash drawer, he thrust himself closer to the specter by my side. "This'll pay for what you ate last time. Don't think you're eating on the cuff again. You go to church for charity, Malcolm. Here you pay in cash, and if this is all the cash you've got..." He shook his fist full of coins under the boy's nose. "...you better trot your sorry ass out to the street right now, because no one here is going to foot your bill."

Skid stomped off to his cash drawer. The clink of spoons on bowls rose all up and down the greasy counter. A bowl of chili appeared in front of me, and I would have added my own clink to that cheerless chorus but the sadness of the boy, now sliding off his stool to shuffle toward the door, kept me from digging into my steaming bowl.

I did not know Malcolm except as a mooch. He had the same look as greasy smoke snaking up from a hobo's meager fire. He looked like a shower of gravel kicked out from under a railroad tie by the roaring wheel of a speeding train. Malcom looked uprooted and alone.

Uprooted and alone are words of desolation. You don't hear mothers using them to describe their snot-nosed kids. But mothers get uprooted, too, and carted off to whatever dumping ground for derelicts their skinflint city governments provide. A dumping ground for derelicts would be Malcom's destination, too. I knew that just by looking at him. And perhaps, simply by taking a glance at my saggy pants and shapeless jacket, he knew the same about me. Bums don't wear uniforms, because they don't have to. The world knows them by their slouch and shuffle. I saw myself in Malcolm, and I guessed he really, really needed that bowl of chili he had wandered in for. At a cost to myself of one-hundred and twenty-five pennies, I could make sure he ate. He then could make his way back to the sorry bed that was his consolation in the night.

I am not John D. Rockefeller, but I figured I could spring for one-hundred and twenty-five pennies. I pulled out my wallet. I slapped a buck on the counter. I fished a quarter out of my raggedy pocket. "Feed him," I said to Skid, and I jerked my thumb toward Malcolm.

I had not become, by that small gesture, a registered establishment figure in Boon, a man of public benevolence. The establishment, for the memberships it stingily doles out, exacts a higher price than a buck twenty-five. I became a benefactor in one bum's opinion, though. And one bum here, one bum there, pretty soon it starts adding up.

Don't buy tickets to my canonization ceremony, though. That' probably a long way off.

The clinking of spoons at the long counter ceased. Diners watched Skid drop a steaming bowl of chili in front of Malcolm. The boy began to slurp. The clink, clink, clink resumed, and Miniature Mike, from the far end of the counter, flashed a thumbs-up sign at me, at Malcolm, at the bowls of chili, at a cock-roach on the stained, weepy-looking wall, at the rain slanting its way down the windows, at the darkness of the night. Who knows what-all the cretin was celebrating with the signal from his thumb. Good luck? Good hope? Charity, perhaps?

Perhaps a better world, though that seems a bit far-fetched.

I awoke in my shabby lodging place next morning to the terrifying sound of Mrs. Tinsel banging on my door. She shouted that she had another prospect looking for a room—and if I planned on moving, she wanted me to do so right away.

I immediately yelled back to say I'd be taking advantage of her hundred-dcllar gift to return to the joyful haunts of my youth.

"In the meantime, Mrs. T, if you need some copper piping stolen, please don't hesitate to ask."

That same morning, I hurried to the Pan-Am office and plunked down the cash Mrs. Meringue-Head had given me for a ticket out of town.

On my way to the seaplane terminal, where I would catch the shuttle to the grown-up airport, I stopped to give bad news to Mr. Pinkham. "The band must learn to do without me. I'm on my way south."

He said, "Oh no," and told me he was sorry. "Is there something I can do to make you change your mind?"

"I'll miss dipping ice-cream bars in chocolate, Mr. P."

"Be nice if you could stick around and train Richie in that work."

"True, Mr. Pinkham, but we'd have to wait for spring. No need to crank out ice-cream bars in the dead of winter."

My ex-employer nodded, but he didn't do it to agree. He gave a nod of resignation, as if the dead of winter were a planetary fact he'd reluctantly come to terms with. I extended my hand. We shook and exchanged our farewells.

Rain was still falling with icy indifference when I reached the seaplane terminal. My shoulders and my seat both were soaked. I was shaking raindrops off my prison-issue hat when who should I run into but Celeste the Ample, the woman I had shared a seat-row with on my long flight north.

"Hi, Sam," she said in her breezy way.

"I'm not Sam."

She paid no attention to my dour reply. She said she hated winter. The long dark made her blue, and her cure for the blues was to fly to Seattle and spend a week at the Bon Marché and Frederick & Nelson's.

"Not the whole week, naturally," she said. "I have to eat. I like to get my hair done. The best part is the shopping, though. When I'm in Frederick's shoe department I'm in heaven. I once bought sixteen pair, all on the same day. My husband doesn't care, because I always look for bargains. I am one smart shopper. They don't pull their fancy sales tricks on me."

She paused just long enough to breathe luster on her ring, the one with a diamond the size of a baby's little toe. She polished it against her coat of Persian wool.

"Let me tell you something, Sam: Money talks. Let the boys behind the counter know you've got the dough and they'll tumble over backwards doing favors. Look at this coat. How much do you think it cost? If you say eight hundred dollars I'm going to laugh right in your face. Five-twenty-five. A bargain. And they ate the sales tax. I told them I didn't live in their damn sales-tax state so

I shouldn't have to pay it. 'Yes, Ma'am. Yes, Ma'am.' They actually bow when they say it. Let them know you've got the money and it's like you've got them on a string."

She paused to purse her lips and stare off into space, contemplating, I imagine, sales clerks on strings. Then she shot me a puzzled look. "What did you say your name was? How is it I know you?"

"We met on the plane coming north."

"You aren't the Stevens boy, are you? You've got the Stevens' ears."

I said my name wasn't Stevens but Sweetcheeks.

I should have known how she'd react. She had the hallmarks of a brayer. Her female ancestors, all brayers, had been scientifically mated with males of good braying stock. They had brayed through wars and revolutions and the Great Depression of the recent past. Celeste brayed now. She brayed with a vigor that did credit to her ancestry. She brayed with such exertion she had to fish in her expensive purse for her lace-trimmed hanky. I watched her dab her eyes.

"You're kidding, aren't you," she said when she could finally choke out those four words. "Your name is Sam. I know it is. And you're right about us meeting on that plane. You had your head all wrapped in bandages. Don't tell me why. I think I can remember. You'd had a run-in with—I may be wrong here; stop me if I am—you'd had a run-in with the charming Cal, the gal who keeps the cat house on the corner of the creek."

She tucked her delicate hanky back in her black purse. "You don't want to mess with Cal." Celeste spoke in a more sober tone. "You'll be mincemeat if you do. Cal had to grow up on the street. Her sister, too. Because her old man boozed up every dime he made. But hard knocks didn't hurt old Cal. Not one bit. Cal could buy and sell her daddy now, a hundred times over, if the poor old sot hadn't seen what he had sired and drunk himself to death."

Celeste spoke as if she were under contract to denigrate dead sots. She put her heart and soul into condemning that particular deceased. Delivered of the burden of what she owed the dead, she let her gaze drift through the crowded terminal until she caught sight of a bulk wrapped in the flayed skins of about four dozen mink. She navigated in the other bulk's direction, and the other bulk navigated in hers. They grappled when they met, and in a matter of mere seconds, they were guffawing.

I didn't regret the loss of my companion. My thoughts were not on Fredrick & Nelson or the Bon Marché. I was standing in a crowded, seaplane terminal surrounded by the wholesome kind of citizens who would square dance at your funeral if the opportunity arose. They had faces so broad you could cook lasagna in them. They wore expensive, dressy clothes, and the kind of shoes that probably cost what a dipper of ice-cream bars earns in a week. The hundred dollars I had shelled out for my airplane ticket wouldn't be enough to last Celeste for thirty seconds on one of her sweeps through the Bon Marché. I had never made a sweep through the Bon Marché. Had never even thought about it. I was a felon specializing in the theft of scrap metal. Copper pipes. Copper wires. Ten-penny nails by the gross. Chevy bumpers, or the bumpers of Fords. As a felon, I would arrive in Seattle with barely enough money for streetcar fare.

What I was truly was a punk. I was a punk, and society had dealt with me in its firmest manner. It had locked me up, and I would still have been locked up if the Second World War hadn't broken out in all its glory, and a broadcast call gone out inviting volunteers to bare their arms and line up for experiments to thwart blood-sucking bugs.

I was a punk, and being a punk had gotten me a kiss from a male dental hygienist. I am not going to say that being kissed by Chip, the dental hygienist well-versed in what causes flatulence, had anything to do with the thought taking shape in my rain-soaked skull. In the overheated terminal of a small-town flight provider, on the day my terrier landlady had told me to hie myself off. No sad thoughts like those tiptoed into my consciousness while I stood, clutching my sorrowful suitcase, with rainwater running off my clothes and puddling up on the floor.

But I couldn't fail to notice, in my desolation, a sly look sent my way from the woman in the martyred minks Celeste the Fleshy had corralled. More jokes, I imagined, about the ancient name of Sweetcheeks. More cruel laughter. I didn't have to hear the feeble witticisms the two gorgons exchanged. I knew what kind of personality delights in snide remarks.

I also knew—of course I knew—what kind of personality rounds up a team of criminals to assault gallant dippers of ice cream in chocolate sauce. It was a personality of fox fur casually shrugged off, a personality of Champagne on the house, a personality of gratuitous insults.

And it was a personality of hiding money from the IRS. Whoever beat the government to sniffing out Cal's hidden profits could commit the almost perfect crime. Who could the ogress complain to when she learned someone had gotten his hands on her tucked-away assets? She certainly couldn't complain to the law.

I returned post-haste to the Pan-Am office. An agent there with lips of cherry red listened to me tell a lie about a sudden illness striking down a brother, forcing me to cancel travel plans. "We thought at first it was merely indigestion, but he woke up with his whole left side stiffer than a frozen fish."

"Stroke?" she asked as she returned my money.

"And he's only twenty-four. He's younger than I am."

My story made cherry-lips sad, or she feigned sadness with professional skill. Her dark eyes turned liquid, as if she might shed tears except for fear of ruining her mascara. I planned to linger at the counter and tell the lady with fruit-tinted labials my stricken brother was a big-time skier and we feared he'd never take to the trails again. Also, that he was engaged to marry a young woman who'd lost the lobe of her left ear to frostbite at a campsite close to Yellowstone when she was only three. I didn't have a chance to engage her with those lies because a high-pitched, whiney voice drew me to an inner doorway at the far-end of the airline company's sleek office. The doorway, for the convenience of travelers, connected the Pan-Am office to the lobby of a hotel. There, chambermaids were standing at polite attention for instructions streaming from prissy Warren Arsenault, the same excessively dainty man who had accompanied Miss Sandusky to my performance at the free-drinks-for-pouring-on-the-floor bar. Warren stood behind his counter in pedicured glory telling a work-weary quartet the order of the vacant rooms to which they'd be required to lug their toilet brushes next.

Seeing Mr. Arsenault reminded me of what I'd told Darlene I'd do. I had promised Miss Sandusky she'd be the first to know my plan to stay in Boon or go. I had made that promise under the intoxication of crab-salad sandwiches. I probably would have written it off, except Miss Sandusky had rewarded what I'd said with a gentle kiss.

Chip, the dental hygienist, had done the same. I had no intention of telling Chip anything. I hadn't yet worked out in my own mind why he had kissed me. Perhaps there's a Coast Guard tradition, like drinking grog for breakfast, that tells a sailor he should kiss goodbye any soul who falls in kissing range. I'm not sure, of course, about grog traditions in the Coast Guard. They seem to go with saying, 'Matey,' and pulling on a lot of ropes to make the sails go up or down. My views on Coast Guard service may be dated. Let us leave the matter there and devote attention to the keeping of a promise made under the influence of crab-salad sandwiches.

I knew a promise of that sort need not be honored. Day in and day out, people make crab-salad promises. Such promises are like white lies. They are a social convention. One can discard a promise that gossamer like the wrapper of a stick of chewing gum. Miss Sandusky would not have taken seriously what she'd heard me say. She knew I was a felon, recently paroled, the killer of a scrap-yard owner, and the insulter of a hardened whore. No logical chain of thought would compel her to expect to see me trip into her office and proclaim my stay-in-Boon decision.

But is there any logic in sitting out the absence of a gentleman who has declared that he must leave the room for a flatulence emergency. I don't know why I even mention logic when it comes to young women and young men. I had a *wish* to trek once more to the green Federal Building and let Miss Sandusky know what I'd decided. Wishes are not kept in the logic compartment. In the cabinet of human capacities, wishes are kept in the drawer labeled *Will*. It was simply the *will* that told me, after leaving the Pan-Am office, where I should direct my steps.

In a matter of maybe six minutes, I stood puddling up Darlene's office floor. I stood in line behind a woman with a pixie haircut, her arms full of file folders, interminably chatting Darlene up. She blocked Miss Sandusky's view, until the second sense receptionists must have caused Darlene to peek around her pixie-headed friend, to check to see who new might be hidden by that friend's shoulders and her bosom and her butt.

Instantly, one of those receptionist alarms went off. The pixie-cut woman glanced over her shoulder, saw me, and launched an apology. "Sorry, sorry, sorry," she said on her way to the door.

Darlene called after her, "It's okay, Maisie." She meant that Maisie didn't have to hasten off. But that *isn't* what she meant. What she said was communication of a different kind, a communication, like a happy song, meant entirely for me.

I dragged off my hat, and then I couldn't stop pulling its brim through my fingers. It was like I had won the contract for straightening hat brims and I would fail the terms of that deal unless I persisted.

"Are you leaving, Mr. Sweetcheeks?" Darlene asked. That's how she broke the silence. She had glanced at my suitcase.

"Up until an hour ago I would have told you yes, Miss Sandusky."

Darlene's smile grew so welcoming she had to glance down at her desk to guard her private thoughts. Even so, her smile widened. "Boon is the land of opportunity, isn't it, Mr. Sweetcheeks."

"There are anthems on that subject, Miss Sandusky."

"The land of milk and honey."

"And crab salad sandwiches."

She laughed.

We bantered back and forth. The weather figured large in our exchanges before the weight of awkwardness sent our little bridge of conversation crashing.

"Will I see you again, Mr. Sweetcheeks?" As she spoke, Darlene offered her hand. I let it rest in my own, rough hand, like the petal of a rose. It seemed to me weightless, but as strong as steel cable. Something butterflyish happened to my heart. I felt a flutter. It seemed to me the flutter must communicate to Miss Sandusky my expectation of a kiss. If so, the flutter failed miserably to carry out the duty I had assigned it. Darlene let her hand float out of mine What lingered was a smile stretching those very pretty lips which had once been touched to mine in a gesture probably innocent on her part but helplessly wanton on mine.

I say nothing about Chip's kiss. I hadn't dared to try to cataloged that.

Darlene and I said goodbye. We promised that we'd see each other. I didn't leave intoxicated, but after I'd been standing in front of the closed elevator doors for a few minutes it occurred to me I couldn't remember if I had pushed the button that would summon the conveyance to Miss Sandusky's floor.

I pushed, but before I stepped inside the cage I looked to see if Darlene had poked her head out of her office to wave me a final goodbye.

In my heart and mind, she did, although in the drab, Federal Building corridor no such farewell was tendered.

Outdoors again, blasted by wind, blasted by rain, quickly zipping up my flimsy jacket, I looked left and right. The fact is, I had no place to go to rest my head. To my left was what Boon called its downtown. Grocery stores. Hardware stores. Emporiums selling men's clothing and intimate garments for women. In that direction, too, lay the dusty-smelling rooming house where Mr. Tinsel had accommodated me until his wife bargained my bed right out from under me and booted me out on the street.

In the other direction lay the lair of the fox-furred harlot who had issued orders detrimental to the health and beauty of my head. It occurred to me that were I to stay in Boon—as my new plan dictated—I ought to come to some understanding with Cal. She was, I had been warned, not a person to tangle with. I had scars to prove the wisdom of that warning.

On the other hand, I was a convicted killer, and a warning to others not to tangle with me might be a courteous thing to deliver.

I am putting matters a little mildly here. If I were to continue my life in Boon, I could not assume Cal might not again assign her goons to use my head for batting practice. I could politely advise her against doing that.

That was the fuzzy logic that shaped my determination.

I turned to the right and set off in the direction of the bar I knew Cal owned.

It was the worst decision I have made in my entire life.

I hauled my sorry suitcase two blocks down the dreary, rainy street to the bar where Cal the Cruel housed her harlots and her goons. Metaphysically speaking, I went armored with sass. Professors of Sass at renowned institutions will tell you sass is an artificial armor. It's worn for its appearance, not its fighting strength. It's composed of disdain and derision. Its buckles are plastic and its breastplates are tin. It crumples up when darts are thrown at it. Against the sword of stalwartness and righteousness it offers no protection whatsoever. You might as well sally forth to battle hardened whores armored in gift wrap. It's like you're making a little present of yourself to them. I knew all that, and after my moment of reflection, I nevertheless determined to sally with brio and dash. Brio and dash were what I had brought with me from Chicago's nighttime streets. They had been my wardrobe during all my prison years. The other name for qualities that chintzy is bravado. But my middle name has always been bravado.

A short bridge I halted before spanned a creek where that creek entered one of Boon's small-boat harbors. The creek flowed past a couple dozen houses lining both its banks. The houses were unsavory in both their moral reputation and physical fact. They were reputed to be occupied by workers in the sex trade. I had had to eye them wistfully on that account because I'd never accumulated enough un-earmarked cash to test the sex-worker hypothesis. The physical unsavoriness of those houses on the creek's stone banks, however, was unmistakable. They discharged their waste water—toilet paper and all—directly into the stream they straddled on their skinny piling legs.

That stream was green and fat and oily looking when the tide was high, but let ebb tide come and the same stream became a briny, foam-specked youngster, volatile and agitated. It was like having two streams in the middle of your town for the price of one. I'm sure the citizens of Boon appreciated the economy of that. They had awarded the stream the name 'Boon Creek.' It was a stream of different guises, a chameleon creek. At one moment sluggish and lazy, at the next full of flash and dazzle. It could inspire moods of contemplation in a person viewing it, and an hour later unsettle and roil him with thoughts of scampiness and having fun. How like the human being in that regard Boon Creek was. How unanchored and changeable. Inconsistent, too. It was a stream of swinging moods, eager at one second for excitement and reluctant the next to expend the energy it takes to even sigh. It was a philosopher's creek. That's what it was, and I might have called it the Creek of Common Humanity. Except for the toilet paper, of course. Except for the god-damned toilet paper.

When I raised my head from the meditations I had been indulging, I saw not Common Humanity suspiciously eyeballing me but Common Sub-Humanity. Mike, the moral equivalent of what I thought of in my more light-hearted moments as toilet paper, had taken up a watch-dog stance beneath the wood marquee of the bar I knew was Cal's, a bar called the Bayside. A watch-puppy stance, actually. He fixed his dopey gaze on me just long enough for it to register he ought to run and warn his boss. Where his boss was, heaven knows. Poisoning apples, probably. At any rate, Mike's squirrel brain made a connection. He quit his post to dart into the Bayside's dim interior.

I would have been known to Mike as the victim of a professional conking. If he was a reasonably efficient watchman, he might suspect my ratty suitcase held a Thompson sub-machine gun fully loaded. 'No such luck, Sweetcheeks,' I told myself. No automatic weapon tucked in among my socks and underwear. Even so, I strode purposefully toward the Bayside as if I went armed. I did not have mass murder on my mind. What principally propelled me toward my fate was a normal person's natural wish not to cringe and truckle during the coming months he'd spend in rainy Boon.

I puffed my chest. I squared my shoulders. And I stepped inside the bar.

Before my eyes adjusted to the dimness, my nose let me know I'd found a bar with a long heritage. I had entered a space redolent of spilled beer and ten million cigarettes. In a room rectangular and rich in shadows, I faced a bar well stocked in the classic fashion with bottles of Old Grand-Dad and Wild Turkey shelved against a mirror. The mirror and the bar in front of it ran the length of a long wall. Behind the bar, a bartender kept himself busy polishing glassware. He had the husky look of someone who, in his spare time, might swing a baseball bat at some unsuspecting person's head. Others in the room were shadows to me. They lolled in attitudes of relaxation, one or two on stools and one or two afoot in casual stances, propped up against the bar with the appearance of sobriety.

I had stepped on something crunchy before I'd even closed the door. It could have been a peanut shell, or it could have been the tooth of someone who'd crossed Cal. To me, it represented the sanitary standards to which the proprietor adhered. I was trying to pick the proprietor out of the smoky figures lounging at the bar when one of those figures twisted around to face me.

I saw Fresh Beauty in the flesh, a slender someone maybe only twenty-one but with enough experience of men to have mastered the erotic glance—the briefness of it, the indirectness, the half-lowered lashes made to bank the smolder in the eyes, the turning away that follows, and then the industry of indolence, the tapping of a cigarette or the idle stirring of a drink.

One glance like that—one glance is all it takes—and the imagination begins to throw its lurid images on the mind's invisible screen. A young man's self-control melts like a snow pack in the springtime Rockies. If not the Rockies, then in the small-potato foothills that are most young males' moral self. I said yes to all my sluices and my freshets. I said yes to the sweet power of the sun. And as I was assenting to that quick defrosting of what you might think of as my moral rectitude, I heard another lounger call out a mocking welcome, "Look who's here. Prince Charming."

The speaker was Cal. The smirking whore's scrawny throat was covered with a chiffon scarf of very nearly the same powdery blue as her pastel pants-suit. She would have been a handsome woman if she didn't have a face so sharp a homesteader in need of firewood might have picked her up by a skinny shank and used her to split logs.

"Hoping for a damsel in distress, bub?" she said. "You won't find distressed damsels here. My damsels take care of themselves. They're all two-fisted."

She sipped her drink and then she added, "I hope you've come to kiss my ass. I deserve it after what you did with the drink I sent. Wasn't good enough for your high moral standards, I suppose. Sunday school standards, if my guess is right. How proud your mother's going to be. I hope you write her soon to let her know you indignantly spurned my offer of a drink. In her evening prayers she'll offer up her thanks for allowing her to raise a son superior to vice."

"I am not superior to vice, Cal, and I have the documentation to prove it. That's what I've come to talk about."

She dropped her eyes from mine to give a smirking glance at her pinkish drink. She lifted them again with a look that dared me to go on.

"I did some dental work on the owner of a scrap-metal yard back east. He didn't volunteer for dental work, nor did I have any experience providing that service. As a result of my perhaps clumsy administrations he died, I'm sad to say."

Cal listened with a smile. She sipped her drink and set it carefully down. "I'll register what you've said as a threat, son. If it will help you to think of me as shaking in my boots, please feel free to do so. There isn't any harm in what you think. Although, you ought to know, while we're on the subject, I had my dental work all done a dozen years ago, so you're a little late with your offer. The dentist hurt like hell. Dental work always does. But then, you yourself have probably learned a lot about what hurts. No need to trade documentation on that. We'd end up in a draw, I'm pretty sure."

She smiled, and the mere fact that she had stopped speaking was enough to make her burly bartender perk his ears in our direction. He might have reached for a bat at a signal from his master but Cal didn't signal. She spoke again instead. "It always raises a person, in my estimation, when I can assume he's a crook. Be proud of your distinction. Flaunt your documentation, son. I'm sure it will impress a lot of people. What I should tell you, though, is that a person sinks—again this is merely my personal opinion—if I suspect that he's a chump. And anyone who rides around on a white horse defending a damsel as plain as potato blight, or any damsel at all for that matter, falls into the chump category. You set yourself up. Not that I would hold your chumpness against you. You probably can't help it. It's your training at your mother's knee. What you *can* help, however, is what you did with my politely offered drink. You embarrassed me, young fellow, and it's only out of the goodness of my heart that I am not going to ask Jerry here, my bartender, to make applesauce out of what you call your brain. I'm going to give you a chance to make good. Get out a dollar. No, get out two. Wave them so Jerry can see."

I hadn't any intention of reaching for my wallet. Cal must have known that. She snapped her fingers and her bartender came trotting up. When he loomed over us Cal nodded toward me. "He wants to buy someone a drink," she told him.

"Not you," I hastened to say. I imagined a replay of our earlier scene, only this time Cal would pour out the proffered drink.

The silver-haired harlot didn't bother to answer. She shouted to a shadowed figure at the far end of the bar. "Breen, honey. This cowboy here would feel honored if you'd let him treat you to a drink."

A slender woman—the one I had christened 'Fresh Beauty'—snaked her way along the bar in our direction.

"Her tits are small but exquisite," Cal whispered in my ear. "And if you've got the money, son, she can show you a good time."

The old whore slid off her stool. At almost the same time the beauty she called Breen brushed her body against mine, her touch as delicate as smoke.

I've never been one to knock sex, but Breen brought me to a tiny room above the Bayside Bar that was so cold I told her, when I handed my ten dollars over, she should complain to Cal.

"She don't like that," Breen said, and she jumped beneath the covers before her skin turned blue.

The fireworks that followed were probably better than the standard-issue fireworks. Not that I had much I could compare them to. Also I was so eager for the joy of what I'll call the primal act I wasn't weighing merits and demerits as we went through all the pleasant motions of the deed. I will say this, however—the bed was much too short, and the big toe of my left foot cramped up against the footboard in such an awkward way it launched shooting pains all up my leg when what we did was over and Breen was asking if I had a cigarette.

I said I didn't smoke.

"Never mind, then, honey. Reach into that drawer there and see if I got any Chesterfields left."

The drawer she meant, in the nightstand by her bed, stuck when I jerked to pull it open. The lamp on top, the only light in the small room, teetered and might have fallen if I hadn't steadied it.

Chesterfields in their wrinkled package lay in the drawer with a few condoms and a lighter in the shape of someone's middle finger being raised.

"Isn't that cute?" Breen had touched the lighter's flame to the tip of her cigarette. "Somebody gave it to me. Some guys are really, really nice. Some are jerks, of course. Say, aren't you hungry? Would you like a drink? We could order something. We wouldn't even have to leave the room. Just you and me. Romantic. But could I put your jacket on? I'm freezing."

The 'something' we ordered turned out to be steaks brought to the room by the diminutive and suggestively smirking Mike. One steak for her and one for me. They came with French fries. After Breen had eaten all of her fries, she ate most of mine. She made up for it, she said, by sharing her drink. The truth is, I drank all of mine and most of hers. She didn't seem to be a liquor kind of woman, but she was ravenous for food.

The bedside lamp was shaded in such a heavy way the shabbiness in which we'd screwed was somewhat hidden. But even shadows couldn't quite disguise the water-stains that streaked the ancient wallpaper, or the cracks in the ceiling's creamy plaster. On four wall hooks near the door, Breen's wispy-looking frocks and chemises hung. On the wall behind the headboard hung a mirror so cheap it gave a fun-house-like distortion to the shabbiness it showed.

Breen must have done her make-up in that mirror, because, sitting beside her in bed while she wolfed down everything the shrimp factotum brought, I had a chance to see a stretch of wrinkles as her jawbone worked and to notice that her scalp showed pinkish underneath her thin, bleached hair.

The Fresh Beauty I had seen downstairs had been my own invention. Not that Breen was homely. I would hesitate to even suggest such a thought. But I can say, from close observation, her nose and ears were mouse-sized, and her fingers were the fingers of a child. She kept her thin lips mostly pressed together. When she parted them to smile her incisors on top protruded in a way that might have made a man more critical than I recall the ability of beavers to gnaw through the trunks of birch and alder trees.

I didn't think of those aquatic mammals when I looked at her scalp through her thin hair. The thought came to me that this young woman had crawled out of some hovel in an Appalachian coal town and had had to scramble for enough to eat all the way to Cal's. She was, in terms of scrambling, probably a lot like me, so when she purred, "You want to stay the night, hon?" and snuggled up against me, adding, almost in a whisper, "We could have some fun," I shelled out the additional twenty she said the night would cost. She squealed when she saw it and traced a line with her cold finger from the hollow of my collar bone down to between my legs.

Morning came, and she told me Mike knew a place that made the best breakfasts in Boon. "Hash browns and eggs any way you like them. Bacon, too. The works. Or they can give you pancakes with real maple syrup if you want."

Breakfast it was, and then more mattress athletics. When Breen suggested dinner again, about mid-afternoon, I had to tell her I was broke.

She found thirteen dollars in my wallet. She had asked if she could look. Two more in change showed up in the pocket of my pants. She said I didn't have to spend it if I didn't want. "You can make your mind up later. First, we'll do a walk, and while we're out I'll tell you about all the fun things we could do for fifteen bucks."

She didn't have a heavy coat so she borrowed my ratty sweater and put her light raincoat on over it. She clung to my arm and wobbled on her heels across the street. We stood on the same steel bridge where I had meditated on the meaning of the toilet paper I had seen coiling toward the harbor. When she tired of watching slips of steam rise from the slime-green waters, Breen said she wanted to show me a dress she wished some nice guy would buy her. To reach the dress store we had to walk toward the Federal Building.

Breen held tight to my right arm and rested her head on my shoulders. She must have majored in clinging at Prostitution U. That's how close we were together. She snuggled so tight you couldn't have squeezed a dime in between us, and in that intimate pairing we rounded the Federal Building bend.

Right around that corner, we ran into Darlene. "Oh, Mr. Sweetcheeks." Miss Sandusky gasped. "I was on my way to Yakamoto's. I didn't think I'd see you. I was going for green tea."

She had rushed out on her errand with her little hat, its flimsy and inadequate veil doing whatever veils of that sort were invented to do. The odd thing is—I mean odd from my unsophisticated point-of-view—I liked it. I saw a woman in a hat reminiscent of the hats once worn by Eleanor Roosevelt, and I knew the woman wearing that old-fashioned hat had kissed me. It hadn't been the kind of kiss Breen the Nearly Hairless had lavished on parts of my anatomy I'm not even going to mention. It had been a kinship kind of kiss—the kiss a mother bestows on a child or a sister on a brother. It was a kiss that said, 'I like you, and I wish you well.'

Although, from the look on Darlene's face, it seemed immediately clear I wasn't going to get that kind of kiss again. She wore an unhappy and guarded look. Her eyes had locked on Breen's, but her expression of revulsion didn't say Breen was a young woman. If Darlene's expression was an accurate guide, what she saw clinging to my arm was as soiled as a well-worn butcher's apron or as disgusting as a just-removed appendix gleaming in its operating room's convenient bucket of blood.

I watched Darlene do a thing I'd never seen her do before. With two trembling fingers, she touched her diminutive veil. The touch must have confirmed for her the reality of what she saw. The reality was that the man who'd shined his shoes to impress her when he'd come to call—the man to whom she'd fed crab-salad sandwiches—the man who'd gobbled down at least a half a dozen of those delicious treats—stood before her with a hooker on his arm.

Miss Sandusky let her hand fall from her veil.

She immediately fled.

"She doesn't always wear that hat, does she?" Breen did not ask her question in kindness. "I hope she doesn't think that thing looks cute." Kindness would have been a foreign language to a woman of Breen's delicacy. Yet she didn't speak in malice, either. She spoke our species' mother tongue—the thoughtlessness language in its stupidity dialect.

"I don't think I've got the time to look at that dress, Breen."

"You don't have to *buy* it."

I had never said I'd buy her the dress she wanted, nor any dress. If we had gone to look at a dress that cost sixteen ninety-five, I would have been about two dollars short. I don't know what dresses cost so I can only make a guess about its price. But Breen had spoken in a way that told me two things. She was letting me off the hook, for one thing. 'You don't have to buy it,' means exactly what it says. But she was speaking out of contempt, too. Contempt for what she must have seen as my cheapness, and contempt for a frame of mind that made me think—correctly, I am sure—she was only clinging to my arm and cooing in my ear in hopes such subtle tactics would charm me into adding to her wardrobe.

"You want to keep my sweater while we walk back to the bar, Breen?"

What I said wasn't subtle. I was letting her know our outing was over. The bloom was off the blemished rose.

"And that hat you're referring to, Breen, is not old-fashioned or out of date. It is not something unsophisticated, if by *that* hat you mean headgear a young woman of your exquisite taste would never wear herself. The hat Miss Sandusky wore looked to me much like the hats worn by a former first-lady. When I say 'first-lady' I'm referring, of course to the wife of a president. I hope you understand that honorific. The former first-lady wore it when she visited hospitals with wounded soldiers in them, or visited the tenements she had vowed would not continue their flea-ridden service to our nation's poor. Those are the kind of things I associate with hats like Darlene wore. Although I guess those concepts might be difficult for someone with buck teeth to comprehend."

Breen came back fighting. "Was that name she called you your real name or is it one she made up? It's a very funny name. A pet name, I guess. Is she a girlfriend or something?"

"It's my real name. I've got a funny name, just like some people have thin hair. You think that's a big deal?"

"You're sore at me, aren't you."

"If I was sore at you, I'd take my sweater back right now. I'd let you shiver in your dirty raincoat and your bargain-basement frock all the way back to your shabby room."

Breen stopped. Her look let me know that saying *bargain-basement frock* hurt. The words violated whatever contract linked her and me. It was very much like calling her a bargain-basement whore. It was mean and cheap and wounding. "Let's not talk about who's sore and who isn't, Breen." I took her arm to hurry her along. "I'm cold. I've got a lot of things to do. I have to find a job. I have to find a place to live. Other things like that."

"You're going back to find the lady with the hat."

"If you have to call her anything, call her a lady with class, Breen. That's what she is. She's a classy person, so do you think a bum like me would go chasing after her? I'm surprised she noticed me. She's got better things to do."

"She noticed, all right."

Breen had gotten even, and when we reached the bar, she pulled my sweater off. I took it from her hand. She put one foot on the raised stoop. Before she climbed, she turned with a question: "Did you get your money's worth?"

She hadn't put her raincoat back on. She looked scrawny in her skimpy dress, and she had to hug herself to keep from shivering. Rain had plastered her hair down. She had asked her question for vengeance. She was weighing everything we'd done together in dollar terms. What we'd done I'd bought in dollars. There's no doubt about the truth of that. But I had thought, 'Fresh Beauty.' And she had talked of fun.

What I replied to her was not sour-motivated. I said, "You bet, Breen."

She laughed, because *you bet* is not an answer. It left the answer up to her. She could think, if she took it in her mind to spare a generous thought, that she had made me happy.

She quick-stepped up the outdoor stairs to the carnality suite above. I stood thinking toilet-paper thoughts and was surprised when she came hurrying back down. I should not have been surprised. She brought my beat-up suitcase and dropped it at my feet. With squirrel-like dexterity, she scampered up and out of sight again.

I was left out in the rain with no companion except self-disgust. Miss Carnality, on her high heels, had gone tottering away. I had spent nearly everything I had on her. Worse than that, I had lost my chance to woo, if I ever had the nerve to take that chance, Our Lady of the Hat Like Eleanor Roosevelt's.

On my way to Mr. Pinkham's, imagining creative ways in which I might beg for my job back, I came across the carcass of a wolf. The beast hung suspended from the wood marquee that protected the recessed entrance of a waterfront sporting-goods store. It was not unusual for that particular store to display dead wolves. Wolves were the island's outlaws, four-legged competitors for the white-tailed deer that sportsmen with rifles considered it solely their privilege to slaughter. The store I approached was one of several in Boon authorized to pay the fifty-dollar bounty the territory dished out to killers of wolves. I had passed similar displays on earlier occasions. Each time I saw a different wolf hung up by its hind legs, left to dangle for a day while the wind rippled through its black or silver fur. The animal had lived a savage life in dells and bogs and hidden places of the woods. One might, by thinking hard, imagine him bringing down a doe or fawn and spilling out its steaming entrails like wet jewels on the frost-tinged, forest moss. Such savagery. It has the stamp of the convicted killer. The wolf obeys no law except the law of his own making. He doesn't care if chipmunks don't like him or if blue jays in their raucous conversations condemn his slashing and ripping of tender deer flesh. He doesn't care if he comes around a corner with a lady wolf of shady reputation hanging on his arm and encounters a female of more decorous reputation with whom he is acquainted. Yet here hangs Mr. Wolf, brought down by a bullet no bigger than a bee. A dolt with a Remington or Winchester had robbed the splendid animal of his carefree, cunning life.

I had stooped to admire the incisors and molars in the beast's frightful mouth when two boys, about fourth-graders by my guess, with their school books under their arms, stopped to confront the wolf of their nightmares, the big, bad wolf, the one they would have fled screaming had they come upon him in the woods. One boy dared the other to touch the dreadful teeth. The dared boy extended a skinny finger but withdrew it before he made contact. He passed the dare back to the second boy, as pre-pubescent custom dictated. The second boy had just put out a tentative finger when a commanding voice said, "Don't touch."

A man in shirt sleeves had stepped out from the store. I guessed the store was where he worked. Anyone else—any passerby or customer making a store visit—would have had a winter jacket on, and a stocking cap, and mittens. "Run along," he said, and when the boys failed to trot off as quickly as he wished, he waggled his fingers at them in a way that said, "Skedaddle."

"Varmints," the man said to me when the boys had hurried off.

I asked him if he needed help at the store. I said I was looking for a job.

The man was wiry and bald. What fringe of hair he had around his ears was pepper colored. He had a hungry-looking face. If he'd been turned loose in the woods, I could imagine him bringing down a doe or two himself, armed with nothing more than fangs and claws. Not that he was clothed in fur. He wore ordinary pants, and a flannel shirt, and he sported gold suspenders.

"I'm of a very mixed mind about paying money for these wolves," he said. "Of course, I have to do it. I'm the agent for a government that wants the wolf eliminated. It's the government that pays the bounty. All I do is hand the money out—which sportsmen like, and I'm in the sportsmen-pleasing business."

He said all this in a voice of challenge, as if he hoped I'd disagree and argue. But I was in a job-supplicant's position. I had thrown a job-seeker's cloak of politeness and submission over my wet shoulders. So all I did was stand and look expectant, as if I hoped for more enlightenment on the subject of dead wolves.

"Come here," the man said. "I want to show you something." He led me just a few steps from his door and pointed to a sign on display in his shop's window. "I sell these signs," he said. "I sell a lot of them." The sign was of a size to be easily read from dozens of paces away. It said, "Property of ______________. Trespassers will be shot." The blank was where a homeowner would ink in his name.

"I've got this sign posted at my hunting cabin. I won't tell you where my cabin is. You'd probably go help yourself to my supplies. You might even wreck my cabin. People have done that before. God damn them. The sign will give them second thoughts. If not, they know the consequences. They'll know they have been warned."

I asked him if his sign had worked so far.

He looked at me like my question didn't make sense, or that he couldn't remember how our conversation had started. If he felt confusion, though, it only lasted for a couple seconds. Almost at once, he started in again. "I call myself 'Lone Wolf,' and if I could sprout a coat of fur warm enough to see me through the winter, I'd take off for the woods. I'd hunt with my brothers, and when a bullet eventually brought me down, I'd go down noble. It wouldn't bother me to die. I'd have lived free."

Perhaps, when he stopped speaking, he expected me to say, 'Congratulations.' He had stuck out his chin and struck the assertive pose of someone proud of his philosophy. But he also wore gold-colored suspenders, and I had not, in my admittedly limited experience with wolves, ever met a wolf who held his pants up with those over-the-shoulder straps.

"No job?" I meant my question to remind him our entire discussion—or rather his entire monologue—had launched from a different harbor. I had asked him about work.

"I haven't been that busy, mac. I can't put someone on." As soon as he spoke, he brushed past me. In a second or so, he was back inside his store.

I had places to go. I couldn't stand around and admire his no-trespassing sign. What he had told me certainly put me in a punk frame of mind, because a punk can sympathize with wolves as much as a middle-aged man in suspenders can. If I had been a wolf, and not simply a human punk, I would have bit him when he shooed the boys away. His bossiness seemed rude, and worthy of a fang and claw response.

As luck would have it, when I reached a candy store, my punk nature was rewarded. The same two boys whom the wolf had attracted stepped out to the street sharing a pack of Necco Wafers. I threw back my head and howled at them the way a wolf would. They did the same to me at once, as if we three had rehearsed our mutual howling. Only we didn't do it to bring the pack in on its prey. We did it for absurdity, which is the natural condition of pre-pubescent boys and out-of-work punks. They chuckled, just a little, then they offered me a Necco Wafer. It was like I'd struck a pact with fellow worshippers of wolves. They would depart with their Necco Wafers. And I would rob a hardened whore.

I found Mr. Pinkham at his desk, seated in the glow from a small lamp resting on his business papers. "I suppose you heard what happened," he said as soon as he saw me.

"To who?" From his woeful expression I would have guessed a stray hair had made its way into a vat of milk.

"To the band, Alan. To our poor band. Grumbs and Delilah. They're gone. Seems they had a little secret something going between the two of them. Did you know? Richie didn't know. Never crossed my mind there might be hanky-panky. And now, all of a sudden, the two of them are down in Pasco, Washington. Seems she's got a cousin there—someone they can stay with until the worst of this blows over. He'll have to start a brand-new dentist practice, won't he. Buzz-buzz, just like before. You can't live on love. Not in Pasco. And both of them have family here. He's got a wall-eyed little boy, not well. How will that play out, I'd like to know. Who's going to pay for all those special glasses? It makes you want to weep, the things some people do. But what about you, Alan? You were leaving, I thought. You miss your plane? You changed your mind? What happened?"

"Something came up, Mr. Pinkham."

"Girl?"

"I'll spare you the details."

Mr. Pinkham didn't smile but he grimaced in a mournful way, as if to say smiling would have hurt. "Are you broke?"

Before he could reach for his wallet, which I knew he would have done, I said I had fifteen dollars, but if Richie didn't want to keep my job, I hoped I could return to dipping ice-cream bars in chocolate sauce, once that season blossomed, as of course it would, because even in Alaska the winter ogre shuffles back inside his cave, and the sprites and elves and fairies of spring come shivering forth.

"Ah." Mr. Pinkham drew the sound out like a sigh. From that sympathetic noise I knew what answer he'd be forced to give. I also knew that what he'd say would pain him.

I had pained him earlier when I'd told him I'd be leaving Boon. He'd nodded at that. He'd said leaving made sense, especially when sticking around meant suffering conks to the head, perhaps repeatedly.

"Richie!" He didn't shout until he'd given me an apologetic glance. "Richie, can you come here for a second?"

Speaking of sprites and elves and fairies, the skinny trumpet quasi-virtuoso who popped into the office to answer Mr. Pinkham's call was spiritually one of those, but not one in appearance. Richie wore the professional hairnet and professional smock of an attendant in a stainless-steel dairy. He didn't look like a sprite. He looked—I hate to say this, but it's true—he looked like a dental hygienist. He knew as soon as he saw me, he had not been called to commiserate about the flight of our musical love birds.

"I fear my days of dipping ice-cream bars are gone," I said.

"What?" That was Richie's entire answer. I must learn to love those immune to irony. The puzzled. The perplexed. Those who wonder what the joke is. They're sheltered from the storms of caustic wit. Not that what I said was very caustic. It probably wasn't even wit. A wiser child than Richie would have told me, "Sorry." He would have shrugged to let me know that what had happened was no one's fault and had no remedy. Such fatalism. An attitude endorsed, I'm sure, by learned faculties in prize-wining philosophy departments at world-famous universities. Books written on the subject win awards.

And here was Richie in his lab coat and his hair net, defying all that academic wisdom, refusing to return a fatalistic answer, mired in his homely ignorance.

Pinkham glanced at Richie and Richie glanced at Pinkham. Neither wished to speak. I was the one who broke the silence. "If the job's been taken, that's okay, Mr. Pinkham. It's plain you've got a business and you have to carry on. Richie, the job was open and you took it. I'm glad. And let me tell you this—you got any questions about chocolate sauce or ice cream bars you come ask the champ." I pumped my thumb against my chest so he'd know what champ I meant.

Mr. Pinkham sighed again, but this time his *Ah* came on a rising note. "And just when we thought the band would be no more," he exclaimed. "What a week this has been, Alan. We lost you—or at least we thought you'd be headed south and would be gone for good. And then Old Grumbs and poor Delilah. Lah-di-dah together. They might be making beautiful music but they won't come back to make it here. I was ready to throw in the towel. Richie was, too. He said so. Trumpet and bass can't make a band but now we've got our drummer, too. I could talk to Junior Pine. Accordion. He might sit in."

"Before I start to bang the drums again, I better find a paying job," I told my former boss. "You hear of anything, you let me know."

Mr. Pinkham and I shook hands. He assured me he'd be on the lookout, jobwise, for me. When I extended my hand to Richie, who was breathing through his mouth in the traditional way the flummoxed of the world have practiced for probably centuries, I said to him what I'd said to Mr. Pinkham about hoping for a job. No response came until I was nearly out the door, then Richie perked up suddenly to say, "Well, maybe..."

He paused because it was his nature not to be precipitous. Pinkham had to prod him. "Speak up, Rich."

"This guy named Mint—he's looking for some help."

"Mint?" Pinkham spoke after a moment when he and I had waited to hear if Richie would say more. "Who's Mint? What does he do?"

"He's got that little place where he sells hamburgers downtown."

Mr. Pinkham slapped his hand loudly on his desk. "Oh *that* Mint. The hamburger Mint." My former boss rose from his rickety chair and did the rubber-legged dance he always did when something made him happy. He seized me by the elbow. He led me out the door. In the frigid street he fired out directions I should follow to reach the hamburger emporium overseen by Mr. Mint.

Off I went, retracing all the steps I'd taken on the sleety streets, past the shops and bars and the carcass of a wolf I thought of as my brother, possessed of only fifteen dollars and a set of prison-issue clothes, homeless, wet, and idiotically happy, for Mint's diner, where I might find work, lay, I knew, within harlot-stoning distance of the bar owned by the woman who was hiding money from the IRS.

"**M**r. Mint?" I said when I walked into the Burger Barn. The man behind the counter had been bent over a crossword puzzle. He took his time about looking up, but when he did, I said, "I heard you're looking for help."

Mint—for the counterman *was* Mint—eyed my battered suitcase. His look was suspicious, but not hostile. I saw a kind of languor in the way he let his eyes slide over me, as if it was his habit to analyze and weigh whatever ragamuffin popped up in his diner and asked him for a job.

"I'm also looking for a place to stay," I told him.

The counterman nodded very slowly, letting me know he would take his time to digest my words. To fill that time, he wiped his fingers on his baggy undershirt. He had the build of someone in the also-ran division. If you ever saw a newspaper picture of the handing out of medals after a high-school track meet you would have seen a plumpish guy like Mint standing in the back. He wouldn't have won any athletic medal, but he would have copped the good-sportsmanship award. His effort would have been earnest, and he'd have shown the meet officials his heart was free from any taint of bitterness.

Mint's dark hair was thinning, and on his chipmunk cheeks he wore a scruffy, four-day beard. He lifted his eyes from my suitcase. He let them rest on my shapeless hat. From its soaking in the frequent rain my hat looked like paste slopped on my head. "What qualifies you to cook hamburgers?" he asked.

"My father cooked for the last queen of Hawaii."

"I met your father once." Mint didn't speak with a drawl exactly, but he had a way of drawing out his words as if he savored them. "And a very fine cook he was. He told me I should never be ashamed of serving Campbell's soup." Saying that, he smiled, knowing, I imagine, his lie had trumped mine, and in his thoughtful and languorous way he had taken that hand. He nodded when he spoke again. "But I was hoping to hire someone who knows a six-letter word for a means of transportation over ice and snow."

"Try *Sledge.*"

"Spell it."

As I did, he slowly filled the puzzle's blanks. "Fits," he said when he had finished. He admired his neat lettering a moment then he looked up and met my eye. "How did you know that?"

"It came up at my trial."

"Not a trial for robbing hamburger places, I hope."

"It was more like a trial for murder."

The scruffy-looking man in the greasy tee-shirt took pause. He let his gaze travel all over my scarecrow appearance, clear down to my clodhopper shoes and then slowly back up. "That's serious, too," he said when his eyes again rested on mine.

"If you want to hear the mitigating circumstances, Mr. Mint. I have an account of them somewhere in my suitcase, stamped and notarized."

His smile let me know that what I'd said had registered as funny. "One thing you should know, young fellow, is that my last name is not Mint. Mint is a nickname. Dispense with the *Mister* in addressing me, please."

"What *is* your last name?"

"It is Slotkin, son. What's yours/"

"You'll laugh if I tell you."

"I promise I won't."

"It is Sweetcheeks. My name is Alan Sweetcheeks.

Mint didn't laugh. He didn't smile. He didn't even let a twinkle light his eyes. "A name doesn't matter much in the cooking of hamburgers, does it, Alan."

"I hope convictions for murder don't either."

The look I'd seen before—a look of detached amusement—flitted across the counterman's face. "Should I flee in terror, Alan?"

He didn't look like anyone ready to run out his back door screaming for help. He looked like someone joking.

"Fleeing in terror is up to you, Mint."

He closed his crossword magazine and fitted it into the back pocket of his jeans. He spent a second pulling on his nose, then he gazed out the window, though there was no traffic on the street, afoot or on wheels, to capture his attention. After several seconds, he sighed. "Well, I have employed drunks aplenty, Alan. Addicts, too. I've employed persons whose moral crimes, if I were to recite them, would most likely turn your hair white. So what's a murderer, more or less? I have to ask myself that question. And people aren't exactly breaking down my door to apply for the job I've advertised."

He paused to wipe the counter with a stain-blotched rag. "Though you may be interested to know, Alan, the opening I have is on the graveyard shift. I keep my diner open twenty-four hours a day. I can't say tips are very good between midnight and 8 a.m. but you'll have the opportunity to improve your crossword skills. You'll tidy up the counter and you'll keep the tables clean. Sweep and do the dishes. I'm sure that goes without saying. Some chopping of onions is required, and I count on my graveyard clerk to run a daily inventory in the bun and patty warehouse."

"When can I start?" I asked.

In reply, Mint offered his hand. Without hesitation, I took it.

Mint, when I asked him again about a place to live, steered me to a boarding house in the alley right behind his all-hours diner. The alley was more like a path than a street, and because of Boon's almost constant rain it was rich in rivulets, puddles and mud. Houses clothed in weepy, weathered shakes crowded the path, few of them bigger than a single-car garage. Tin chimneys, all atilt at drunken angles, sent threads of timid smoke snaking toward the charcoal sky. Porches sheltered dogs too dispirited to bark.

The owner of the boarding house, Molly Baskins, was the human equivalent of rivulets, puddles and mud, of weathered shakes and chimneys all atilt. Not the equivalent of dogs too dispirited to bark, though. Mrs. Baskins—a well-known sloven, I was soon to learn—barked with the best of them.

On my first trip to Chez Baskins, I climbed plank steps to her front door, where I found a hand-lettered sign: *Use Back*. Underneath that homely message an arrow pointed the way I'd have to go. To make that detour I had to thread my way between the edge of the decaying house and Mrs. Baskins' eternally parked Studebaker. When I had navigated past that sorry vehicle, I came to a set of rickety stairs rising to a patched door. A sheet of plywood covered where the door's window once had been. I knocked and waited, knocked again, and repeated that futile performance. I had given up and turned away when Mrs. Baskins, a steaming cup of coffee in her shaky hand, pulled open her repaired door. She wore a ratty housedress and had not devoted much attention to her grey hair, I supposed, since puberty. She asked if I'd come to fix her Studebaker. I said I'd come about a room. At that, she snarled, "I wish someone would fix my god-damn car."

"What's wrong with it?"

"Take a look and see."

"I gave up fixing cars to study for the priesthood."

The fishy look she shot me indicated doubt.

"I gave up the priesthood, too."

"Thank God," she said as she stepped aside so I could squeeze into her tiny kitchen and escape her city's constant rain.

Mrs. B and I did not have our Studebaker conversation every morning. Not even most mornings. Most mornings, Mrs. Baskins was what her only other roomer, a man named Taggs, called *indisposed*. Taggs hadn't worked for several years because, he said, of a heart condition. His rent was often in arrears. Before I'd enjoyed Mrs. Baskins' hospitality even for a fortnight, I'd twice heard that formidable woman bellow through his bedroom door that—if she didn't see some money soon—she would boot his skinny ass out in the street. Maybe because of her yelled threat, Taggs stayed mostly out of sight. But when I jiggered the back door open one February morning, I found him in the kitchen.

"My nerves can't take much more of this," he said.

I asked if I could help.

He whispered it was kind of me to offer. Then he tapped his chest and softly said, "The ticker."

Taggs wore what was more or less a uniform for him—a silk, paisley robe and soft-cloth slippers. He looked like someone who had enlisted in the invalid army. He only hesitated long enough to get a reading on how sympathetic I might be before he said, "I shouldn't even mention cigarettes because I know the scientific evidence about the harm smoking does. I would quit in an instant if I were out and about more. One does tend to indulge one's self when one's not feeling well. You have probably never had that problem, Mr. Sweetcheeks. You are such a husky-looking individual. I congratulate you on your health. I envy what it must mean for you—access to the wider world, freedom to go and come as you please. The only reason I feel bold enough to beg a favor is because you have your health, your strength, your wholesomeness, and you might, by chance, accommodate a person older than yourself who finds he's not in tip-top shape."

"You want cigarettes?" I had to risk being blunt to stall further verbiage.

"Pall Malls. And I'll pay for them, of course. If you'll follow me, I have the money in my room. Not a word of this to Mrs. B. I'm afraid I'm in her debt this month the teeniest, tiny amount, so mum's the word, please. Mum's the word on all of this."

He fluttered his way back toward his room and I strode in his wake. Curiosity, as much as anything, made me want to go. I rarely saw Taggs, mostly only when he scuttled to the bathroom, but I often heard grand opera records playing in his room. The music made me want to know what lay behind his door.

What I found when I followed him into his room was a hoarder's paradise. Most of what I saw was magazines. They filled up cardboard boxes and flowed out to spill across the floor. He had crammed them onto bookcase shelves where they stood in tilted stacks. They rose in piles from the messy floor, and they peeked out of his closet like they were planning an escape.

"Forgive the disarray," he told me as he opened the drawer in a bedside table and took a leather change-purse out. "I intend to do a major housekeeping but I'm so anxious for my health."

He glanced my way to see how much of that I believed. Whatever he saw made him wave toward some photographs framed for display on the wall behind his bed. "That's me when I was better," he said. "Jaunty in those days. Much, I might say, like you."

If I had impressed him as jaunty it hadn't been on purpose. The only time he saw me, generally speaking, was when I dragged myself home from the Burger Barn and found him in the kitchen hovering over the percolator in hopes of speeding its work. The pictures on the wall, though, showed me quite a different Taggs. He looked calm and self-confident, as a man should be when he's habitually photographed—or so it seemed—at resorts and villas on romantic coasts. He rested his hand on a roadster in one of the pictures and sat behind an automobile's wheel in another. Pretty women at his side grinned at the photographer. Taggs' flawless jackets and slacks spoke not so much of money as of style. He was what he had declared himself; he was jaunty.

"Did I mention Pall Malls?" he asked when he turned to me with his money. "I don't have quite enough for a carton but you can buy, I think, five packs."

The favor I did for Mr. Taggs was the first of many I'd perform to help the timid man. I don't know why I did them. I could think of no self-serving motive. At least, I could not think of one at first.

The graveyard shift served a graveyard world; and if that world waved a flag, it would have waved it upside down like a signal of distress. The forces abroad in daylight are the forces of convention and propriety, but those forces retire before twelve a.m. Longshoremen sleep, and soda jerks sleep, as do the presidents of chambers of commerce. Teachers of math and teachers of biology pillow their heads beside the pin-curled heads of their wives. In nearby bedrooms their children sleep. Their cousins sleep. Their aunts and uncles slumber. In rooms of their own—quite separate rooms—protestant preachers and men ordained as Roman Catholic priests gently snore. Protestant snores disturb protestant spouses just enough to earn a sharp poke in the ribs. Then the snoring ceases, but in time begins again. The celibate priests don't suffer nocturnal elbows in the rib. They snore in perfect peace.

It is only after midnight that vigilant propriety dissolves. From their burrows and their dens come the natural inhabitants of dark. The late-shift DJ, after he has played the national anthem and put his station off the air, complains to his favorite short-order cook about how few fans he has in his listener pool for the music of Django Reinhardt. He sips his Coke and drums his fingers on the counter while I fry his hamburger. Teenage boys in their buccaneer cadres play with their food and tell one another they are going to get laid. Taxi drivers dart out of their still-running cabs and dash across the rain-slick street for the coffee I pour in paper cups to go. A young Coast Guardsman who must have won the Homely-Sailor Sweepstakes drifts in from time to time to look for love. *God help you, lad,* is what I would tell him if he stayed to buy a hamburger and the chance came up to speak. The Burger Barn is not the place to look for lovely ladies. The only ladies who drift in have no place else to go. They've enlisted in the derelict army and march into the Burger Barn wearing uniforms of dirty clothes. What they own they tote around in shopping bags, and as they dawdle over coffee they unroll their brown-cloth bandages and expose their blue-veined legs.

I became, at Mint's Burger Barn, a connoisseur of what is hopeless and unkempt. Souls distilled into their alcoholic essence flowed in and out: Tin-Ear Tweet, an always startled-looking man; the bum named Whiskey Pete who never spoke but only growled. I put coffee in the shaky hands of a pioneer called Hard-Rock who searched and searched to find the nickel it would take to pay.

Often enough, if Mint was present when this charade took place, my boss would place his hand on the trembling paw of the grizzled derelict and shake his head to tell him his money wasn't any good. His coffee, this time, would be on the house. My boss's generosity amounted only to a nickel, but it unsettled me, nonetheless. "You should boot Hard-Rock's sorry ass out in the rain, boss. If you keep being nice to him, he'll only mooch more."

"I'm not being nice to *him*, Alan. I'm being nice to me."

"Storing up treasures in heaven?"

"Don't go all supernatural on me, please."

"I'm right about the mooching, though. You know that."

"Maybe I know that, Alan, and maybe I don't care. Maybe a nickel is a cheap price to pay. I'd pay more to get my shoes shined. And what makes a person feel better—shined shoes or a poor bum's gratitude?"

"I've rarely earned a poor bum's gratitude, and I've never had shined shoes, so I'm not really the person to ask profound questions of, boss."

"I'm setting you a good example, aren't I."

"I should contribute cups of coffee to all the bums who wander in?"

"Don't be a wiseass, Sweetcheeks. The coffee is mine, not yours. Contribute your consideration. Contribute patience and wisdom. Those things won't cost anything. Contribute your human kindness. Maybe that's what I employ you for."

"If I do all that, Mint, can I put in for a raise?"

My boss laughed. He had hung up his apron. Now he shrugged his jacket on. He was zipping it up before he thought of a reply. "Yeah," he said. "Put in for a raise. A nickel an hour. I'd be willing to pay it if the bums were happier."

His hand was on the door latch, but he hesitated about pulling the door open. He looked lost in thought. The wise guy in me wanted to crack jokes about how nice to bums I'd have to be to get that extra nickel in my pay. Offer them a paper napkin so they can blow their dripping noses? Keep dry socks underneath the counter for their poor, frozen feet? I think it's a mark of my progress in the moral measure of things that I did not make those silly suggestions. My boss seemed serious in the offer he was making. A nickel an hour for happier bums. How many bums were worth that nickel, and how unhappy did they have to be? I could picture the Burger Barn crammed to the walls with despair's midnight crop. Maybe Mint could picture the same thing.

He didn't speak again, but he nodded very kindly as a way to say goodbye, then he was out into the rainy night and gone.

Mint's hamburger emporium stood kitty-corner across the street from Darlene's Federal Building. I say 'Darlene's Federal Building' as if she owned that monumental structure and didn't merely work there. I never saw Darlene. Our hours of employment did not overlap. Perhaps that's just as well. I don't know what I would have said.

I did see, occasionally, the toothpick Breen hanging on another's young man's arm. I can't say I sympathized with whoever the youngster was. Breen had worked her will on me, but I had had to cooperate. And if in my counterman's apron I was metaphorically hung up in front of a sporting-goods store, the equivalent in human flesh of the carcass of a wolf, what right had I to harbor resentful feelings?

I fried hamburgers. I poured Cokes. And one night, when a familiar derelict, the one shaped much like a pear, waddled past the Burger Barn I scooped up some crumbles of left-over hamburger and hurried outside to offer them to Pear-Shape's charcoal-colored cat. The cat trusted me enough to eat out of my hand. Pear-Shape smiled his appreciation, but when his sawed-off friend, Fence-Post Mike, full-time shrimp and part-time basher-in-of-heads, strolled into sight to join him I closed my hand on the last few crumbles and straightened up to my full height.

Height is a wonderful thing for a human being to have. It imparts a kind of gravitas that runts can only envy. I am not spectacularly tall. I am six-feet-one. But if sawed-off Mike hit four-feet-ten I would have been surprised. He had to crane to see how baleful I looked. Not that he was daunted by my balefulness. His dopey grin had been surgically implanted. He bestowed it on the cat, on Pear-Shape, on the string that served as the cat's leash, on the slightly steamed up windows of the Burger Barn, on the rivulet-rich gutter gurgling beside the curb, and on the splash a passing pick-up truck threw almost on his shoes. He was a grinner *par excellence*, and he might have melted a softer heart than mine. Every time I saw him, though, my scars began to keen. Their chorus cried for vengeance. I probably would have strangled Mike with the god-damned cat's string leash except for the natural respect I have for the majesty of the law.

The cat, as cats are wont to do, nosed its way around my ankles as if to say, "Cough up the other crumbles, buddy."

I stooped again. I opened my palm to the little animal's exploring tongue. He lapped the hamburger crumbles away and then turned his feline face to try to read my still-stern expression, either saying thanks or telling me he wanted more. The mystery of what cats mean remains unsolved to this day. Pondering that mystery, I looked up and saw two gifts of the night invisible to me before: one of them was a single star, and the other was Malcolm, the natural-born mooch. The clouds had parted just enough to let the star show off its sparkle. Malcolm, on the other hand, had no sparkle. In his mopeyness, he could claim to be the World's Least Sparkly Human.

Mendicant Malcolm. Sparkly star. And, of course, me, a petty thief and flipper of hamburger patties.

I am not a trained astrologer, so I have no way of knowing if stars command invisible and weightless reins they tug and slacken to give direction to our lives. If a team of stars could take turns twitching me in this direction or that direction, I might never have insulted a harlot or felt the weight of strong feelings tugging me in the direction of a woman who chose hats based on the ones commonly worn by Eleanor Roosevelt. Astrological sign posts would know better than to steer a person in either of those directions. What we screw-up, we screw-up for ourselves. I had had to put my shoulder to the wheel. I had poured out Cal's proffered drink without any assistance from heaven.

And here was Malcolm, by degrees of magnitude much more miserable than I. We traded glances, silently assessing each other. The glance was all. Neither of us spoke. The glance spoke for us, not of friendship, not even of companionship, but of silence and solemnity, as if, on this parched earth, we shared some secret bond, forged in dimes and bowls of chili, and defying all the regulations requiring a punk—like me—to sneer.

Forty-seven days went by, and I had come no closer to finding where Cal kept the money she hid from the IRS. I had sleuthed her the best I could. I had spied. I had snooped. I had minutely examined every crumb of information luck brought my way. I saw her gold De Soto parked close to the Bayside Bar almost to the midnight hour most nights of the week. I knew she sometimes had Mike drive her home and sometimes drove herself. I could clock her regular visits to André's, from which she emerged newly silvered.

Customers, when they bellied-up to the Burger Barn's counter, sometimes cursed her in the limited vocabulary of the perpetually dim. When they did, I eavesdropped. She was bitchy. She was vicious. I knew all that. The commonest complaint I heard was how skilled she was at reeling suckers in, hooking them, playing them, and when she had milked them of their final dime tossing them back in the street. Good times at the Bayside Bar belonged just to those with money. The Bayside, in that respect, was a microcosm of the macrocosm my nose had been rubbed in for all the years of my carefree youth. I had a well-rubbed nose, but that was my own business, no one else's. I was silently resentful. I could do my cause no good by telling the whole world I was sore. I had a secret plan—to rob the hardened whore—which, it seemed to me self-evident, no else should know.

Patience, Sweetcheeks, I said to myself. It took the Lord Jehovah forty days to drown the cavorting world. And the father of the universe has powers up his sleeve the average convicted killer lacks. He can part the waters and raise the dead. Multiply the loaves and fishes. At his mere touch, lepers get certifiably cured. I had nowhere near such powers. I could not even make Mrs. Baskins shut up. If I had a proverbial nickel for every time that sloven asked me to fix her damned Studebaker, I wouldn't have needed to steal Cal's money. I could have retired to the Florida Keys and treated Ernest Hemingway to fishing expeditions aboard my private yacht.

"Tell Mr. Taggs to fix your Studebaker," I told her on the morning of Day Forty-Eight. "He knows more about cars than I do. He's got all those pictures in his room."

"Does Taggs look like a mechanic? No. Not in those pictures he doesn't. He looks like a fairy, his clothes are so clean."

"My clothes aren't clean?"

"You're a man, Mr. Sweetcheeks. That's all I'm saying. You're a man and you should know about cars."

I had not come home from my graveyard shift in a mood of unalloyed happiness. I had had to dodge back into the Burger Barn as soon as I'd turned things over to the day-shift man. I had seen Mr. Tinsel. He appeared to be on an early morning dash to the post office. It was my good fortune to see him before he caught sight of me. I still owed the Tinsels a hundred bucks. At the rate I was saving my nickels and dimes, I could count on paying that debt the same year I started collecting Social Security. I skulked in the Burger Barn until Mr. Tinsel had deposited his letters and bustled back in the direction of his store.

Mrs. Baskins knew none of this, of course. I was not in arrears with Mrs. Baskins. Nor did I wish to be. She had greeted me from her kitchen table, with a pack of Lucky Strikes close to her pudgy hand. She let herself toy with the cigarettes while she gathered in her fuzzy mind what else she wished to say. "Taggs is not the only one with pictures," she finally announced. "Let me tell you that. You like pictures? Come see mine."

She heaved herself up from her chrome-plated chair and waddled toward a room I rarely visited, her parlor. An oil furnace with a little mica window sat against one wall. Behind the furnace, a display of framed photographs and newspaper clippings, also framed, gathered dust, as I imagine saintly relics must in alcoves of European cathedrals. I don't speak from experience. I have never been to Europe. And if I went, I doubt I'd visit cathedrals. Blue, my cellmate, on his honeymoon, had taken his bride on a tour of every cathedral in the province of Quebec. Their marriage ended in Blue pushing his wife off one of Illinois' rare cliffs, so my opinion about cathedrals was tinged with a punk's habitual sneer.

"See that?" my landlady bellowed when she had wormed me around the muttering furnace and we stood hip to hip before the dusty display on the wall. She pointed to a framed newspaper photo featuring a mob of pre-pubescent girls shivering in their bathing suits. Each wore a rubber cap that made her look like an invader of earth from outer space. Missing baby teeth gave most of the girls a jack-o-lantern grin. With their bony shoulders and skinny limbs, they might have been stick-figures, drawn with crayons, not real human children captured with a camera. "Tadpoles Test New Swim Hole," the clipping's headline read.

Mrs. Baskins cast a coy glance across her shoulder. "I was one of those tadpoles, Mr. Sweetcheeks. Can you guess which one is me?"

I peered—or I should say I put on a good imitation of peering. I knew at a glance I would never be able to tell one of those homely urchins from another. They looked like elbow macaroni dressed in bathing suits. The picture had been taken before the Coolidge administration had been sworn into office. The slattern beside me now displayed, through her carelessly pulled-together bathrobe, a chest as wrinkled as the ankle of an elephant. While I squinted at the uniformly homely tadpoles, Mrs. Baskins sighed. "My father was a swimming champion in Steubenville, Ohio. He once met Johnny Weissmuller. I've got a Tarzan picture—autographed. There wasn't any place to swim when Dad first came to Boon. He had to get Rotarians to help him make a pool. They raised a ton of money and built a dam across a cove. The dam made a pond. Everybody swims there now. It's where I learned to swim myself. And I'm just like my dad. I love to swim. I swam across the Narrows back and forth one time. It turned me blue, but I did it. I've got a photograph to prove it. I can show you. Or we could drive out to the pond and you could see what daddy did. It isn't very far—about three miles."

She batted her lashes at the weak smile I gave. It was not the kind of smile she could expect from a Tarzan. I did not have Tarzan's chest, nor his calves or thighs. I was redolent of onion odors, and the grease from hamburgers. Tarzan, I'm pretty sure, never fried a hamburger in his entire life. Mrs. Baskin may have had the same thought. She yawned in visible boredom and wandered off to poke her coffee pot into bubbling hot water up over fragrant grounds. She tapped the photo's glass with her fat finger before she hied herself away, however. In demented flirtatiousness, she smiled up in my direction and said again, "Try to guess which one is me."

My landlady disappeared. Crockery in the kitchen must have known she was coming. I could hear it tremble.

She left me contemplating a nugget of new information she had quite casually let drop.

Before bad luck, good luck.

That's practically a scientific formula. Bad luck came at the end of my next graveyard shift, but the whole shift had not been bad. Very nearly the opposite, in fact, André, hairdresser to the stars, whom I had never expected to see in the Burger Barn, stepped in from the rain about five-fifteen a.m. and said, "Ah ha," on seeing me behind the counter with my somewhat greasy apron on. I hadn't seen him since he'd cut my hair, and because more than two months had passed since then, his first glance went to my ginger-colored locks. I caught the frown of disapproval that flashed across his face. My locks had been cut, but not by him. Mrs. Baskins had volunteered to be my barber. She had more than volunteered. She had pushed me down into a kitchen chair, tied a somewhat sanitary sheet around my neck, and tackled my scalp with a needle-nosed pair of scissors, relatively sober as she clipped, although not sober enough to keep me from flinching each time her weaponized hand came close to my eyes.

"I've been meaning to stop by your shop," I said to André.

Whatever he'd been thinking, he let a smile bloom on his plump face, and when he'd taken a seat at the counter he said, "I'm never, ever up this late, but I've been keeping company with a sick friend. A bronchial affliction. Or that's what I believe. I hope it's not contagious. If you're worried, Mr. Sweetcheeks, I can trot myself right off."

"Not worried in the least, André. I'd count it as an honor to be bronchially infected by a person who once cut the hair of José Ferrer."

He laughed. I poked his hamburger with my spatula to test its sizzle. "I hope your friend is resting comfortably, André. Do you know him from the shop? Is he somebody whose hair you style and shape?"

These were conversational questions. They didn't require me to turn from my duties at the grill. I heard André sigh. "Charlie is bald, so there isn't really any reason for him to drop by the shop. When I used to play canasta, he was part of our little group. Then he started getting these attacks of pleurisy." He sighed again. "But you don't want to hear about somebody's troubles. Everyone has troubles of their own. I should tell you instead about my triumph yesterday."

"José Ferrer again?"

He smiled indulgently at my weak joke. "I helped a customer—a long-time customer who never wanted to change the way she wore her hair. It wasn't even a style, the way she wore it. It was only braids, like a child's braids, but pinned in a crown on top of her head. She looked like one of those Swedish girls who wear candles in their hair at Christmas time. Something medieval about hair worn like that, that's how it always looks to me."

I knew someone whose golden hair, in braids, made her look like a medieval queen.

"Not that I'd ever volunteer anything about the way a person wears her hair, Mr. Sweetcheeks. It's such a personal choice, don't you think? I like to talk around that sort of topic. I'll suggest a fuller style or perhaps a more layered look. Side-swept bangs can sometimes help.

"Not that this young woman had a problem. It's not a *problem* to choose to wear your hair in braids, the way I've said. There are better choices, though. On that topic, I will say no more. I've said too much already. What I'll say very simply is that I could have gone on for a hundred years doing her hair as she wanted and keeping my mouth shut. She would have been happy. I would have been happy. But yesterday I just happened to say, in a casual manner, 'Same style?' For a long time, I didn't get an answer. It was like she'd gone off into her own little world, thinking her own thoughts. So I showed her some magazine pictures. Nothing radical. I hate hair-dos too-too, if you know what I mean. I showed her a picture in which the model happened to be a brunette. This lady I'm speaking of, my customer, is a honey blonde, a very rich color. The model I showed her had auburn-colored hair. Before I could turn the page, my customer stopped me. 'Could you do me like this?' she wondered. 'You mean this cut?' I asked. The model's hair was just a little bit severe. No wave to it. No bounce. Very little curl. 'The shape,' she said. 'Could you do a shape like hers?'

"Well, Mr. Sweetcheeks, I have to say I was flabbergasted. I could see exactly what she had in mind. We thumbed through more of my magazines, and we found a style frillier and freer than the braids she'd always worn. With bangs, of course, but then a kind of brush along the cheeks. A more flattering look than the one she'd come into my shop with—she had come in many, many times. And in all her visits I never said anything. We handicap ourselves when we refrain from speaking out, keeping mum for fear we might offend. Don't you think so, Mr. Sweetcheeks?"

I had toasted the hamburger bun. I mayonnaised it up. Lettuce. Tomato. Pickle. I added the whole works. And when I tilted the can of potato chips to shake out a supply I was very, very generous to my friend. I thought of potato chips as his reward for tact and human decency. I tried to picture what Darlene must look like with wings of hair fluffed out beside her cheeks, with side-swept bangs. I hoped she had gone straight to her cheerful Coast Guard friend, whether he was aboard his ship or out giving toothbrush lessons to attentive little children.

Or even at her house. Did I know if he stayed there when the call of duty didn't take him off to island villages? No. I did not know that. I did not want to know. But I wished it had been I who had suggested to Darlene that she adopt a different style for her hair. We would have talked at length about it. When she saw results she liked, she might have given me a kiss. We might have kissed longer than we had before. We might have touched all over.

Of course, I had—in case you've forgotten—let myself be glimpsed with a hooker on my arm. So when we want to talk about pain, we could talk about that. Other than that—other than evidence that proved I was a lecher—I am a run-of-the-mill convicted killer and unreformed felon who had not done one single thing nice that entire, cold night except reward André with extra potato chips.

I'd given him the extra chips for his kindness to Darlene. He'd given her a hairdo that improved the way she looked. I let myself get lost in daydreams about Miss Sandusky. Those dreams shattered when Santos stepped in from the cold. He handed me a note from Mrs. Tinsel.

"You owe me a hundred bucks," it said.

I would personally be ashamed to write a note to a convicted killer and tell him he owed me a hundred bucks. Convicted killers know what their debts are. But this particular convicted killer could only pay his debt off at about twenty cents a week. Two dimes was the margin I had between being broke each weekend and not being broke. It was what remained in my pocket after deductions for rent and meals, other than the burger Mint allowed me, one a night. If I had dropped two dimes in Mrs. Tinsel's hand on Friday every week, I could have paid my hundred-dollar debt in about ten years. But I hoarded my twenty cents. Or I spent it frivolously. So Mrs. Tinsel had every right to imply I was a deadbeat, and it depressed me to think I'd earned that reputation.

I was penniless, but I was not a deadbeat. I had been, for several months, a model of sobriety and a saint of incorruptibility. The owners of Fords and Chevrolets in Boon went to bed each night comfortably sure that when they rose the next morning their bumpers would be where they'd left them. I had religiously toed the proverbial line, and I had absolutely nothing to show for it except several stitches on my head and a smell of hamburger grease that clung to my tee-shirts despite vigorous washings.

But here's one of the adverse things that popped into my mind because of Mrs. Tinsel's dunning: People who plan to rob hardened old whores shouldn't fret about their penny-ante debts. If

I wasn't worried about burglarizing the keeper of a bawdy house, why should I worry about repaying a debt of a hundred-dollars to a woman whose hair looked like whipped cream?

"I shouldn't let it bother me for even one minute," I said to Mr. Taggs. "I got that hundred dollars as a gift. It wasn't offered as a loan."

"That's certainly one way of looking at it," Mr. Taggs told me. I had made another surreptitious purchase of Pall Malls for him. He owed me the duty of a courteous answer. Even so, he didn't stick around to hear more of my third-rate rationalizations. As soon as he had his coffee cup in his shaking hand, he shuffled back to the safety of his nest. He had seen the moth holes in my garment of self-righteousness. I had been told I must repay the hundred dollars Mrs. Puff-Ball Tinsel had thrown into my lap. The hundred dollars may have been, at one time, a gift. But the gift came with strings, and *string* is a code word, in Mrs. Tinsel's vocabulary, for saying, "Get out of town." Convicted killers are the kind of people you can issue that command to. You couldn't tell the wife of your Baptist minister to get out of town, nor could you say it to the always pleasant owner of a corner stationary store.

I took my own cup of coffee into the parlor and squeezed behind the smelly furnace to gaze at the Tadpole clipping. I asked myself, as I did so, why I let my alcoholic landlady's coy question bug me. "Can you guess which one is me?" What I saw was twelve Tadpoles, all in bathing caps, looking as identical as bullets. How was I to tell which of them had morphed into the gargoyle who rented me my room?

In perplexity on that particular question, I squeezed back around the ever-burning furnace and tapped quietly on Mr. Tagg's closed door.

"Come help me guess which Tadpole is our landlady," I whispered.

Taggs must have put his ear to the door when he'd heard my tap. Relieved that the tapper had not been Mrs. B, he opened his door and responded at once "I haven't the foggiest, Mr. Sweetcheeks. Why do you want to know?"

"I have no answer to your question, Mr. Taggs."

He looked at me *askance.*

Don't you love that word *askance.* I think it comes to American usage from some aboriginal language. Athabaskan, perhaps. Or Cheyenne. Or Crow. I knew as soon as I saw 'askance' on my fellow roomer's face I owed Taggs a further explanation. On the spot, I made one up.

"If I win the Name-that-Moppet competition, Mr. Taggs, I win the thousand-dollar first prize. And what might I do with a thousand dollars? Let me ask you that."

No more *askance. Annoyed,* rather.

 "You're never serious, Mr. Sweetcheeks. You make it difficult to carry on an adult conversation. I'm sorry I asked you why you needed to certify Mrs. Baskins in that photograph, But if you really want to know what little girl might be she, you ought to take the picture to someone raised in Boon, someone who knows the city's history. You'd be much better off asking a person like that than asking me."

He had clutched his silk bathrobe tight at his throat, and he spoke with surprising finality. He didn't even wait to hear my answer. He scuffed backward in his cloth slippers, closed his door, and disappeared.

I hadn't shared with him my reasons for identifying Baskins as a tot because I didn't know myself what my reason was. Among my many other faults—and I have a lot of other faults—I am often prey to vague motivations. Compared to stealing copper pipes and bumping off scrap-yard merchants, following vague motivations is a trivial failing. It's a fault no bigger than a pimple, but humor me in it, please. I sometimes find vague motivations preternatural.

Preternatural is another borrowing from the Athabaskan tongue.

I went to the front room, coffee in hand, and contemplated the picture from a distance of about eight feet, calling to mind all those I'd met in Boon and wondering which of them might hold in memory the identity of one or more of those shivering youngsters. Mint would have been a child then. He might even have been a child Rotarian. As a Rotarian, the boy Mint would have helped pour concrete for the swimming hole the gap-toothed youngsters frolicked in until their skin turned blue.

Mint would know, I told myself. My landlady had completed her afternoon debauch and was passed out behind her bedroom door. *Mint would know.* With that thought, I slipped the framed clipping off its nail hanger and carried it to the Burger Barn.

My boss had spread his crossword-puzzle magazine open on the counter. He was not yet taxing his brain with the clues, however. He was in conversation with one of the neighborhood's champion loafers, a man named Spinks who toyed with a cigarette he couldn't quite bring to his lips because he would have had to interrupt his constant stream of talk. Spinks made the effort, though. He lifted the cigarette between two fingers to right below his nose and let the smoke drift up until he had to squint to see my patient boss. When he squinted, he moved his cigarette away and batted at the smoke with his free hand, all the while relating some droll story, the point of which was lost on Mint. My boss's eyes kept wandering to his puzzle, but that signal of disinterest did not silence Spinks. After forty-nine seconds, my patience had grown short. I interrupted Spinks to tell my boss, "Refresh this fellow's coffee, Mint. We want to keep our cherished customers coming back."

Mr. Spinks must have heard sarcasm. He came to a full stop. He turned his red-veined eyes on me. I took advantage of the silence to hand Mint the clipping in its dusty frame. "Which of these kids is Mrs. Baskins?" I asked. "She is bugging me and bugging me. My instinct is to guess the one most homely. She might take that amiss."

Spinks finally drew on his cigarette. The smoke he exhaled wafted up my nose. When he was satisfied with the irritation he had caused, he scooped up his package of Old Golds. He might have left his matchbook lying on the counter but Mint pointed to it as Spinks rose. "Ah," the departing man said. He tucked his matchbook into the tight pocket of his vest, a brocade vest like a riverboat gambler's, with a fleck of something shiny on its rounded lapel. The fleck could have been a diamond stick-pin, or it could have been just snot. Spinks headed for the door before I had a chance to ascertain. He stopped with his hand on the latch. "One of those urchins is the harlot Cal," he said.

That was the fact I'd learned from Mrs. Baskins, a fact eventually transforming in my life.

Spinks, as soon has he had spoken, stepped out into the rain.

What makes me think of something shiny on a man's lapel as snot? I suppose it's my punk nature. Spinks loped off and I had barely begun my mental *mea culpas* when Mint spoke. "What's the big deal about knowing who's who in that picture, Alan?"

"I want to flatter Mrs. Baskins, Mint. I want her to remember me when she comes to write her will."

"She'll remember you, Alan. Don't worry about that. You're young and good-looking and sarcastic. I'm sure you bring a sparkle to her life."

"And I don't wear brocade vests."

"Well, there you have it, Alan. Give yourself credit. You may actually be a better person than you think. Test that thesis. Go see Mrs. Tinsel, why don't you. She's an old-timer in Boon. Take her an IOU. Let her know you haven't forgotten. Butter the old biddy up. Turn on your thousand-watt charm. Say you know she's the prettiest one in the picture but you want to know which one is your landlady. People like to talk about the old days. I'll bet she'll help you out."

Mint returned to work on his crossword puzzle. The blanks he filled in spelled 'demented.'

I must have been demented. The madness of what I'd heard Mint say made sense.

I undertook my errand on April Fools' Day, an irony not lost on me.

I found Mrs. T, her meringue hair baked solid, behind the desk in her husband's authentic store. She fixed me with a sniper's look as soon as the bell above the door announced my presence. "Ellery's not here." She spoke in a knife-edged voice.

"I haven't come to see Mr. Tinsel. I've come with this, for you."

I had taken the trouble to print out in block letters the kind of debtor's note that's called an IOU. I had signed it with my full and legal name, and before I'd scrawled that signature, I had asked myself if I ought not to write above it, 'Love.' I had spared Mrs. Tinsel that sarcasm, and ignoring the balefulness of the steel lady's stare, I took my IOU out of my shirt pocket, unfolded it, and did my best to smooth its wrinkles away.

I laid it in front of Mrs. T.

She studied it a moment before she returned her gaze to me.

"What am I supposed to do with this, Mr. Sweetcheeks?"

"What you do with it is your own business, Mrs. Tinsel. I offer it as evidence I do not intend to skip out on my debt."

"I told you to leave town."

"A woman made me change my mind, Mrs. Tinsel."

"Spare me the details, Mr. Sweetcheeks." She spoke with an undisguised look of horror.

I said immediately, "Of course." Then I unwrapped the framed clipping. "But while we're still on speaking terms, I'd like your help with this." I put the clipping in its clumsy frame down in front of her. "One of the moppets pictured here is Mrs. Baskins, currently my landlady. If you can tell me which one she is, you will help me avoid a mistake. She constantly asks me to pick her out from this crowd. Between me and you—and I hope this goes no further—Mrs. Baskins' only flaw is that she is a trifle vain. If I were to pick a homely moppet and say it looks like her, the worthy woman might resent my error. I do not want my land-lady—any of my landladies—bearing me resentment."

Mrs. Tinsel sighed at what I'd said. She knew more about re-sentment than I could learn through years of supervised study. I watched her fit to her nose the prescription glasses she wore on a chain around her neck. It might have been curiosity about the picture that made her do that. But it might have been my charm offensive, too. She might have seen, in the sincerity I oozed, some of the *better me* Mint felt certain must be there.

Mrs. Tinsel bent above the clipping, every curl on her snowball head a study in rigidity. As it dawned on her what the long-ago photographer had captured, she first gaped, and then she gasped. Her glasses dropped and swung back and forth on their chain. She turned a look on me of astonishment, indignation, and per-haps a dozen other maniacal, wild emotions. She rose to her feet.

"*She* put you up to this! I know she did!" she roared. "Get out. Go! Right now. I'm sick of you, Sweetcheeks. Sick of seeing you. Sick of hearing you. You and your smart mouth—you make my skin crawl. Take the picture. Get out of my husband's store."

She pulled open a door behind her, the door to the stairs climbing toward her upstairs living quarters. I heard her clomp her way to the lair above my head. She slammed the door to em-phasize everything she'd yelled. When she was gone, the silence was profound. The store got unnaturally still, like a room in which a corpse is readied for the grave.

I had a feeling I was being watched. I saw, out of the corner of my eye, the carving on the shaman's wand, with its knowing, cynical sneer.

At the glimpse I got of it—only a glimpse because I hurried from the store—perception, no bigger than the point of a pin, started slowly drilling toward my brain.

The Studebaker at Baskin Arms had long since surrounded itself with salmonberry bushes and almost disappeared, like Sleeping Beauty's castle. All winter the stalks of the bushes had been as bare as bones, but late in April leaves the size of teardrops began to show. Mrs. B had urged me, from around the autumn equinox, to get the car repaired. The next time she repeated her complaint about no male of her acquaintance being man enough to fix her car, I said I'd see that it got fixed providing she'd let Mr. Taggs teach me how to drive.

We were in her kitchen. I had just returned from work. She was burning eggs for me. I hesitate to describe burnt eggs as a love offering, but I believe that was what she intended them to be.

"That car was my husband's." Her terraced chin trembled.

"Deceased?" I had never heard her mention a husband before.

Mrs. Baskins had her blackened eggs to worry about. They kept her from responding until she'd opened the door and waved out the smoke. Then she craned into the wet morning to pick out among the bushes her parked Studebaker. "He won it in a card game. The only thing he ever won in his whole life."

"New?"

"So he was told." Mrs. Baskins closed the door and ran a hand through her wiry curls to shake off the rain. "And he believed it. The fool. He was the trusting type. I would have guessed the odometer had been trifled with. Not that I know about such things, but the tires were all bare. He had to monkey with the gear shift if he didn't want to drive around in first. The heater needed fixing. The windshield wipers kept going on strike. And the ignition didn't do its duty. It still doesn't. I told you that before. You're as gullible as he was if you think that's almost new. And Mr. Baskins is *not* deceased. He went to Sacramento for a convention of the Moose in February, 1948. A red-head with big tits reeled him in like a halibut. I hope she checked on *his* odometer. I'm sure he set it back."

She let her gaze drift in my direction. She wanted my sympathy. I extemporized. "You have cause to be aggrieved," I gently told her.

A distant look came to her eyes. I thought, "Oh dear," for the hearts of wounded ladies are very much a mystery to me. Not that I've made a study of the subject. In prison, I would have had to learn through correspondence courses. Nevertheless, I'm as human as most other men and if you bring me your sad feelings, I'll lend you half an ear. Repetition mars the telling of a tale, though, and repetition sets in soon when the story is of a lover's wounds, blah blah blah.

Yet if one wants to get his hands on a Studebaker's keys one has to buckle down and charm. And I did want to get my hands on the Studebaker's keys. I wanted to learn where Cal the Cruel kept her hidden gains. And I want to drive to wherever the horde lay hidden and dig it up.

Which plan I put in motion as Mrs. Baskins told me more of all the good years she had wasted on a two-faced, playboy bum, I said, 'That's awful.' I assured my landlady she was a saint for putting up with so much crap. I cursed the red-haired woman and for good measure I threw the Moose Club into the cursing pot as well. When Mrs. Baskins rested her head on the table and let her tears pool up on the oilcloth, I fetched the toilet paper roll so she could blow her nose.

A calculated tenderness, of course, but the upshot of it all was her grudging agreement: If I could get the Studebaker running, she'd let Mr. Taggs teach me how to drive.

"I don't know what you want to drive for, though. We live on an island. Where do you think you can go?"

She blew her nose dramatically, and the exertion seemed to cheer her up. "But you want to see my beach, of course." Her spirits lifted by the mention she'd made of the island's man-made swimming hole, the one her beloved father had constructed, she plopped her despicable eggs on a plate, which she then placed before me. Next, she wandered into the living room to worship at the altar of the framed clipping. "You never said which one is me, Sweetcheeks. Come here."

I slid my dreadful eggs into a trash can underneath the sink and joined her in front of the sooty wall. I spent a minute pretending to study the scrawny would-be swimmers. "You'd have to be the prettiest one," I said.

A giggle. "Which one's that?"

I had no idea which one that was. If there was a pretty child among that scraggy crew, she had escaped my scrutiny. But I made a guess. I pointed to the child who looked least like she had scuttled out of an inter-tidal pool. My reward was a smothering hug, and in the fleshy vise of Mrs. Baskins' suggestively amorous embrace I heard her whisper in my ear, "You just get that car fixed, Sweetcheeks, and we'll go visit my dad's pond."

I would have gladly visited her late father's septic tank or cesspool or his deteriorating corpse if I thought doing so would enlighten me as to where Cal kept her hidden money. I would have trod where Rotarians had trod before me. But what do Rotarians know about hidden treasure? Rotarians are gregarious creatures of energetic good will. They'll happily build swimming holes everywhere you look. They'll build a couple of them in your yard, or where your grandmother lies buried. But ask them where a treasure is buried and they'll gape at you like Richie and say, "Huh?"

What would I learn by picnicking with Mrs. Baskins on the shore of her father's bucolic pond? I might learn, eventually, how to drive a Studebaker with a sticky gear shift. I knew that wouldn't be a big achievement. But when you're out to rob a hardened whore, you must go step by step.

I didn't know anyone who fixed Studebakers. I mentioned the problem to Mint one night when he had just hung up his greasy apron and was putting on the jacket he'd walk home in. He grunted the way a guy grunts when he's listening to someone else's problem while pondering a problem of his own. To me, that meant he hadn't paid attention, but two days later, after the doughnut-delivery man had regaled me, as he always did, with obscene tales about his amorous adventures, but before the morning's frantic coffee crowd ripped through, a boy bicycled up and spent a long moment peering in the Burger Barn's steam-hazed windows.

The boy was of average height and average weight and not particularly handsome. His only distinguishing feature, as far as I could tell through the steamy window, was his look of wholesomeness. *Put that boy in khaki shorts*, I told myself, *slap a campaign hat on his blond head and you could pose him for a Boy Scout calendar.*

If he wasn't a Boy Scout, he could have been a Mormon missionary. I was afraid he might proselytize, and I'd begun rehearsing blasphemous things to tell him about buried books inscribed on plates of solid gold, but when he finally parked his bike and pushed the door open what he said from the threshold in his cracking, teen-age voice had nothing to do with upstate New York revelations.

"I can fix cars."

He looked too young to make that claim. I delayed responding while I looked him over. He wore the chinos and cloth jacket that were practically the uniform of Boon's schoolboys. His sandy hair was freshly plastered down, as if he had showered and carefully combed it before he'd set off on his bike.

"Are you even old enough to drive?" The bicycle prompted my question.

"Almost." The boy's voice cracked when he said it.

"Show me your hands, son."

The boy promptly approached the counter with his arms extended. I only had to glance at the backs and palms of them, and at his youthful thumbs and fingers, to see nicks and gouges and scratches and abrasions, evidence of application to the mechanic arts. Black grime seemed permanently caked under his fingernails. Stains of grease had worked their way into the wrinkles of his knuckles, too. His hands were the hands of someone who had spent a lot of time bent over an engine. After I had studied his hands to my satisfaction, I eyed the youth and asked, "So, what's your name?"

"Cheek Moskanovitch."

"Did I hear you say *Cheek*?"

Had Mint told him my surname? Did the boy consider his first name an abbreviation of my last name? Did he know my last name and had he invented a nickname in hopes of flattering me? I am naturally a trusting individual, so I didn't dwell on my suspicions. Plus, cherubs don't premeditate their monikers. That's against their union's rules.

The boy blushed and in his child's voice he said, "It's really Cornelius."

I felt like I'd been trusted with a secret. I nodded very solemnly and after a few seconds I spoke with pompous authority. "I'll call you Cheek," I said.

Mrs. Baskins had splashed on cologne, no more than a bucketful but enough to make young Cheek reel as if he had been clobbered with a hammer. He had come to make a study of the balky Studebaker, and he did not expect, I'm sure, to be seduced by someone forty years his senior.

Cheek needn't have worried. Mrs. B had augmented her attractions solely for my benefit. The bashful boy was incidental.

I had joined the young mechanic at the side of the ailing car, and my head, like his, was under its raised hood when my landlady put in her aromatic appearance.

I can't say I was surprised. Increasing signs of amorous inclinations had been emanating from the antique siren ever since I'd correctly guessed which snot-nosed tot was she. She had fixed me breakfast on two mornings she'd been sober. Not a breakfast of burnt eggs, either, but a healthy one of bacon, toast and carefully fried eggs, eggs of perfect freshness served sunny-side up.

She hadn't targeted Cheek in the same way, of course, so when a smell like one you might expect from the floral arrangements surrounding a Mafia casket came wafting his way, he raised his head so suddenly he banged it on the underside of the Studebaker's hood.

Cheek didn't swear. That was one of the nice things about the boy. He grimaced, and his eyes teared-up, but no vulgarity or blasphemy escaped him. When I asked if he was okay, he smiled. After that, with just a nod to acknowledge my blowsy landlady's presence, he ducked back under the raised hood to continue studying the engine while Mrs. B, after trilling about how smart he was to know so many things concerning cars, waddled back to her house for yet another nip, I'm sure, from her pint of Four Roses.

May had turned the halfway mark, and May in Boon is as wet and miserable a month as October or any of the soggy months in between. I stood across the Studebaker from Cheek shivering in my damp jacket. I offered moral support because I couldn't offer any support of a technical nature. I had to rely on the teenage wizard entirely, and when he finally completed his preliminary survey and lifted his dented head, I asked him what he thought.

The answer came in a language barely English. I heard about bezels and things called solenoids. I was required only to nod, as if I knew exactly what the merit-badge mechanic meant. I had to keep that pretense up for only a few minutes because after Cheek had cleaned his hands on a rag, he said he'd have to look for parts. Then he climbed aboard his bike and wheeled away.

That began what turned out to be a half-month of sporadic visits. Cheek most often came alone, but occasionally he arrived with a companion, a tubby youngster, also on a bike, named Eugene who seemed to function as squire to Cheek's shining knight. Eugene served as sounding board to Cheek's ideas about what the Studebaker needed. He assisted sometimes like a surgical nurse, slapping tools into Cheek's greasy hand at the young wizard's whispered requests. He offered Cheek his unquestioning loyalty. Given Cheek's sterling character, that fidelity seemed appropriate. It also made me wonder about the sources of Cheek's moral strength. Who were his parents? What was their background? How had the boy come by his inner resources?

Mint's answer to those questions—when I halted him before he left one rainy night—began wryly. "Cheek's the proverbial rose on the metaphorical pile of manure," he said. "His dad is more or less a con man, though he owns Star Point Cannery now and contracts with Libby, McNeil & Libby to supply their salmon. Came out of East Bayonne, I think. He got hold of the cannery by marrying the original owner's daughter. That mating produced two children. The other one's a girl, much like her mother in terms of snooty deportment. Cheek is the family's gentlemanly exception. He told me once he hoped heaven would have an auto-repair garage. I asked him about his hopes for a celestial Burger Barn. He missed the drift of what I said and told me he'd be happy with a soft-serve ice-cream place. That's when he became a friend."

Mint was still spilling out details of young Cheek's manure background when the pear-shaped man, whose name I'd learned was Morris, sauntered into view with his grey cat on its dirty string. Mike, the natural-born fence post, again was with him.

"Give the cat some crumbles," Mint told me. He'd scrubbed his hands and didn't want hamburger grease to stain them.

I had, on occasion, treated the cat to hamburger leftovers. I'd only done it on nights when Morris the Pear walked the animal alone. I had never consciously said to myself, *I don't want to stoop down in front of moron Mike because his natural instinct to bash strangers on the head might overwhelm his more humanitarian instincts.* I didn't want to think in such a formal way about Cal's midget minion. I had no evidence that Mike had been the wielder of the bat that laid me low. On the other hand, I didn't need evidence. I hated him anyway. Hatred, sometimes, is such a satisfying emotion. It concentrates your thoughts and helps you devise insulting monikers—like *natural-born fence-post* and *moron Mike.*

Rather than stoop down and feed a cat associated with Cal's cretin helper, I would have preferred to conk *him* on the head. That would have been, to me, a noble deed. I pictured myself handing out business cards bearing the legend, *Noble Deeds Performed at Bargain Rates*, with a line-drawing illustration of me knocking Mike for a loop.

But my boss was watching. Mint, I had learned, had fought his way from Anzio up the Italian boot to liberate the city of Rome from the fascists. Never mind that he had topped that military exploit by trading bootleg nylons to Roman matrons for nights of love. Mint was still a darn nice guy.

In response to his order, I filled my palm with the charred and crumbled remains of somebody's half-eaten hamburger, and—as if I bore the dimwit Mike no ill-will—stooped down near his feet to serve the cat. I would not like to make a career out of kneeling down in front of pocket-sized thugs. If I did, I would lose what little self-respect I'd managed to accumulate through my years of poverty, incarceration, and parole. Precious little self-respect, in the grander scheme of things. I had no money. I had a flunky's job. I locked my bedroom door against the amorous assaults of my landlady. I planned to rob a whore who'd had her thugette participate in beating me up. That thugette stood over me. I won't say he *loomed* because looming was beyond Mike's physical capacities. But he was up and I was down. I glanced at him over my shoulder and saw him pleasantly beaming. He beamed at me as much as at the cat. I could tell from the way his button eyes blinked he wanted to be nice. I then had a thought I knew at once might transform my life. *Be nice to Mike, Sweetcheeks. He well may know where the old whore hides her loot.*

Dr. Cheek kept showing up for house calls on the recovering Studebaker, bringing the equivalent of prescription pills in the form of rubber do-hickeys and metal thing-a-ma-bobs. He continued his work under the hood, taking the equivalent of the car's temperature and checking on its automotive pulse. When Eugene accompanied him, they stepped aside from time to time for murmured consultations. In my chilly forays to the sickroom, I had heard the word 'bezel' often enough to recognize it when the two spoke. I had no idea what it meant. If Cheek had told me it was a hard-shelled nut that grew only in marshy places in Brazil, I would have nodded, as if knowingly.

Meanwhile, Mrs. Baskins made her scented assaults from the house, trilling optimistic sentiments and regaling me with plans for a glorious picnic at her father's swimming hole in celebration of Cheek's expected achievement.

Summer was edging its timid way toward Boon, and the city was shaking off its winter torpor. Boats from the halibut fleet steamed into port. Loggers stumbled from one bar to the next drinking themselves full before their dry spell in the woods. Trollers stocked up on canned hams and Campbell's soup. They then braved late spring's gusty winds to reach the fishing grounds.

The sun did not exactly beam, but it poked a ray or two between cloud patches often enough to assure rain-weary citizens it hadn't gone out.

In the Burger Barn I served my premium midnight hamburgers and six a.m. coffees. I listened to endless pornographic anecdotes from the jolly doughnut man, and heard from the late-night DJ more complaints about the abysmal musical taste of the audience his airborne broadcasts reached.

On the last day of May, Cheek took me aside and confided that he hoped he could have the car running by the fifth of June. He said Eugene, who enjoyed the use of the high school auto-crafts shop because his father was the school janitor, was milling a final part, and if it came off the lathe the way they hoped it should complete the car's repairs.

The reason he requested privacy to convey this information remains a mystery. It may be that he feared Mrs. Baskins, in her exuberance at hearing such good news, might plant a sloppy kiss on his chin or jaw, as she frequently stretched up on tiptoe to plant on mine.

Whatever his reason, Cheek did show up, with his friend Eugene, in bright sunshine on the fifth of June. They brought, wrapped in what looked like toilet paper, a ring of fine metal they said was the bezel and held it up for me and Mrs. Baskins to admire.

It looked like a crown for the king of the squirrels, but of course I didn't say that to the boys. They were proud of their achievement and eager to fix it in place.

Cheek already had the hood up and a screwdriver in his hand when Mrs. Baskins exclaimed, "Wait! Wait!" She wobbled into her kitchen and returned mere seconds later waving a screwdriver and shouting, "Use this!" The screwdriver she offered had the S from the Studebaker signature stamped on its handle.

"It came with the car," she told us, and she fluttered her eyes in my direction as if her words were words of love.

Both boys worked at getting the bezel secured. Into it they clamped the Studebaker's ignition. Or I believe that's what they clamped. Their words escaped from under the hood and were subject to misinterpretation.

With the bezel secure and the ignition in place, Cheek and Eugene tackled the corroded battery terminals. When the terminals were clean, they hooked the battery up again.

Mr. Taggs, perhaps because of his motoring past, found himself shoved by Mrs. Baskins out of the house, still in his paisley bathrobe, and made to take a seat behind the Studebaker's wheel.

As he turned the key, the engine caught and purred to life.

I shook the grinning Cheek's begrimed right hand. Then he was assaulted from behind by the rapturous Mrs. Baskins who seized on the moment of triumph not only to surprise him with a warm embrace but to plant a wealth of kisses on the back of his left ear.

I might never have seen Darlene Sandusky again if Mr. Taggs hadn't followed through on his promise to teach me to drive. I was behind the Studebaker's wheel, with Mr. Taggs cringing at my side, when I slowed to a stop at the Harbor Street corner to let four pedestrians hurry past. One of them, I saw, was Darlene. My instinct was to roll the window down and yell, 'I like your hair.' The wavy shape Andre had given her hair had transformed Miss Sandusky so completely I had to glance a second time to make sure it was she. The woman I saw was shapely, modestly dressed, and animated in the conversation she was having with the woman at her side. My very first thought when I saw her was 'I'm glad she's not with Chip.' I could pleasantly think of Chip off at some island village teaching up-on-the-down-teeth and down-on-the-up-teeth to attentive little children. I could not wish that a tidal wave would come and sweep Chip out to sea. A disaster of that magnitude would sweep the little children away, too, and even I am not a moral monster enough to wish for that.

Might I have wished that were Miss Sandusky not with Chip she would be with me? Miss Sandusky had last seen me with a hooker on my arm. 'A hooker clinging to my arm' is what I should say. A hooker like an alien life-form growing from my rib cage. A Siamese-twin hooker permanently attached. A defect of character made flesh.

I also could not think thoughts linking me to Miss Sandusky because I had Mrs. Baskins in her back-seat lair constantly advising me, in a voice of rising alarm, "Eyes on the road, Sweetcheeks. Please! Eyes on the road." To emphasize her order or command, my landlady finger-snapped the back of my head. To finger-snap, you trap your index finger with your thumb, and then you strain the finger forward until it escapes and slaps the object you have aimed at with all the force a finger has. It is an efficient and be-littling correction. It is used on boys ten-years-old or younger. It stings just perfectly enough to remind them they are small and someone else is giving orders.

I drove on, with Mr. Taggs in the passenger seat, pleading, "Slow... Slow..."

We passed the spot on the street where Darlene had crossed. I inhaled deeply, as if she might have left some scent behind. Essence of crab-salad, I might say, but what an inadequate and punk description that would have been.

It was a more-than-misty morning, and Darlene seemed to have been hurrying to work. As she reached the left side of the street, the lights came on in a men's shop she was approaching. Mannequins in suits and ties jumped suddenly out of their off-duty gloom, prepared, as it were, to sing and dance in a Technicolor movie, a chorus greeting Darlene's step onto the curb. I would have sung and dance myself, but I lacked the talent and the nerve.

"Go...Go. . ." Mr. Taggs whispered, hoarse and desperate.

The street had cleared. Darlene had tripped away. I stepped on the gas.

I was with Mr. Taggs at a later date when fate ordained that I should see Darlene a second time. I had convinced my nervous instructor I needed driving lessons in the dark. What I didn't tell him was I needed nighttime skills because I planned to burglarize the horrible Cal as soon as I learned what secret safe or vault or robber cave the venerable procuress tiptoed to in the dark of night to squirrel her unreported profits away. Darlene, when I saw her this time, was with fussy little Warren, who, on a snowy night some months before, had brought her to the Windward Bar. On my driver-education night, she and Mr. Prissy were in the flow of a crowd streaming out of a movie where the feature must have been something comical. Faces were aglow, and guys were repeating to their dates the movie's best jokes.

Streetlights glowed and shop windows threw their scant illumination where couples and friend-groups walked. I was gloating at the thought of little Warren Arsenault as Miss Sandusky's escort. He did not represent a rival the way the politely flatulent Chip did. I had only an instant to treasure that understanding. Mrs. Baskins, a guardful and observant backseat passenger, leaned forward for a glimpse of the theater's marquee. "Is that the Clifton Webb picture," I heard her ask Mr. Taggs. "If it is, I want to see it. I hear it's really good."

Mr. Taggs had flattened himself against his seat cushion. He kept whispering, "Slow," in a choked voice, because the movie crowd, as such crowds do, streamed out to cross the street without regard for traffic.

As I pulled to a halt, Darlene strolled into the beam of our headlights, her hair in its new arrangement, darkness hiding her face. She passed like a lighthouse beacon, brilliant for one second and then swallowed by the dark.

I hoped she was happy. I sincerely, devoutly, and deliriously hoped she was happy.

"Drive," Mr. Taggs whimpered in his cringing voice.

And Mrs. Baskins—*always* Mrs. Baskins—whispered in my ear. "It *is* the Clifton Webb movie. I'd love to see it but I'd have to find someone to go with. I hate to go to movies by myself."

Again—insistent—the drumming fingers on the flat part of my neck, much like, I imagine, an executioner's exploratory touch before he swings his fatal blade.

To those who know my history of failures to be nice it may come as a surprise to learn I eventually *did* escort Mrs. Baskins to the movie starring the always dapper Clifton Webb. I enjoyed what I saw. There's nothing wrong with a few laughs. Walking home, I allowed the Studebaker's owner to hang on my arm. I listened to her blather about Esther Williams. Esther Williams had not been in the movie we had seen but Esther, because of her swimming prowess, was one of Mrs. Baskins' favorite stars. I agreed with every superlative Mrs. Baskins uttered about Esther's looks, and swimming talent, and acting skills. I even agreed when Mrs. Baskins said a lot of people told her she was the Esther Williams of Boon. I saw no harm in being agreeable. I had two examples of agreeable people as models for behavior. One was the extremely helpful Cheek. The other was the always kind Darlene—the sole two stars in my skimpy moral firmament.

Not counting Mr. Tinsel. Mr. Tinsel had done an unselfish thing. He had invited a former felon to Boon and promised to help him start life anew. There'd been a bit of duplicity to his offer, of course. He wanted a criminal's assistance in ending the career of the owner of a brothel and employer of thugs. All for a good cause, all for the advancement of Protestant civilization with its emphasis on industry and thrift.

Mr. Tinsel, with his somewhat devious plan for my off-hours employment, represented for me the morally fudging mass of men and women to which I acknowledge myself as rather grudgingly belonging. I know I can be as upstanding a citizen as anyone else if I see something to be gained from it. I was already busy in the kindness vineyards. I regularly fed a thankless cat crumbled bits of hamburger, stooping down in the wet street to do it. I offered pleasantries to the pear-shaped walker of the beast and refrained, by some superhuman effort, from kicking Pear-Shape's dopey, sawed-off, grinning, doltish, thuggish, slightly simian companion. By being nice to Mike, perhaps I'd help Mr. Tinsel advance the anti-Cal cause close to his heart. I might at least be doing the harlot damage. One hand rubs the other, as the old saying tells us. But there's a complicated choreography to that. It involves the part of us that's crooked, and the part that Sunday School teachers give gold stars to. The gold-star person has to hide the crooked person, and the crooked person has to tolerate the platitudes of virtue. I say all this knowing almost nothing of the complicated moral plumbing that keeps human beings functioning. Books on that subject crowd scholarly shelves. They say nothing about love. They go on and on and on about psychology, but they say nothing whatsoever about an imperfect human being and the remote possibility of convicted killers triumphing at love.

CHAPTER

XX

I don't want to give the impression Mrs. Baskins accompanied me on all my driver-training trips. She stayed home soused much of the time, and it was very nearly the end of June before she spoke of what she called our 'date.' She meant the trip she had proposed to the beach her father had helped build.

"We'll make it a picnic," she trilled as she wrapped egg-salad sandwiches in waxed paper and put them in a wicker basket with two apples, four cookies and two bottles of beer. She also put a blanket in the car. "Just in case," she said.

I knew she would have giggled if I asked her what *just in case* meant. She made almost all her picnic preparations giggling. It was like forty years had vanished from her age, and her jelly flesh had been replaced by the sinews and cartilage and firm muscles of Esther Williams.

The transformation was only metaphorical. The jelly flesh sagged and wrinkled as before. The jowls drooped. The same bruised-looking bags pouched up beneath her eyes. I heard her coy *just in case* with the dead feeling I would have had if a black-robed judge pronounced on me a life-time sentence of hard labor, and on the cloudy morning of our adventure day, I sullenly soaked in the tub, hearing my soon-to-be companion singing in the kitchen as she shelled the eggs and chopped them up with mayonnaise. By the time I was dressed and drinking coffee in the kitchen, clouds, which eternally hovered on Boon's horizon, had drifted across the sky like herds of bison.

"It's going to rain," I said to Mrs. Baskins.

She dashed to the door and pulled it open to squint at the sky. "It might get a little dewy, but we'll be having fun, so we won't pay any attention."

They play baseball in Boon in the rain. They marry. They bury. They brawl. Whatever gamboling they do takes place in meadows so drenched in dew they soak their sorry asses right through their woolen underwear.

As it turned out, the day did dew-up a bit. "It's kind of romantic. We'll have the beach to ourselves," Mrs. Baskins tittered. She made it sound salacious, like everything she said. I had to ask myself at this last minute if the pleasure of plotting a burglary outweighed the obligation Mrs. Baskins' curdling insinuations predicted. I didn't for a single moment doubt it did, and in between my sips of steaming coffee I rewarded my landlady, my possible paramour and doughy inamorata, with my best imitation of a smile.

"South out of town and then straight to the beach," Mrs. Baskins sang to me as I steered out of the alley in which her house squatted.

I had a reasonable command of the vehicle I had only recently learned to drive, but I was not self-assured enough to more than glance at the sights my landlady eagerly pointed out.

"That's the Teal Brothers cannery."

I saw a purple wall slide by.

"There's the cold storage."

White walls and a glimpse of blue water between what looked like storage sheds.

"Coast Guard base."

A helmeted man in a comic-opera guard post stood sentinel over what looked, from our hillside vantage point, like a huddle of grey roofs.

We passed through a native village, and Mrs. Baskins suggested we come out and take pictures of the totem poles someday. More egg-salad sandwiches, I assumed. All the pitty-patty silliness of love. The grins and goosings. The baby-talk baloney put to carnal purposes. Science tells us there are cells that reproduce just by dividing. How much more time than we those cells must have for pondering the mysteries of physics and finding meaning in the stars. Not that I'm opposed to sex. I am just opposed to nuisance, which a fifty-year-old fatty with egg salad sandwiches is very close to representing in the ample flesh.

Nevertheless, there was Cal. There was her home. There was the secret place in which she kept her profits hidden from the IRS. So bring on the Mrs. Baskins of the world. I had the grit for anything if it would help me reach my goal.

That was my thought as Mrs. B leaned out into the wind and gleefully yelled, "The beach!"

I did not see a single grain of sand. A grain of sand would have had to walk all the way from California to find this lousy beach. It would set its suitcases down and bawl, and as soon as it could dry its eyes it would send postcards to its fellow grains back on California's sun-kissed shores and tell them to stay home.

I parked in a packed-dirt lot defined by massive timbers dragged in place to form a barrier just off the road. The Studebaker stood, the solitary vehicle in that circle of gravel and dirt. I saw glimpses of water through a curtain of hemlocks and spruces. My companion, carrying the nuance-laden blanket, chirped, "This way," and I followed her down a path so rich in fallen needles from the swaying evergreens it was like a scented carpet, commercially piney.

When I stepped out of the shelter of the trees, I saw a dimple-sized cove walled off from the restless outer waters by a concrete wall. The wall trapped a pool shaped like a coffee cup. Three of its banks were rock tailings and the fourth was the famous concrete dam Mrs. Baskins' late father, with the help of the Rotarians, had conjured into place. The swimming water in the cup's depression looked sludgy and lifeless, but Mrs. Baskins, who dropped the blanket and skipped down to the water's edge to heave a rock and squeal like a girl, explained that when the tide was high strong freshets from the sea poured in. "It's nature's way of sanitation," she explained. Then she smiled at the scenery to let nature know how proud of it she was. "My father's name is on a plaque. Come on. I'll show you."

What I said about tailings mostly was true. There may have been, in times before the pick-axe and explosives, a natural shoreline of kelp-slick rocks as ridden with hummocks and hills as nature intends. Reports, erroneous, as it turned out, of hillside veins of gold a half a century ago had sent Hard-Rock Nelson and his palsied like panting up slender trails. On their donkey-powered rail-carts they ferried tons of tailings to the beach, and now those tailings, rich in the gleaming ore called fool's gold, made up about half the pool's lip. On the bank above the water, scrubby brush had put in a determined reappearance, and it was through that scrubby brush Mrs. Baskins led me.

We had barely reached the grassy ridge of one of the defining slopes when what looked like the moss-covered roof of a wicked witch's house blinked into sight. It nestled within a stand of evergreens a stone's throw to our left.

"Cal's," Mrs. Baskins called out in a derisive voice. She jerked her thumb in the direction of the roof, and I pretended no more interest than I would have had in a briar or the desiccated carcass of a crab. All the time we picked our way closer to the commemorative plaque, however, I had my eye on the dwelling, which, step by step, came more clearly into sight.

What I saw was not a single house but a compound of buildings that looked tacked together as need demanded. The place had grown from what might have been a fishing hut into some sort of seasonal dwelling and then into a place of year-round occupancy with room for relatives visiting from Duluth. I saw no sign of life except the gold DeSoto, a car of recent vintage, parked on a gravel apron near the front door. No shadow passed before a window. I heard no thump from someone chopping wood nor the screams of anybody being beaten with a club. I did not want to stop and stare in a way that would have made the interest I took in Cal's dwelling obvious, but as I stumbled after Mrs. Baskins on a path that brought me to a stand of hemlock trees, I saw a pastel flash pop from a front door and disappear inside the DeSoto.

I froze in the stillness of the hemlock arbor and saw a second figure, the troll-sized Mike, emerge in a bustle and scurry to the car. He climbed into the driver's seat, sitting, I'm sure, on an egg crate to allow him to reach the wheel. In a moment the DeSoto was gone. The house sat in tempting solitude.

Mrs. Baskins broke the spell the stillness cast. "Here it is," she shouted. "Here's the plaque." She waved me over to a pillar anchoring the concrete wall. On a greened-up plate of bronze or brass I saw a list of names engraved. The elements had not been kind to the cheap metal, but with my landlady's eager help and with my own imagination I read, down near the bottom of the list, the name Adolph Lowell.

"That was Daddy," Mrs. Baskins sighed.

"It's beautiful."

"Isn't it nice here." She turned in a nearly complete circle to take in the isolated panorama.

After that came kisses. And the stripping off of clothes.

The sex, I must admit, except for the rocks and the mosquitoes, wasn't bad. Except for the rocks and the mosquitoes and the companion, of course. But probably the companion goes without mentioning. So the sex was good except for the aforementioned and also except for the fear I had all during the act that a hectic mother and her chirping children would pull up in the parking lot and a bug-eyed horde would swarm down on our dalliance.

Mosquitoes. Rocks. Companion. The possibility of bug-eyed toddlers. That's the complete list of exceptions to my sex-act pleasure not counting the egg-salad sandwiches which I would have to trudge my way to the picnic basket and pretend to enjoy, despite the fact that the smell of an egg-salad sandwich when it first emerges from its wax-paper wrapper almost always makes me gag. I know I am a very sorry human being because not only current disagreeableness but the prospect of disagreeableness-yet-to-come distracts me from the ecstasies of sex.

Well, what is sex for? Let us ask ourselves that question. It is certainly for reproduction and the preservation of the species through eons yet to come. It can be the subject for a lot of really funny jokes. It gives a person something to do when the electricity fails on a Sunday evening and he can't turn his radio on and laugh at Jack Benny's jokes. It is also a commercial enterprise which involves, at one extreme, people with the moral caliber of the cruel procuress Cal employing the young but hardened vixen known professionally as Breen, and at the other extreme a lot of blue-nosed, church-going, stalwart, respectable, pillar-of-the-community types—e.g. Ellery Tinsel—who, in addition to being moral role models, are also somebody's wife or somebody's husband with all the give and take and horse-trading husbandry and wifery involves.

Yes, sex plays a role in the domestic power structure, too. While, let us say, Male A in any given set of married couples is plotting and hoping and praying to get his rocks off, his wife, Female A, is calculating what it is going to cost to re-upholster the armchair, and how she's going to make her husband pony up.

There's always going to be tension between a man's freedom to goof off and whatever domestic arrangements the female believes are the very *minimum* requirements for respectable standing among her housewife peers. I am not saying there's anything wrong with this. I am merely saying that the thought of it comes swiftly after climax, and once the male's spent, as the poets speak of this experience, he's also depressed.

Or at least I am.

Plus, the mosquitoes depressed me. The rocks. The possibility of being spied upon by some gap-toothed six-year-old and his prepubescent sister. The god-damn sandwiches, etc.

Also the companion, who didn't even try to roll her satisfied self off the rocks and put her clothes on but who plopped fully out like a great white whale of love stranded on the kelp-wracked shores of sex. I heard her speak in rapturous sentences of the future we might have. I *hope* her sentences were rapturous. I do not like to be unmannerly about the episode I might delicately call the encounter on the beach. Even over-ripe landladies deserve a little rapture, and I am justified in looking on the service I'd performed as a good deed. Ordinarily, of course, I do not congratulate myself on my philanthropic qualities, but the duty I'd performed benefitted Mrs. Baskins. It perked her up. Rejuvenated her. Her frowsiness, her dowdiness, I might even say her habitual sourness faded. She trilled and chirped, and since I had played a prominent part in bringing those chirps and trills up from the basement of her soul I could tell myself, or so I believed, that I had performed a deed in keeping with benevolent principles and charitable instincts.

Imagine my surprise, then, when Mrs. B began to speak about a leaky toilet at her god-damn house. "They say it can rot out the floorboards unless something gets done right away."

I suggested she call a professional plumber because I had no toilet-fixing skills.

She said it wasn't hard to fix a little leak.

"Where is the leak, Mrs. Baskins?"

"It's at that ring of wax around the base where the toilet connects with the soil pipe."

"What's a soil pipe?"

She propped herself up on one elbow and cast a baleful glance at me. "You don't want to do it, do you?"

"I wouldn't have the least idea how."

"Mr. Taggs did it once."

"Have Mr. Taggs do it again, then. Let him work off some of his rent."

I stood up. I pulled my underpants on. I would have put my pants on, too, but Mrs. Baskins grabbed them, whining as she did, "I was nice to you, Alan. Don't you think you owe me one small favor?"

"Give me my pants, please."

"I planned this whole day just so you could come and see the wonderful work my father did for children. No one in Boon thought of building a pool before he did. There was hardly any place to swim except to jump off the docks. It wasn't safe for children. My father saw that right away. And he didn't have much money either. He had to talk the Rotarians into helping out."

"Please, Mrs. Baskins, my pants."

She didn't hand them over. She sat on them instead. "I knew right away you would take advantage of me. That's exactly the kind of person you are. You'd probably run off to Sacramento with the Moose Club if I gave you half the chance. You're just like him. You're just like every man. It's *wham* and *bam* and *thank you, ma'am*. To you I'm just another easy lay."

"Not with those god-damn sandwiches," I said. "Egg salad makes me puke. But let's not spoil things, shall we, Mrs. B. It's been a lovely picnic. It's been a lovely day. I will shed some god-damn tears about your father if you like, but I will not fix your fucking toilet. Call in the Rotarians for that."

I stormed down to the water's edge, although storm is the wrong word to use for walking barefoot over stones. I didn't want to see Mrs. Baskins bawl, even if turning my back on her opened up the possibility she might throw a rock. I took that risk. I reached the water's edge. I stood and faced her father's fetid pond. *Let her throw*, I thought. *Conk me good and knock me cold. I'll drift along the shore until the kiddies come to romp.*

I enjoyed picturing my corpse afloat in the scummy pool. I saw it floating very much at peace. *How serene the dead must be*, I thought. *How fortunate they are. No fifty-year-old fatties with broken toilets to be fixed.* I closed my eyes and wished away the world's soil pipes. I wished away the wax rings that connected them to toilets. I thought that somewhere on this earth there must exist an Eden where people can plan to rob a hardened whore without complications from sex and peanut-butter cookies. I longed for such a paradise. I would drift in calm contentment there, more like vapor than like flesh, a thing with no more substance than a cloud.

I entertained this dream for a long minute, and when I turned to reason again with my landlady, I found she was gone.

So were my pants.

Gap-tooth and his pre-pubescent sister, just as I had feared, showed up almost on cue. They popped out of their mother's Packard at exactly the same minute I walked up from the beach and brought my pantsless self into their view. Mother screamed, of course. I launched, as nonchalantly as I could, my near-nude walk to town, but before I'd gone a quarter of a mile I heard sirens.

One good thing—I didn't have to eat Mrs. Baskins' god-damn sandwiches. I had kicked her wicker basket into her father's fetid pool. She didn't ask me about her basket because she wasn't sober enough to even answer the door when I showed up with my Territorial Trooper chauffeur. The door-answering duty fell to Mr. Taggs in his damned paisley robe. I could tell by his craven attitude he had reason to fear an encounter with the law. Moral lapses, I assumed. I guessed it was his conscience that made him flinch. And yet I was the one standing on the saggy porch in my Jockey underpants. Taggs summoned up the courage to confirm my residence at Mrs. Baskins' sour little dump. The wooden-faced Trooper departed. The blue light blinking on his patrol car's roof had drawn every ragamuffin in the alley. The crowd parted to let the law put itself into reverse and crawl back to the street, but by that time I was already in my Baskins' cell kicking my bed, and punching the walls, and bulleting curses at the world in general for treating a convicted killer in such a shoddy way.

Worse was to come.

"Hah!" Mrs. Baskins bellowed when I slunk out of my room on my way to find a bite for dinner. She had commandeered the kitchen passageway. She waved Boon's daily paper in my face. "Read this, Sweetcheeks. I hope it makes you proud."

What she showed me was not a front-page story. For that I can be grateful. But on an inside page, about halfway to the bottom, under the heading Police Report, I had made the news for walking down a highway *sans* trousers.

I snatched the paper and devoured the paragraph. Mrs. Baskins didn't wait for me to finish. "And where's my wicker basket?" She yanked the paper from my hands to roar her question in my face.

"Your cheap, goddamn basket is disintegrating in your father's foul swimming hole, Mrs. B. You can find it there with the beer bottles and condoms and all the other assorted trash. May the tide perform its sanitary duty and wash the gimcrack thing away. Let the ocean carry it to China. Tell China it's a god-damn family heirloom. The entire Chinese nation would laugh right in your face."

The diatribe I let fly carried me out the door. I scooted past the Studebaker, composing more insults. The Moose Club, for example, and the red-head with big tits. I reached the Frontier Café still fuming, and when Malcom the Apprentice Mooch sidled up and begged for change the only thing preventing me from snapping off his head was his forlorn homeliness. He had a sodden look about the eyes, and the very best scraggly whiskers a boy of his tender years could manage. He didn't ask for change as if he expected to get some. He asked his timid question as if afraid he might be punched and driven away.

I found a quarter in my pocket. I handed it to him. He closed his fist around it and hurried off. I watched his hunched back vanish out the door before I took my nearly habitual seat at the counter. There I found, close to my right hand, someone's discarded copy of the Boon Daily News. While I waited for my chili, I read again the paragraph about my run-in with the law.

It was, thankfully, only a paragraph, and it was buried inside. It didn't even lead the column. I could almost convince myself no one would read it, except as I spooned up my dreadful chili, I began to imagine District Attorney Richard Chambers picking his teeth and reading. He was a person born to gloat over another's misfortune. He would shout to Miss Sandusky, in his outer office: "Come see this! Our little friend." He'd poke the paragraph with his fat finger when Miss Sandusky reached for the page he would be offering her.

'Little friend' was exactly the sort of sarcasm a brute of Chambers' limited vocabulary would employ. The two words would imply that Miss Sandusky should have known better than to exchange pleasantries with me at her receptionist's desk. The words would inform her his judgment of human beings was superior to hers, and that he could have told her that anyone who shot a scrap-metal merchant in Illinois would naturally take off his pants and stroll down a highway in Alaska.

Though that's something Miss Sandusky probably knew herself. She knew, at least, that a person who had shot a scrap-metal merchant had linked arms with a frail hooker and trotted around the corner of the post office looking very much like someone who had just crawled out of a love-soiled bed and was eager to crawl back in.

Breen and I had rounded that corner just as Miss Sandusky had set off for Yakamoto's and its specialty green tea.

Oh horrible green tea! Oh twigs and leaves of musty, stale aroma. Concoction of weak color and very nearly indiscernible taste. Can I blame green tea for all my problems?

No. Green tea had nothing to do with my little frolic on the beach, nor with wax-ring dams for soil-pipe connections. I was in the paper for faults entirely my own. And my reward was loathsome chili and mooching Malcolm. My loss—crab-salad sand-wiches and the warmth and wonder crab-salad sandwiches suggest.

What was I to do? I asked myself that question, and in a flash of inspiration a voice in my somewhat-healed head said, "Go to Yakamoto's. Buy a package of their best green tea. Mail it to Miss Sandusky with a card signed, "Your friend, Alan."

I *did* go to Yakamoto's.

I *did* buy the green tea.

I did not mail it.

My nerve failed me.

I planned to be indifferent to the notoriety the gap-toothed child and his screaming mom had brought me, but before I could show indifference to the sneers of the people of Boon, the people of Boon, sneering or not, showed indifference to me. Citizens had more pressing matters on their minds—mainly getting very, very drunk. We had reached the eve of that national festival celebrated annually on the fourth day of the seventh month, and in the run-up to that patriotic holiday people practiced their swigging and their tippling and guzzling so that, on the immortal anniversary itself, they could play their parts with pride, many of them peaking in their stupor well before the fireworks went off.

"You missed all the fun," Mint told me while I tied my white apron on. "Two fist-fights, a half-dozen cussings-out, one public urination, and a frozen halibut used as a weapon in what ap-peared to be a parking-place dispute."

"A spectacle worth selling tickets for, boss."

"Your buddy Mike came by."

"I hope he asked what I was doing in my underwear two miles out of town."

"I don't remember that subject coming up, Alan. Should it have?"

"What should have come up, boss, is the generous pension package my employment here provides. By my calculations, that package will furnish me with all the resources I'll need to lead a life of comfort for about thirty-two seconds after I hang up my greasy apron on my last day as a short-order cook. I have enjoyed the hospitality of Boon for almost one full year, and in those three-hundred-sixty-plus days I have been bashed on the head, on one occasion, and deprived of my dignity by a hooting eight-year-old on another. I won't offend your delicate ears with the story that disgrace involves. Suffice it to say, boss, that the incident has left me what I will call out-of-sorts. Not-entirely-pleased, in other words. *Dissatisfied* might be the best coloring I can put on the mood to which I've sunk. I see no profit in virtue. Not that virtue, with her little magic wand, has tapped me on the head and gilded me from head to toe. But I have been a reason-ably pleasant, usually reliable, and even somewhat honest Burger Barn employee, and it's hard for me to understand why my re-wards aren't greater than the privilege I enjoy of frying hamburg-ers for drunks."

Mint moved to the door and didn't speak until his hand was on the handle. "If they canonized people for self-pity, Alan, I would probably be a saint myself. I am sorry if your compensation pack-age does not permit you to vacation in Hawaii. Richer rewards may await you, and I hope they do, though I have to say I do not think you'll reap them by striding in your underwear down the main highway of our town. Be kind. Be good. Be generous. Those traits become their own reward. And you've got some goodness credits on your scorecard now. Look at the way you feed that cat. Be happy with that. Mike or Morris, for all we know, might re-member you in their wills." He waved in the way a person does to forestall a reply. "They might be writing their wills exactly at this moment." He liked his own eloquence, I guess, and didn't want to hear sarcasm from me. He gave a grave nod, pulled open the door, and strode away into the noisy night.

What revolutionary thinking. That was my first thought. *Why had no one before ever told me to be good?*

Well, actually, the State of Illinois—with its wardens and its guards and its panopticon prison—had made a mighty try. And in his own charming way, Richard Chambers, the district attorney, had attempted the same thing. Illinois and the D.A. had coercion on their side, and coercion is a strong inducement for a felon to behave. I shuddered at the threat coercion, in my case, implied. I had not stolen, nor had I, to best of my recollection, murdered anyone during the nearly entire year since I'd stepped on Boon's wet shore. But that didn't leave me blameless, not in Mr. Chambers' eyes.

A drunk stumbled in. I put his patty on to fry. I tried to decipher his request for a beverage. When I put a Coke in front of him, he insisted on paying at once. I took his dime and nickel to the cash drawer. I rang the transaction up and when the drawer slid open, I saw Mint had not removed the day's receipts. The drawer was full of money. I don't know how much. I slammed it shut too quickly to even try to count. I didn't want to be a tempted. I had to think, nonetheless, why Mint had forgotten, on this holiday eve, to bag up his take and remove it for deposit in the bank. The bank would not be open on the Fourth, of course. Perhaps his reasoning was that he'd do his banking on the Fifth. Still, the drawer held lots of money. Call that the holiday effect. I knew I'd need a hundred dollars to buy a ticket out of town. I'd gone through that exercise before. A ticket cost four times what my weekly wages were.

I was not saying to myself that I would steal. I could view whatever I might do as withdrawing what was owed me. Not that I believed that shallow rationalization for even one second. What

I was contemplating—despite my best intentions and my conscious avowal *not* to entertain even the thought of a crime as vile as theft from a friend—what I was contemplating was to pocket the hamburger money and fly out of town the next day.

It would be a crime against Mint, who'd employed and befriended me. It would not be as innocent a thing as trotting off to sell the bumper of a stranger's Chevrolet. I enjoyed my boss's trust. That's what I should have been thinking, and perhaps, on a certain level, that's what I *was* thinking. But uppermost in my thoughts were the logistics of my very roughly sketched-out crime. Could I buy an airplane ticket on July the Fourth? How soon would Mint know the money was missing? What if he called the police in Seattle and they were waiting when I arrived?

Those are the problems a well-schooled thief should apply himself to before sticking his hand in a cash drawer. I qualify as a well-schooled thief, and I weighed those problems with appropriate gravity.

At the same time as I weighed them, though—I weighed what Mint had done for me. Except that's not quite the abstraction that occurred to me. I pictured instead my grease-stained boss on his knees feeding crumbles of left-over hamburger to a charcoal-colored cat. That example of kindness—a brutal example if you look at it from a thief's point of view—kept me from immediately helping myself to Mint's money.

Mint's example stayed my hand, plus the patty I was frying for the drunk required my attention. I took great pains with the presentation of that inebriate's fifty-cent meal—the spreading on of mayonnaise, the selection of the crispest lettuce leaf, symmetry in placing the pickle, the generous heaping up of chips. I slid the plate in front of the bum, and while he labored to bring his eyes to focus, I silently prayed for some sign or clue or omen about what I ought to do—betray my boss and, I must say, my friend, or resign myself to a perpetual life of putting artistically arranged hamburger sandwiches in front of clueless souses.

That's what I was thinking when the cat-walking Morris appeared. Framed beside him in my emporium's front window was Cal's diminutive factotum, Mike.

Outside, I knelt. "The obligation to indulge one's self on national holidays—how nobly the patriots of Boon rise to these occasions," I said to the cat. "I have seen them stagger. I have seen them totter and pass out in the street."

I didn't *actually* say that to the cat. I said it to the cat's two scarecrow handlers.

"Hoorah for the flag. Hoorah for the national anthem. Hoorah for Santa Claus and Christmas. I believe, gentlemen, those holidays are the only thing that separate us from tigers and wolves. We'd be disemboweling one another in publicly funded arenas if it weren't for Independence Day and the god-damn star of Bethlehem. What is the consensus on that thought? What do the two of you think?"

I stayed on my knees, with crumbles in my hand. The cat tickled my palm with his soft nose. I had knelt to launch my charm offensive, and by kneeling I proclaimed as an article of faith that I believed the flesh mountain Morris and his subhuman companion had been sent to this sad corner of Boon by the angel in charge of preventing felons from stealing the hamburger profits of their kindhearted employers.

Morris responded with a ponderous nod. Mike's only answer came in the form of a simian grin. To other simians the spreading of lips and wrinkling of cheeks might suggest profundities. I did not expect profundities from Mike. I had never had any proof that he even understood English. If I had said to him, "Fetch," or if I'd said, "Sit," I might shrewdly guess how he'd respond. To reward him, I could let him feed out of my hand. That was my only thought about Mike.

The walkers of the cat watched me rise and brush the last of the crumbles off my greasy palms. I kept my smile friendly, as if kneeling in the rain-soaked street and pampering a cat was the highlight of my day. Morris began his glacial glide away. Mike fell in step beside him. I called out, "So long," to the departing pair. The only sign they'd heard came from miniature Mike. Before he disappeared, he turned and waved goodbye.

I strolled back to my cuisine duties. I punched open the cash drawer and spent a long moment contemplating the greenbacks and silver. Then I turned to the fragrant drunk I'd left gumming down the hamburger I'd put in front of him. "Good?" I said in my kindest voice. The task of chewing demanded all his attention. Concentration kept him from replying. I didn't care. I had said *Good* more for reasons of my own than to ascertain his satisfaction. What did I care about the satisfaction of a bum? The word *good* had many meanings for me. It reflected on my own behavior and my own character. Where did those qualities fall on the scale of goodness? That's a perennial question, I think, even for convicted killers. *Good* also refers, in the conversational use of that word, to prospects. Good hope. Good chance, and so forth. The prospects of a graveyard-shift short-order cook are never what most daylight people would describe as *good*. The short-order cook is not suddenly going to be made bank president or be elected to a term in the legislature. What *good* means becomes a bit more relative under circumstances of poverty and near despair like mine.

I might have succumbed to temptation. I might have pocketed the day's receipts and snuck out of town. That may have been the thought I entertained when I popped the cash drawer open one more time. The money grinned up at me. It said, "Take me. I am yours."

I slid the drawer shut again.

I told myself I didn't need Mint's money.

I set my thoughts instead on Mike. Mike of the farewell wave. Mike the flunky. Mike the errand runner and driver and possibly the sharer in the secrets of the horrible Cal.

I could be nice to Mike in a million endearing ways if being nice meant he might offer me some clue to hidden money.

The very next night, divine intervention came like clockwork. It was the night of the grand and glorious. Mike, by the grace of God, came sidling back. No cat this time. No Morris, either. His companion on his holiday stroll was the chronically twitchy inebriate with the curious name of Tin-Ear Tweet.

"What's the secret of your nickname," I asked when the pair plunked down their money for coffee. "If it's a matter of singing ever-so slightly off-key, can you serenade us with the *Star-Spangled Banner* and let us judge for ourselves?"

What an appropriate occasion to bring up the *Star-Spangled Banner*. The night had just barely passed its peak of patriotic fervor. Fireworks had been shot into ever-present clouds. The somewhat frosted result had drawn appropriate oohs and aahs. The band had packed up and gone home. Dignitaries had departed. Mommies and daddies had tucked assorted toddlers under their arms and lurched away. Noise was subsiding in the city's many bars. The patriotic orgy was coming to its end. We three in the Burger Barn—me and Mike and the wonderfully nicknamed Tin-Ear—seemed to be the only celebrants still standing in the entire town. The clock had struck two. The most dedicated drinkers, after giving it their best for three solid days, were falling into bed, congratulating themselves, I would imagine, on a job well done.

I had spoken about singing to show my friendly side. I didn't think a derelict—even one as dedicated to the profession as Tin-Ear—had it in him to burst into song, but to my surprise he opened his mouth and poured forth the first few bars of the national anthem. He sang atrociously. He curdled the cream in its miniature pitchers. He would have cracked Mint's plate-glass window if he'd had the chance to yodel to the end, but a black and white Ford with lettering on its doors that said 'Police' prowled by at a stegosaurus pace. The clean-up squad. The paddy wagon. The law on the lookout for late-night hooligans. I don't know if Tin-Ear Tweet qualified as a hooligan but he may have feared he had that reputation. His reaction was Pavlovian. He knew the back-door way to the alley behind the Burger Barn. He ducked out through Mint's minuscule storeroom, aborting his concert and leaving behind little Mike the Moron, as homely as an orthopedic shoe.

Oh, let the sluices of my sympathy not open for this wart. That's what I told myself. *Let me not pity his sawed-offness. Speak, stitches. I have one task which I must focus on, and that is charm, charm, charm, charm, charm.*

"A man can't be too careful, can he, Mike." I smiled as I said it. His grin stayed stapled in place.

"I'd refresh your coffee, Mike, but I know Cal keeps you hopping and you've got a million things to do."

Not a whisker of change in the simian expression.

"It makes me break out in a sweat to even think of all the work she piles on."

His eyes gleamed.

"Driving here and driving there and running errands and keeping watch. I hope she pays you plenty."

The smile wavered just a bit.

"She rakes it in, though. That's what I hear. She should be glad for all your help. I hope she shows her gratitude. A little extra something at the end of every month?"

There are light bulbs you can dial down to a dull glow. Mike's incandescence went through a similar fading.

"Do you ever ask her for a raise?"

A sadder expression, not dour but on the dour end of the emotional scale.

"She's got so much, and she owes you, Mike. That's what everybody says. Do you know where she hides it? I hope you do because nobody would blame you if you took some. You'd only be taking your due, Mike. No one in the world would even say tsk-tsk."

The runt slid down from his chrome stool and turned to go. I tried to hook him back with one final question: "Does it ever make you mad the way she bosses you around?"

No nod. No chuckle. No sign he'd even heard. He would have stepped out into the post-holiday night except as he stood for a second eyeing the darkness, he caught sight of Malcolm. Malcolm, the apprentice derelict, had come trailing his habitual misery. His shoulders slumped. His head was such a burden to his skinny neck it trembled. His expression a studied replication of the expressions of all sufferers inured to all the blows and sneers and insults of this cruel world. He had shuffled up to the Burger Barn's window, not as a human being but as the standard bearer for the world's dispossessed, its mentally afflicted, all those wounded through their own stupidities and follies. He had been standing where he could take in the little drama in the Burger Barn. His eyes, it seemed to me, stayed fixed on the Burger Barn's round coffee pot warming its glass bottom on the well-worn hot plate behind our establishment's chrome-edged counter. Malcolm's stance said *penniless*, but there was nothing unusual in that. His stance always said *penniless.* His eyes said it. His hair said it. His scruffy cheeks and fleshless hands said it.

I had saved poor Malcolm from starvation once. I didn't want to go to all that trouble again, but I was moved by his abjectness and filled a paper cup with coffee. I handed it to Mike. "Give it to him, please," was all I said.

From Mike's punctual reaction one would think he and I went through a similar routine seven nights a week. Feed the hungry. Clothe the naked. Get on with the job of human kindness and don't pester the indifferent universe with questions asking why. That's what Mike's reaction seemed to say. He pulled the door open and offered the steaming cup out into the rainy night. Malcolm glanced in terror at me. He seemed to think I must be pulling off an awful trick that would drive his misery past the *Bingo* point and wipe him off the earth. Mike gave the proffered cup a gentle forward shove, softly speaking to Mr. Misery as he did, saying things I do not know. The emaciated boy accepted with a trembling hand the steaming cup of coffee.

Mike grinned to watch the emblem of despair sip his gift of coffee. I stood in the doorway. Another night of scraping the blackened grill and disposing of congealed fat awaited me. "You deserve the best, Michael." I used his formal name because a great formal feeling had come over me, a feeling of cosmic sadness, as if the sufferings of all people from all time had been condensed into one hour of desolation on the post-celebration streets of a tiny town on an insignificant island in the northern reaches of the largest ocean on earth. "Keep your wits about you. Find out where Cal is hiding her money. Think about her chintziness. Think about how hard you work."

Mike turned his smile from Malcolm to me. Then he turned it back on Malcolm, and Malcolm smiled, too. Their shared smiles, briefer in duration than the twinkle of a star, bore secrets. They seemed to me, for that brief second, to be secrets of affection.

That's pure speculation on my part. I would not apply what little I know of affection to sawed-off runts and scrawny bums. What form would affection take between specimens as adrift as that? I make no guesses. Discretion draws its curtain, and I will let discretion do its work. Happiness is rare on earth. and whatever form it comes in—licit or illicit, normal or abnormal, celebrated or kept secret—men should seize it with both hands and clasp it to their bosoms to fondle and cradle and sniff.

Mike let his happy smile fade. He shuffled away. Malcolm, silent as a star, spoke from his friendship with the midget, or from his billion years of suffering, or from causes I have not been cleared to learn. But what I heard was vital.

"She hides it in her freezer."

Malcolm spoke that single sentence, then he turned and disappeared.

ad I been a married man, I would have run home to my wife and whispered, "I have happy news." If I had been a drunk, I would have sung in celebration to my buddies in a bar. I did not have the advantage of being either married or a drunk. I was the carcass of a wolf hung up on display for the edification of fourth graders. I was that wolf before the ceremony of the hanging and display. I made my home in hidden dells and had no one with whom I could share the secret triumph I'd achieved.

But convicted killers don't complain. They go about their business as if they had learned no secrets that stirred their shriveled hearts into springtime giddiness. I fried more hamburgers. I served more Cokes. And when my relief man came at 8 a.m. I returned to Mrs. Baskins' charming domicile with sobriety of purpose. I had solved the problem of where the harlot hid her money. She hid it in her freezer. Of course the woman hid it in her freezer. Common sense would dictate the freezer. I'm sure there's a handbook for hard-hearted whores that includes a chapter on hiding money from the IRS. Such a chapter would certainly recommend the freezer. Would the IRS paw through your pork chops and shove aside your rump roasts on a suspicion you had hidden beneath them funds you'd failed to report to the tax authorities? The IRS, I hope, has better things to do. Cal most likely hoped the same. She surely knew that Mike, her minion, would not blab about her hiding place. But Malcolm had learned that hiding place. And Malcolm—perhaps out of gratitude; perhaps out of some other pump of emotion; the kind of emotion that inspires the most scatterbrained deeds; the most wonderful of scatter-brained deeds; the spilling of secrets—had shared with me, his sometimes benefactor, the single cherished thing he guarded in the entire world.

One problem solved. Next problem—transportation. Mrs. Baskins had put the Studebaker out of reach. In addition to the imagined slights she claimed she'd suffered on the beach, she liked bellowing about a very real oversight of mine—I had left her picnic basket at the scene of our dalliance.

No, that's not quite correct. I hadn't *left* the dilapidated basket, I had kicked it into her father's vile pond.

"What about my wicker basket?" Mrs. B demanded time and time again.

Time and time again I bellowed back I knew exactly where her wicker basket was and if she would hand me the keys to the Studebaker, I would try to fish it out from underneath the scum on her father's pond. I occasionally expanded on the sanitation standards at her father's god-damned water hole, but my words almost always made the hag burst into tears. She blubbered that the basket had been a wedding present from the in-laws she'd acquired when she and her Moose-Club husband plighted their troth. At the thought of her husband, she blew her nose. She dabbed at her tears. "Instead of silverware, which is what they should have given when they married off their two-timing son, my cheapskate in-laws foisted off that lousy basket. They told me it was a family heirloom. Heirloom, my ass. They probably got it at a flea market. Five bucks, top."

More tears after that and then a second thunderbolt. "You're lucky it wasn't a valuable set of silverware, Sweetcheeks. I'd have the cops on you so fast your neck would snap."

She would march off to cry in her bedroom, but she'd shout from the hall that I'd never see the Studebaker keys even if hell froze solid.

I regretted, after my success with Malcolm, my rashness with the wicker basket, but regret could not restore to me the Studebaker's keys. I needed to devise another plan. I ruled out buses because none ran in the direction in which Cal lived. I toyed with the idea of hiring a taxi. But would a driver transport a masked man lugging burglary tools to a dark house on a deserted beach and obey his instructions to wait a few minutes while he tended to some unspecified business? No. The taxi was out of the question. So was stealing a car. That would be tempting fate even beyond the burglary I planned.

I had no further inspiration while a day or two went by, but then, by luck or even by providence, who cycled past the Burger Barn on his Schwinn Phantom (B-17) but the wholesome youngster, Cheek Moskanovitch?

I admired Cheek. I admired, first, his mechanical aptitude, but I also admired his character. He was polite almost to the point of being deferential. He was modest about his mechanical gifts. He was diligent at carrying out what he'd promised he would do. He was resourceful and tidy. But in addition to all his teenage virtues, he owned a sturdy and beautiful bike.

Which I authorized myself to borrow.

The Moskanovitches lived at 124 High Ridge, as anyone could learn by glancing at Boon's skimpy telephone directory. Only one Moskanovitch family was listed. I made it a point, after dinner on an evening of rare sun, to climb to their hilltop address and check out their two-and-a-half story, Queen Anne-style home, plunked down on a lot overlooking Boon's few business blocks.

The view from the generous Moskanovitch veranda must have included sweeping vistas of cloud-wrapped mountains and water-borne traffic up and down the choppy Narrows.

The original Moskanovitch had arrived in Boon a bum like me, but he had married a cannery-owner's daughter. My philosophical employer, Mint, told me Original's chosen bride, though not unlovely, was far from beautiful in any traditional sense. "Bad teeth," Mint said. "She was an only child, though, so she and her East Bayonne bridegroom would inherit the cannery, and the two of them became inordinately wealthy when some bad crab served on their wedding-banquet canapes killed her proud father."

The lamentable death meant the Original Moskanovitch could afford a handsome house. He could trade in his Lincoln Continental on the anniversary of its purchase every second year. He could pamper his daughter with dance lessons even though his own wife told him the girl had no more grace than an alligator.

He could also buy his well-beloved son a Schwinn Phantom (B-17) bicycle.

I left the High Ridge neighborhood not exactly rubbing my hands in the classic manner of comic-strip villains but inwardly gloating. I felt clever enough to outwit whatever guards the Moskanovitch clan placed on their son's handsome bicycle. My transportation problems, I believed, were solved.

Imagine my surprise, then, when I crossed paths with Mrs. Tinsel, hurrying downhill and positively giddy. "It's fireweed," she said about a scraggy mass of blossoms in her arms. "It grows wild on the island. I really shouldn't bring it home. It only lasts a little while. But while it lasts it's like a breath of nature in the house."

She spoke and was gone. I stood and watched her positively gambol down the hill. I wondered if she even knew to whom she had spoken. She was like a robin, programmed to trill her happiness no matter what. She hadn't seen me as a human being. She had only seen me as an ear. And once she'd sung her fireweed ode she skipped away, shedding blossoms, a dowdy phenomenon, surprising me with a joy I had not thought I harbored, a joy for steely matrons singing the praises of weeds. And a concomitant joy, a joy for bums and former felons who could be surprised in an island's sunshine by a lady cast in iron who was trilling like a nightingale and leaping like a fawn.

The world reserves the right to surprise us. That much must be said.

But I had work to do.

Burglary tools required my attention, and burglary-tool materials, fortunately, were almost right at hand. One was the branded screwdriver that had come with Mr. Baskins' Studebaker. That would be my torque wrench. I hope *wrench* does not imply I'd be employing the kind of tool a plumber uses to loosen the pipe ring on a radiator. *Wrench* is a courtesy name. It is given to a blade thin enough to fit among the tumblers inside a lock. I spent many hours at Mrs. Baskins' kitchen table patiently filing the screwdriver tip to the required thinness while the souse herself was passed out in her bed.

My other tool would be a pick. I had commandeered a hacksaw blade, also from Mrs. Baskins' tool drawer. I clipped it with wire cutters to the required length and shape. Clipping with wire cutters is not the recommended way to cut a hacksaw blade. I concentrated over it for three days in a row, always with an ear cocked for the shuffle of Mrs. Baskins' slippers in the hall. By diligent clipping and filing I produced a tapered shank that ended in a nub of steel no bigger than a pimple. Inside any standard lock, the shank would rest on the wrench's slim blade for the sake of leverage, and the pick's pimpled point would press against the tumblers.

The last hour of work involved just enough laborious filing to produce a grating noise somewhat softer than a squeal but louder than a squeak. To mask the noise, I turned the radio on. I kept it playing at a level barely to be heard, but I hadn't counted on the sensitive ears of the semi-invalid who was my fellow roomer. Mr. Taggs tottered into the kitchen with his paisley robe cinched around his skinny waist. I had heard him coming and had just time enough to hide my tools.

"I do hate to complain, Mr. Sweetcheeks," Taggs said, "but I have the tiniest touch of a headache and would like to find escape in sleep, and yet the music from the radio…? It's just exactly loud enough to keep me painfully awake. If it's not too much to ask, I wonder—could you turn it down?"

"Join me instead," I said. "We'll listen to the Django Reinhardt Hour."

I was making this up. I wasn't hearing Django Reinhardt on the radio. Frankie Laine was crooning.

Taggs fluttered his left hand and settled it on his chest. "There's a Django Reinhardt Hour? Oh, Mr. Sweetcheeks, I saw Django once. In Cleveland. In 1946. On the same program as the great Duke Ellington, if you can imagine. What an evening that was! Let me tell you. Exuberant and reverent, both at the same time. Isn't it amazing how that happens?"

He lost himself in rapture for the space of one long breath, then he fluttered his eyes as a memory struck him. "Django lost the use of these two fingers in a fire, did you know?" He held up his left hand and pointed to his pinkie and ring finger. "His wife, because they were so poor, earned money making celluloid roses. Terribly flammable things. A candle got knocked over. Nobody knows how. Django lost the use of those two fingers in the flames. Doctors said he'd never play guitar again. You're a musician yourself, Mr. Sweetcheeks. I'm sure you can appreciate what awful news that was. It would have broken a lesser man, I'm sure, but he went on to world-wide acclaim. Despite his handicap. Despite his crippled hand. Remarkable, the human spirit, don't you think?"

He let his gaze rest on the radio a second. "I didn't know there was a Django Reinhardt Hour," he said.

"I was teasing," I told him. "I'll turn the radio off."

"So kind. So kind," Mr. Taggs murmured, and without waiting to see if I'd keep my promise, he tottered down the hall and shut his door.

We live in a world where grown matrons skip and frolic down the rainy hills of little towns with great bundles of fireweed clutched to their shriveled breasts. A world that shelters invalids recalling with rapture the pleasure of a concert in Cleveland in which the musical giants Duke Ellington and Django Reinhardt generously shared their talents. That's small potatoes, I well know, compared to the poverty, violence, prejudice, contempt, injustice, and assorted other foulnesses the world also shares with us. But still, despite that depressing fact, fireweed and Django Reinhardt cannot be ignored.

I did not have to wait for a moonless night to begin my Schwinn-stealing operation because most nights in Boon are naturally moonless. Clouds cling to frosty mountaintops and Mother Nature wrings them out. Downpours come, and creeks roar through their culverts to shoot into the sea. Mist and drizzle bring their melancholy, but souls inured to rain plunge through showers unperturbed. No mist-and-drizzle melancholy plagued the night of my adventure, but I had to wait till ten for darkness to establish itself.

The reign of night in Boon is short in summer months. Because my graveyard shift began exactly at the Cinderella hour, setting out at 10 p.m. meant I had about one-hundred-twenty minutes to steal young Cheek's bike, pedal out to Mrs. Baskins' poor excuse for a beach, break into the low-roofed dwelling of the monster Cal, discover if among her frozen halibut I could find the money she was hiding from the IRS, bag that loot, pedal back to town, ditch the bike, hide the cash, and present myself at Mint's Burger Barn in time to sizzle a meat patty for the first homely sailor who, forlornly, wandered in.

A large order for what would amount to—give or take—two hours, but I set off in the cloud-enhanced dusk with my hat pulled low, my collar turned up, and my precious burglar tools in my pocket.

The few souls out on Boon's downtown streets, souls recently freed from their burden of patriotic debauchery, paid me no attention. In pairs or alone, people scuttled from one bar to another. The brief, limpid light that flowed to the street when they pulled a saloon door open lent the night an underwater feeling, as if we weren't *people* out and abroad but some sort of hybrid, submarine creature whose feeding spots were ill-lit and raucous and rank with the odor of booze.

The first part of my climb to the hilltop home of the Moskanovitch family was up a flight of wooden stairs built against the face of a bluff. The stairs rose and rose until they brought me to a cluster of homes high over a small-boat harbor. I rested on the landing only long enough to appreciate the twinkle of the lights below—some of them navigation lights in the harbor, others cabin windows gleaming on moored boats.

After that, I followed a street winding up hill until I stood nearly panting across from the house I had identified as that of young Cheek and his family.

Lights burned in second-story windows. Behind one of the windows, surely, were the Moskanovitch parents running through their bedtime ceremonies. I imagined the paternal parent emptying change from his pockets and stacking it on the dresser top. His wife I thought of as brushing her hair. Another room, another light—perhaps that of the Moskanovitch daughter, maybe daydreaming in front of a picture of Tyrone Power she had clipped from a movie magazine.

Then a final lighted window behind which the scrubbed and toothbrushed Cheek might be practicing his Boy Scout knots. Or unraveling his socks to knit mittens for the children of the poor. Maybe on his knees to his Creator.

I sincerely hoped Cheek wasn't praying. You can only pile up so much goodness on a person before his legs give way. Perhaps, though, in contemplating Cheek, sarcasm is out of place. The mechanic prodigy was linked a little bit to me just by the nickname he'd been given—*Cheek*, a diminutive of Sweetcheeks in the language of the Uighars, from which my name derives.

If I had a son, I stood thinking in the dark, I wouldn't let his buddies call him *Cheek*. Sweetcheeks, by itself, would be enough of a problem for him. I'd protect my boy. He might be *Tiger* or he might be *Biff*—some name to let his buddies know they couldn't take him lightly. He'd be kind of like a leader to them, but he wouldn't be a boss. No son of mine is going to order his buddies around and tell them what they have to do. He'd be a leader by example. He wouldn't have to say a word. Whatever he did would be what they would want to do themselves. They would wish they had thought of it first. They'd fall in step. They'd follow. Not that everything he did would be namby-pamby. He'd like to fool around. Fooling around is part of the nature of things. The trick is to have fun and not be some sort of louse. My son might be called *Chief*. Or maybe *Duke*.

He would not be a punk, of course. That job was already taken.

A solemn thought to be contemplating while planning a theft. *Focus, Sweetcheeks*, I told myself, and precisely at that moment one of the second-story windows suddenly went dark. A light had been turned off. The change from bright to black came like a sign from God. It said, 'Come on, Alan. Get your ass in gear.' I stepped out of the shadows and quickly crossed the street. A gate across a narrow path of planks opened without the least sound. The path skirted the side of the Moskanovitch house. At its end, next to a garbage can and almost underneath the platform that held the fuel tank for the Moskanovitch furnace, Cheek's Schwinn Phantom (B-17) angled up against the sidewall of the stairs.

I had one hand on Cheek's bike when a light came on above my head, a signal someone had entered the kitchen. I froze, prepared to bolt at any challenge to my mouse-like presence. No challenge came. No sound at all. Whoever had come to the kitchen didn't rattle crockery or clink glassware. The light went out again. I exhaled slowly, and, expecting that the Schwinn must surely be locked, I ran my hand on a search up and down the bike. I had come with the tools required for picking a lock. Picking wasn't necessary, though. In the sanctuary of his hilltop-home, the wonderfully trusting Cheek had seen no need to lock his bike. I could take it simply by steering it down the plank alley, past the low gate, and out to the deserted street. In the street, I climbed aboard the Phantom to coast down the neighborhood's many hills.

After that, I happily, madly, deliriously pedaled to Cal's.

How nice it is to ride a bike when you're not stealing copper. The encumbrance of tubes and wires—you are free of that. It is you and the night. The speed of the wind ripples your hair and swells your jacket. You grin. You can't help it. You glide downhill. You pedal across flats. You pump on the up-slopes, but to tell the truth there turned out to be precious few up-slopes between High Ridge Street, where Cheek's Schwinn Phantom (B-17) came into my possession, and the destination I eventually arrived at, i.e., Lowell's Beach.

I passed through the nighttime blocks of Boon—the ten-cent store, clothing stores, Western Auto with its peeling, white-washed walls. Sleeping fishermen snored aboard their trollers in a small-boat harbor lying in the shadow of a ridge. Homes stood along the ridge like sentinels. Before I reached the half-block slope rising to those elevated homes, I pedaled past a line of sagging storefronts and the sad, rented rooms above them. After the hillside homes I passed the sheds and bunkhouse of the cannery Mrs. B had pointed out, its purple dormitory for Filipino workers now quiet for the night. I glanced up a road of rutted dirt that led to the final resting place of Boon's lamented deceased. After that, except for a farm of enormous fuel tanks, I rode with the silver Narrows on my right and the forest's velvet blackness on my left. The lighted window of a homesteader here and there gave me my only hint that I was on a populated planet. Those windows, plus the watch-house glare around the entrance to the Coast Guard station, let me know that despite the dark I was not alone. After the Coast Guard station, though, I had no companionable lights until I reached a native village where dogs rose up on their spindly legs to bark in savage warning.

The strange thing is, I welcomed their chorus of snarls and howls. It matched the thirst for freedom my ride aboard a stolen bike had built up in my soul. Far from fearing the dogs, I stopped right in the middle of the village they so loudly defended. A glance up a short incline gave me a glimpse of totem pole monuments majestic in the dark. I felt so strongly the attraction of those exotic carvings I pedaled up the slope they dominated to spend an awed moment gawking.

Here was something new and strange to me. A garden of gargoyles, to my western eye, but gargoyles powerfully alert, gargoyles with an arresting dignity that my underdeveloped aesthetic did not allow me to appreciate as fully as I might. I was surrounded by beasts in stylized form, by bears and wolves and taloned raptors. I got the sense I was surrounded by companions, that the wolf and bear were my clan mates, that I answered to no god except the god that fixed their natures, and that I answered to no code except the code that says to do what nature formed you for, which in my case involved, basically, breaking-and-entering, burglary, and theft.

How nice, I told myself, *to come out to this gargoyle garden.* An aesthetics of distortion. We could learn something from that. But I am not a person given much to profound observations. Thoughts profound sell by the pound. See Bartlett's compilation. Transcendent moments interfere with practical endeavors. I had business to accomplish, so after some kicks at the curs who had the nerve to snarl their way close, I once again mounted my borrowed bike and continued my felonious journey.

I was looking for the dimple in the coastline that would tell me I had reached the beach's parking lot, although I actually pedaled past the gravel-bedded clearing without recognizing what had been the starting point for my tryst with Mrs. B. I had gone too far by maybe half a mile before my *Eureka* moment came. I instantly executed a smooth U-turn and in about a minute I could halt my bike at the side of the road and survey the lot's gravel emptiness behind its barrier of dinged-up logs.

The place had a ghostly quality. Not a spooky kind of ghostliness but a sentimental ghostliness. Had I been a person of a poetic bent and not just a common criminal I might have sat down on one of the parking lot's barrier logs and whipped off a sonnet about the night and the stars, the water and trees, and stealing lots of money. I haven't a poetic bone in my body, though. Plus, I had a mission—breaking into the house of cruel Cal and purloining the cash she'd carefully hidden from the IRS.

First, of course, I had to reach her house. To that purpose I wheeled my bike across the parking lot. I am naturally averse to pedaling a bike across a stretch of gravel. Gravel plays havoc with your steering, and those pesky, sharp-edged pebbles might as well be broken glass for all the damage they can do a tender tire. In the screen of spruce and hemlock trees that separated the parking lot from what can laughingly be called the beach I left my stolen Schwinn leaning on a tree and wound my way through underbrush. I took care to high-step over the root-knuckles of spruce and hemlock on my way down to where the rocky cove embraced its repellant pond.

Clouds shrouded the sky. What I saw appeared in shades of black and silver. The shore was black. So was the wall of trees on each arm of the cove. The fabled dam constructed with the help of Mr. Lowell, now deceased, made a wall of blackness at the far end of the pond. The pond had the same silver color as mercury, but it didn't shine. At best it sort-of glowed, like something toxic in a science-fiction movie. Beyond the dam the same silver glow showed where the Narrows swept by with its hammered-metal look, free to slosh exactly as it wished, the mother-waters, as it were, frolicking past the pup-like pond which Mr. Lowell, with help from Rotarians, had so successfully penned up.

These are the kind of thoughts that come to burglars in the solitude of night. If I had been visiting Lowell's Beach in the light of day, I doubt I would have been thinking of the Narrows as a mother or of the pond as a god-damn pup. But even waxing metaphoric I had pressing duties to perform. The first was finding in the dark the house I could reasonably identify as belonging to the pastel procuress.

Oh, would that hard-hearted whores outlined their roofs with neon or put flashing arrows in their driveways saying, "Here's the place."

Actually, I didn't need the flashing arrow. There was only one dark shape even remotely suggesting somebody's house. It stood not exactly screened by trees but sheltered by a stand of sentinel hemlocks so its entire shape did not jump out against the silver water. Instead, from the brushy verge where I'd halted, I saw a line that slanted with such manufactured regularity I knew it had to be a roof. I moved toward it in the shelter of the trees. I had two reasons for not making my approach a more direct one. The beach was made of rocks the size of peaches. One misstep and I'd have sprained my ankle. That was reason number one. Second reason: secrecy. In the shadow of the trees, I could move with perfect stealth. And with standard burglar caution, I observed the laws of stealth.

I worried about dogs.

None barked.

I looked for lighted windows.

None showed in the assemblage resembling a house that gradually took silhouetted shape against the silver backdrop of the waves.

There are some housing structures you can look at and know without being told that what was once a homely cabin expanded as need required, and each tacked-on room was added helter-skelter in a make-do manner that would have forced the directors of the American Academy of Architects to sink into their padded chairs and weep. Cal's house wasn't rinky-dink. The correct description is probably *slap-dash*. It had an almost jaunty, thrown-together air, and the solitary indication that its owner cared about the way the place appeared was a cardboard sign hung on a stretched-out string blocking the back-porch steps.

"Wet Paint," the small sign said.

I tested the paint with my torque wrench. A torque wrench doesn't leave a fingerprint. The merest touch was all it took. I slid the slim tool's point across an inch or so of the porch's painted floor. It came back dry. Wet paint, of course, does not prevent convicted killers from burglarizing homes, but this paint wasn't even wet. It had dried to glossy perfection. I stepped across the string, stretched knee-high from pillar to pillar on the porch, and in the shadow of the marquee-style roof I tiptoed up to the back door.

With wrench and pick in my gloved hands I went to work on the back-door lock. I deftly lifted interior pins. Pressure astutely applied held the lifted pins in place. I worked by sound and feel. I could have let myself be blindfolded and still have done my job. All the ingenious apparatus of a lock is hidden from the person picking it. One must think of piano tuners when one pictures how an accomplished burglar works. A piano tuner hears, after he's completed his delicate work, perfect harmony and perfect pitch. That is his reward. The rewards for picking locks are much more modest. One hears a series of faint clicks and when he tries the door, the door swings open.

Cal's back door swung open on perfectly silent hinges. Her handyman-troll-simpleton helper, Mike, must have kept them well oiled. An odor not unlike the odor of the waterproofing grease that's applied to winter boots assailed me. I was in a room where raincoats and galoshes and other outdoor wear was kept. I saw also in the room, inexplicably, a set of four automobile tires, plus a wringer-washer in disgraced old age, disconnected from its plumbing and huddled in its misery against the wall graced by the door.

Across from the crippled washer, against the interior wall, a chest freezer sat in all its white-enamel glory, a lid-lock inviting me once again to test my torque-wrench and pick-handling skills.

The refrigerator lock was a post-production addition to the gleaming freezer. The lock itself was a padlock of the most ordinary, dime-store variety. Nothing complicated about that. It could only work, however, if it threaded its arm through a clamp that could keep the freezer lid from being lifted. That clamp came in two matching parts, each one a steel bar with a ring end, each bar welded to a flat, steel plate. The cautious freezer owner, concerned about the safety of his steaks and frozen peas, aligns the bars so the padlock can pass through both the rings. Then he cements the metal plates in place, one on the freezer's lid and one on the freezer's body, with a compound manufactured under the strictest industry standards in the wastelands of Soviet Georgia, a compound sold to people so afraid their Swanson's frozen dinners might be stolen they acquiesce in sacrificing who knows how many Soviet elk so Soviet workers, probably enslaved, can boil down the hooves of said elk for that miracle glue.

I'm only guessing about the elk. Also about Soviet Georgia. Whatever glue cements the metal plates in place is formidable, though. It would defeat the crowbar of the most determined burglar. The only option he has is to pick the padlock, which I did in a laughably short time. A padlock doesn't have the number of pins a door lock has. Padlocks, in fact, are given to baby burglars to practice on. I won't say opening the freezer lock was a cinch, but allow me the privilege of boasting I had it done in just about a minute and a half.

Click and bingo! I could lay, with my gloved hand, the violated lock on the floor of painted wood and lift the freezer's lid to feast my eyes on all the treasure callous Cal was hiding from the government of the United States.

When I did, however, my immediate reaction was to think I must have tuned my intuition to the wrong frequency. What looked like standard freezer fare rested layer after layer in its stiff wrapping. I had to shove aside packages the shape of roasts and steaks and probably briskets, although I have no idea what a brisket's shape is. It was only when I'd clawed through the two top layers that my fingers felt a package more regularly shaped than haunches or ribs. In shape and size, it was much like a construction block. When I brought it out to the dim light, I saw it was wrapped not in butcher paper but in the standard paper bag a grocer will fill with your carrots and green peppers. The package was secured with grocery twine stiff from ice.

I slipped the twine off.

Inside was bundled money. Bill after bill after bill. Twenties. Fifties. Perhaps some hundreds. I was too excited for a thorough examination. This was the treasure. It was the profit Cal hid from the tax authorities. It was more than that, however: It was vengeance for the baseball bat that had bopped me on the head. I was gloating when the trees outside the closed-in porch were swept all of a sudden by a moving headlight beam.

In panic I shoved the frozen, future meals back into some sort of order. I trembled as I clicked the padlock in place. I heard a car door slam. I crouched next to the exiled washing machine. I plotted the murder I'd have to commit on whoever opened the back door.

But the god of burglars smiled on me. The string—the glorious string with its rain-warped *wet paint* sign—intervened. Whoever had arrived was stopped by the now-inaccurate warning that sign bore. I heard a woman bark out something vulgar. I recognized Cal's throaty voice. I heard her stride away on crunchy gravel, a solitary striding. I don't know what she had done with Mike. Dropped him off, most likely, at the kennel. A distant door opened and an interior light flashed on.

I crouched. I waited. I held my breath. There was still a chance that Cal would want to hang her coat up where I trembled in hiding.

Thankfully, the burglar's friend, a home-owner's bladder, intervened. Another interior light flashed on. A fart sound, like a trumpet, indicated bathroom use and told me I had a window of perhaps eleven seconds in which I could escape.

Seize the cash in its cold package.

Secure the package underneath my arm.

Out the door.

Close the door.

Glide across the porch.

Lift one leg across the helpful string.

Lower leg.

Slip ever so slightly on the first step.

Recover from slip without falling.

Lift second leg over the string.

Dash for the hemlock where young Moskanovitch's Schwinn Phantom (B-17) awaited.

I had done it. I had burgled. I wheeled the bike back to the road and flew away, my right hand on the steering bars and my left arm clutching tightly to my chest untold thousands in their frosty paper bag.

I had stolen seven-hundred and thirty-one one-hundred-dollar bills, sixty-four fifty-dollar bills, and twelve-hundred and eighty-nine twenties. If I had also stolen ten pounds of frozen veal and a kielbasa, my haul would have come to one hundred and two thousand, one hundred dollars. Even without the frozen veal I had reason to exult. Since my release I had been living on the piddling amount a dipper of ice-cream bars in chocolate sauce makes and the even more piddling pay offered to a graveyard-shift short-order cook. I paid Mrs. Baskins twelve-fifty a week for my room. Rapid calculations told me that with one hundred and two thousand dollars (give or take) I could enjoy my warty land-lady's hospitality for more than eight thousand years.

Of course I intended to leave Mrs. Baskins' long before that. And I didn't even know, until the morning after, how much loot I'd carried off. I got back to Mrs. Baskins' (minus Cheek's bike, which I dropped off a bridge into the nearby creek) just in time to cram my swag into my second-hand suitcase and hide the suitcase under my bed. I locked my door and double-checked to make sure the lock would hold. I spent my entire shift at Mint's hamburger emporium with agonizing pictures in my mind. I saw Mrs. Baskins working some sort of skeleton key to open the door to my room, and I imagined the same of Mr. Taggs. I entertained as well visions of thugs and rascals and brutes big enough to shoulder my door open by force and make off with the treasure stashed beneath my bed.

I'm afraid I gave short shrift to all the homely sailors who wandered into the Burger Barn that night. I failed to laugh at the droll stories told by the dirty-minded doughnut man. And I held myself taut in suspense all the time the midget, Mike, and pear-shaped Morris, strolled by on cat-walking duty. Had Cal risen in the predawn hours to check her freezer? Had she quizzed her runt-factotum about what was missing from among her frost-tinged beef-pot pies?

Tangled feelings of alarm kept me jittery until I was back in my room with the lock fastened and with my dresser pushed against the door. It was then I finally dumped all the money out across my bed.

I was in awe. I didn't feel like I owned this vast amount. I felt like an acolyte sworn to its service. I handled each bill reverently. I addressed it by its name. As I placed each one in its appropriate stack I said, "Twenty, this is your official pile," or "Hundred, you'll be happy here among your friends."

I postponed, until I had partitioned all the different bills out to their separate corrals, giving my attention to a notebook that had also tumbled from the frost-tinged paper bag. It was a spiral-bound, cardboard-covered notebook of the smallest standard dimensions, about the same size as a deck of cards. When I finally flipped the wrinkled cover open, I saw writing in a hen-scratch hand. Freezer frost had done its work on the cheap, lined paper. I had to stand beneath the naked bulb in my ceiling for light enough to give the pages the close examination they required. Squinting also helped. A pattern emerged to the writings, which looked like hieroglyphics until I brought the notebook almost to my nose.

The hieroglyphics were dollar amounts in page-long wobbly columns. The first said $50, and next to it I could barely make out pinched initials which could have read CG or CC. I had to trace the column downward with my finger to make sure what the second letter was. But then the mystery deepened, because what had re-vealed itself as CG became SG.

CG...SG continued as the dollar amounts grew. On the last damp page, the figure had reached $200.

$200 for what? Sexy get-ups? Several girls? Cheap grub?

Were the amounts income or outgo? And did they indicate ac-tivities or did they mean purchases of silken garments? Chintzy garments? Were CG and SG people? Were they related? Could they be brothers? Or father and son? Or husband and wife?

Was CG 'Coast Guard?' Why would Cal write 'Coast Guard' in a palm-sized notebook she kept in her freezer. The initials didn't tell. They were genderless, if gender was involved, and fleshless, if the story of their origin had to do with flesh. They were odorless as well. They didn't even smell like brisket.

I postponed delving into the mystery. I had a bag full of money, which I had to hide at once. It was exactly 6 p.m. I was starving, and, in the expansive mood I assume all successful burglars en-joy, I intended to treat myself. Ma Duk, in her tiny eatery, served the best spicy spare-ribs in Boon. I had just turned in the direction of her dining palace when the sight of a crowd on the bridge across the creek brought me to a halt. People were craning down at the water. Ma Duk herself, in her lacquered hair, was among the many on-lookers. So was Cheek Moskanovitch. So was a cannon-ball-shaped person I took to be his dad.

Mint had come out of his hamburger emporium to gawk. I asked him what was going on. He said, "Cheek's bike. They found it in the creek."

I looked again at the twittering crowd and this time registered a fire department presence, and a police department one as well. Firemen, in their turnout coats, were hauling ladders to the boardwalk on the far side of the creek. They lowered them into the water from a spot I couldn't see. My view was blocked by the Bayside Bar and its crib-like rooms above.

"What's it doing in the creek?" I asked my boss that question knowing full well Cheek's bike was in the creek because the burglar who had borrowed it had thrown it there. I asked the question as a way of donning my innocence costume. Mint shrugged in answer, but he confirmed my guess about the cannon-ball shape. "That's Cheek's dad." When the door on the patrol car swung open and a uniformed Goliath stepped out, Mint added, unnecessarily, "Here comes Chief Gallant."

I knew Chief Gallant already, as the gushing fan of Mr. Pinkham's now dismantled band. *Gushing fan* exaggerates, slightly, the chief's enthusiasm. I knew him also as Richie's father.

"Tin-Ear found the bike," Mint explained. "Hard-Rock told me. Tin-Ear climbed down the bank behind the boardwalk to try to haul it out. That's why the fire department's here. First they had to haul poor Tin-Ear out. Tide started coming in. He couldn't get the bike and he couldn't scramble back up the bank. Probably would have drowned."

Twice a day, when the tide was low, the creek splashed in white-water gaiety toward the protected harbor. When the tide was high, the creek plumped out, flowing not white but green and sluggish.

"He's lucky," I said.

I was the one who was lucky. At least I wouldn't have a derelict's death on my conscience. I did have the bike on my conscience, of course, and the sight of Cheek, at the rotund side of his father, caused me a twinge of mortification. Cheek had done a service for me. I had repaid him by throwing his bike in the creek. I won't say I suffered pangs of conscience. Pangs of conscience are a luxury for burglars. They're a very rare and occasional treat, like Ma Duk's spicy spare-ribs. I wouldn't be smacking my lips over those spare ribs, though, any more than I'd be tormenting myself with conscience-driven thoughts about iniquity, ingratitude, double-dealing, theft, and lying. Conscience-driven torment is another luxury burglars learn to live without. I bedded Mr. Conscience down in some back room of my mind and concentrated on the crowd and the many people in it whom I knew.

Breen was making her slinky way up and down the railing of the bridge. She stopped for animated conversation with Ma Duk.

Cheek stayed close to his father's side, and the older Moskanovitch seemed to seize the opportunity of father-son closeness to lecture and instruct. I'm sure he was telling his son about nefarious creatures prowling by night, and the need to keep one's bicycle not only locked but chained to a sturdy post.

Cheek looked unnaturally sad, as if his little bubble of illusion about a wholesome world had been cruelly popped. He had been treated to a glimpse into the horribleness which is the actual and real world, a world full of betrayers and ingrates.

Like me.

Not that I wished to dwell on the ingrate and betrayer aspects of my personality. Ingratitude and betrayal paid off. I had a hundred-thousand-dollar proof of that. A blink was all it took to put a hundred thousand dollars foremost in my mind. Goodbye, regrets. Hello, big bucks.

Although I still could not dismiss the voluble crowd. People pondered the mystery of how the bike got in the creek. It sewed them up into a kind of patchwork cloak of curiosity. They shared not-knowing, and because nobody knew, speculation could run rife. Even Mr. Tinsel bustled up and joined in. He cornered Chief Gallant and took advantage of his status as a pillar of the town to inquire and to nod with great sagacity at what he heard the Chief impart.

Oh, sagacity. Oh, speculation. Oh, the reasonable laying out of facts. I could say 'Oh, jokes and witticisms,' too, because I could see grins. I heard guffaws. When the fire department rescuers of bums and bikes appeared on the bridge with Cheek's Schwinn a cheer went up.

Mint, by that time, had left me. He was back at the grill, with its sizzle and enticing aromas. I stayed at the edge of my alley to watch Cheek stroke dampness off the saddle of his bike and bounce it on its black tires to make sure it was still in riding shape.

What I saw next came close to moving me. Chubby Mr. Moskanovitch fished his wallet out of his black pants and handed a bill to Tin-Ear. A finder's fee or something. Some sort of reward the poor old wino certainly did not expect. I watched him stare in wonder at the greenback and then break out his gap-toothed grin.

A cheer went up from Ma Duk and Breen and Mr. Tinsel and all the other members of the crowd. A diminished crowd now; the excitement was over. But a crowd of solidarity, a crowd of shared interest, a crowd of companionship.

Not a crowd for me, of course.

I had no wish for spare-ribs any more. I turned and headed elsewhere for my dinner.

The sacred art of rescuing bicycles from frothy creeks continued to dominate what passed for conversation even at the midnight shift-change in the Burger Barn. The homely sailor had wandered in and was listening to Mint hold forth on the rescue drama. I arrived just in time to hear Mint explain, mistakenly, that Cheek had given Tin-Ear a reward of ten dollars.

"It wasn't Cheek. It was his father," I explained.

"Wrong, Alan." My boss turned from the grill to offer his correction. "Mike was in here earlier. He saw everything that happened. He said it was Cheek."

"He said it was ten bucks?"

"His very words."

"I don't think it was ten bucks. And I know it wasn't Cheek. It was his father."

"Ten bucks. Wow." The homely sailor's only thought came in the form of admiration. He probably knew ten bucks could buy a lot of love. I knew that fact myself. Such generosity—if ten bucks it truly was—would have been a thing to celebrate. It dwarfs, in terms of magnanimity, a dime here and a bowl of chili there. If ten bucks was the going rate for bicycles rescued from creeks, I could pay for the rescue of thousands. I had the ready cash. It was stashed beneath my bed.

Those were sour thoughts. I was certainly not going to devote myself to paying off the rescuers of bikes. Quite the opposite, in fact. I was the one who'd thrown the Schwinn into the god-damned creek in the first place.

The homely sailor, still in awe of the munificence he'd heard described, said "Wow," a second time.

I was putting my apron on. I had a whole, long night to work. I vowed if he said "wow" again, I'd boot his ass out to the street.

I didn't plan to delay my departure from Boon, nor did I plan to rush away in so much haste hundred-dollar bills might float out of my too-hastily fastened cheap suitcase. It wasn't until Tuesday of the week following that I set off at my leisure for an afternoon jaunt to the Pan-American office where I intended to assure the cherry-lipped clerk my brother had advanced so far in his recovery I could now safely leave his care in the hands of incompetent others.

On my way to Pan-Am's office, though, I saw Leonard P. Grumbs supervising a crew bringing dental drills and sanitary bibs down from his second-floor office. Grumbs, when I strolled up, was in the shadows of a rental truck's interior, making sure a scowling man in a dirty cap safely secured a glass-fronted cabinet. I could see him in the cave of the truck's body giving involved instructions to his burly hireling. None of Grumb's gestures were large, and his voice was too soft to carry to where I stood. He stooped; he bent; he made quick and delicate motions with his hands. He could have been, judging by the fineness of the way he moved, scraping tartar off a lion's tooth. I watched him be dentist-ish—I mean small and precise and careful. When I think of dentists, I think of passion on the scale of a toothpaste tube. I wondered how desire had peaked high enough in Grumbs to propel him into infidelity.

The departing dentist gave me a look of surprise when he started down the truck's ramp. Before either of us could speak he extended his hand. His handshake was warm, and he seemed glad to see me. He still didn't speak, though, and I had no conversational ice-breaker to fire off either. Instead I whistled a bar of *Open the Door, Richard*, a song we'd been rehearsing before the band broke up.

Grumbs didn't laugh. He had to step out of the way so two movers could carry another cabinet into the truck. He watched them set their burden down and then, without turning to look at me, he said, "My son is sick."

Did he mean his son the wall-eyed boy? Mr. Pinkham had told me boy wasn't well.

"Bad, Grumbs?"

The philandering dentist sighed. "It isn't easy on a kid, you know." A flutter of emotion played across his face. I caught the flavor of his thought. His mind was on his predicament. He had a soon-to-be-former wife whom he would have to saddle with care for their ailing son. He had a soon-to-be-wed mistress unpacking household goods in Pasco, Washington. His look let me know he had strayed, in the classic erring-husband fashion, and now he didn't have the standing to complain.

He would never have complained to a convicted killer anyway. To me he said, "What the heck is going on? There's cops all over the terminal. They're checking all the luggage before it goes on board."

"Russian spies, undoubtedly. They crawl out of the woodwork about this time of year." I quailed as I said it. It wasn't Russian spies.

Grumbs smiled. He said he hoped none of Boon's atomic secrets fell into Stalin's hands.

"Boon's men in blue are up to their surveillance duties, Grumbs."

"Thank God for that, Alan. Thank God for little things."

With that, we said goodbye. He climbed the ramp again to do more supervising, and I turned my steps not toward the airline office but back the way I'd come.

Cops all over the terminal?

I had seen no news of a daring burglary in Boon's daily paper. But that didn't mean my secret was still safe. Police aren't bees. They don't swarm with the intention of setting off on a search for a better hive. They swarm to catch criminals. Whether they knew it or not, it was me they were looking for. It wasn't any secrets about atomic bombs.

Home held a shock for me even greater than the shock about the scrutiny at the seaplane terminal.

On my arrival, I found Mrs. Baskins surprisingly sober and busy in the kitchen on what looked like appliance repair. Her vacuum cleaner lay prone on the table, some of its fuzz-crusted innards on display. I gave Mrs. B as cheerful a greeting as our post-coital relationship allowed. In reply she growled a question: "Have you seen my little screwdriver?"

I had, of course, seen Mrs. Baskins' little screwdriver. Not only had I seen it but I had filed its working end down to a sliver so it could help me jimmy Cal the Ogre's locks.

"The vacuum cleaner's broken," Mr. Taggs piped up to say. He was seated at the table like a visitor to a sick room. He patted the vacuum's bladder. "Simply stopped working."

I gathered, without being told, that the distinctively stamped screwdriver was needed for vacuum repair. I allowed myself to nod with great solemnity. That established, I believed, appropriate sympathy, but what I said was, "Screwdriver?" as if I'd been baffled by the technical complexity of the question.

Mrs. Baskins eyed me with her gimlet stare. She may have thought the powers of her slightly bloodshot eyes could force me to say more. Also, her look came at me aslant, the common practice of persons trained since infancy to cast suspicious glances. I deserved her suspicious glare. I knew, though she did not, I was the one who had last used the special screwdriver. "I'll look in my room," I said. With that, I bowed my way out of the kitchen.

I hurried to my room.

I closed the door.

I went through the pockets of my other pair of pants.

I shook out the shirt I'd worn on Burglary Night.

I dropped to my knees and searched under the bed.

I went through every drawer in the cheap, stinking, hateful bureau standing in its smugness against my unattractive wall.

When I had done all that I sat on my bed to mournfully digest the possibility I had lost the god-damn screwdriver. In my excitement at the frosted bag of loot had I—madly, insanely—left incriminating evidence on Cal's mud-room floor?

When I stepped into the Burger Barn two nights later Mint handed me a note Mr. Pinkham had left. It said Grumbs' young son had died and there would be a service the next day. Mr. Pinkham, in his note, made a point of telling me where the service would be held. I took that to mean he hoped I'd come.

I had been sleeping about eighteen inches above a hundred and two thousand dollars for several days. The dresser pushed against my door helped me trust I had a margin of safety, should desperadoes come with sledgehammers. But at night, when I was at work, I had to stop myself from rushing home to make sure the door was locked. In my imagination, Mrs. Baskins snuck into my room. So did bums and hoodlums and thugs. Some of them walking charcoal-colored cats. And the cats peed right on my pillow.

But I couldn't even think of cat pee. Cat pee made my head spin. Was I threatened by cat pee? No. Not at all. I did not have the Studebaker screwdriver I had carried to Cal's den. *That* was my most material worry. Mrs. Baskins didn't have it either. Nor did Mr. Taggs. It existed in the nowhere land between crime and discovery. That common, household tool, should it fall into the hands of the law, would connect me to the crime at Cal's. The screwdriver was evidence that could put me back behind bars. Stupid burglars make mistakes, and a wiseass felon cannot afford to be stupid. The danger was tempered only by the fact Cal could not report the loss of her frozen assets without alerting the IRS to the fact they existed. There would be evidence of criminal activity against the harlot as much as there would be against me. In that we were like partners in crime. We might end up cellmates. Could I have stood being cooped up in the same cell as a lady in a pastel pants suit for the rest of my natural life? It seems like cruel and unusual punishment, doesn't it. And I have constitutional rights.

Except that Cal didn't have to reveal her hidden assets to the IRS to wreak revenge on me. She could safely tell the police an amateur burglar had left a screwdriver at the scene of a crime. The police could slap watchdog squadrons on the only exit off the island, i.e. the rinky-dink airport, while they puzzled over the implications of a screwdriver stamped with the Studebaker 'S.' Suspicion eventually would light on the Studebaker parked behind my landlady's house. Police officers can put 'screwdriver' and 'Sweetcheeks' together. The coincidence is too prominent to ignore. Somewhere in the city, even as I sat reviewing what looked like evidence not entirely in my favor, a task force of blue-uniformed enforcers of the law was probably going, 'Ah ha!'

Faced with what was obvious in those dire calculations, I couldn't help but think a funeral might be fun, so at 1:30 p.m. on the third Wednesday in July, I took my place in a parlor-sized chapel among twenty-five or thirty other mourners, including Mr. Pinkham and Richie, but not including Delilah because she was collecting twigs for her new nest in Washington State.

The congregation of mourners split in two. Mr. Pinkham, Richie and I sat on the side of the aisle with the partisans of Mr. Grumbs, and almost everyone else sat on the opposite side among those sympathetic to the dead boy's aggrieved mother.

The theme of the short eulogy, preached by a lanky young man, was the death of innocents. He started with King Herod and that inauguratory slaughter. He went on after that to an army of medieval children marching off to save the Holy Land. The enthusiastic funeral orator summed things up with fresh catastrophes culled from the recently concluded world war.

Much of what I heard was eye-opening because my own experience with innocence had been so limited. And I could tell, by the congregation's sobbing, that the lean, young preacher in his ill-fitting suit was doing his job well. Whose heart would not be touched to think of a child with a cock-eyed view of life—because Grumbs' son's eyes did not quite properly line up—snatched from his playmates at an age when he could barely tie his shoes?

There was weeping on our side of the aisle and weeping on the other side, and I am not going to say it was a competitive weeping because that would mark me as cynical and sarcastic, attributes even punks disdain. Such an ungenerous assessment would also leave me unable to explain the brief hug Leonard P. Grumbs gave his estranged wife, and her reciprocal hug, also brief—a reconciliation of those warring parties, you might say, by the intervention of tragedy. The surprising hug took place in front of their child's small coffin, a coffin the same color as a penny. I knew the reconciliation would be temporary. You can only stretch the death of innocents so far. Folks let the temporary flare blaze up and die away. If grace was what had put the hug in motion, it was not the kind of grace that likes to stick around. Grace has other duties, I imagine. Someone has to save lost souls and lead hardened sinners toward redemption. And even while it's doing that, grace likes to tap its watch and let the fallen know it hasn't got all day. Grace probably glanced at me and rolled its eyes. I had not joined the bier-side crowd. I am not one to mingle at the side of children's coffins. I sat alone, fingering my sorry hat, my eyes on a tableau of tenderness but my thoughts on the god-damn screwdriver, a screwdriver required to repair a faulty vacuuming machine.

I was a faulty vacuuming machine myself. My faulty machine did not suck up tableaus of tenderness and hints of reconciliations. Into the maw in my breast it sucked everything droll and biting and raw. The sarcastic and the snide slid through the works of the machine into my dark interior. I hoovered up the scornful and the jeering and the tart. A sack-shaped bladder inside me held the sour debris of a wiseass world, and Mr. Taggs could have patted my breast till he bruised it, all to no avail. I was a convicted killer, a punk and a felon—all that by my own choice. And the choices I had made had rewarded me with a fortune of a hundred thousand dollars. Not that I could consider my riches surefire safe. I had hidden them in a sad-sack suitcase underneath my bed, and it was to the safety of that hiding place my thoughts returned after ruminations on children's coffins and parental infidelities and burglar errors. Through rumination, too, I knew what I must do, and as soon as the opportunity presented itself—as soon, in other words, as Mr. Taggs had shut himself in the bathroom with his newspaper, a sure sign he meant to spend at least four minutes at his lavatory task—I hid my stolen money in his messy room.

The mess is what made his room a perfect place for hiding something stolen. It was the kind of mess for which the Nobel Prize for Squalor could well have been awarded. If someone had told me Mr. Taggs had collected every magazine published since 1935, I would have believed it. Stacks and heaps and mounds of magazine abounded. They rose in piles against the walls and spilled out in flood force so far across the floor they left only a path for Mr. Taggs to squeeze through to his bed. I shoved my booty under copies of Collier's, 1936-1938, and slipped back to my room, no one being the wiser because Mr. Taggs was moving his bowels and Mrs. B was soused and passed out on her bed.

I had to hope Taggs would be a better hoarder than a reader. What would I do if he suddenly remembered an article of interest from a Collier's magazine of, say, April, 1937?

I didn't know what I'd do, to tell the truth, but I went to a bar to think about it, and going to the bar proved to be a very big mistake.

I dodged into a cubbyhole-sized lounge called the Ambassador. Seated at the bar, nursing a frosted beer and clipping his fingernails, was Standard Gallant, chief of police. He saw me as I made my vain attempt to zip back to the street. "Don't like the company, Sweetcheeks?" he yelled.

The owner of the Ambassador, a matron six-foot-four named Alexandra, stopped polishing a glass to toss in my direction her best commercial smile. She bared her teeth in a wordless invitation. The invitation said, "Yes, don't be frightened of the chief of police even if you've got a professional burglar's customary guilty conscience. Come in and have a drink."

The average tippler, I'm sure, given the choice of bellying up to a bar with a chief of police or taking his trade elsewhere, would not need to spend more than twenty minutes choosing his preferred option.

"Don't stand there with the door wide open. Come in from the rain," the matron Alexandra growled, this time not bothering to smile before she turned her attention yet again to punishing a tumbler with her grimy polish rag.

I took a step inside the bar and closed the door. The strange thing is that in the tiny room's back-lighted dimness I could see a lot of dust motes swimming through the air. It was as if I'd stepped into a universe of baby stars, because each dancing dust mote gleamed when it caught the subdued light.

The massive matron polishing bar glasses was known to enforce the decorum of her modest establishment with a length of iron pipe. Or I should say she was rumored to resort to that iron pipe when customers got rowdy. But had she ever actually wielded it? This touches a point worth examining: What was the reality of decorum at the bar? Was it the actuality of Alexandra's iron club, or was it the belief her patrons had in the club's existence, a belief that put them on their best behavior out of fear of getting whacked?

I saw in that a metaphysical conundrum worth pondering under conditions more appropriate than the ones I then faced. I had no time for pondering. I instantly did what criminals do: I bluffed. "Let me buy you a drink," I said to Chief Gallant as I seated myself on one of the bar's padded stools.

The slow smile he turned in my direction should have given me pause. "I may or may not accept your offer," he said. "First tell me if you recognize this."

He punched his huge hand into his pants pocket and pulled out something he rolled toward me on the polished bar.

When it stopped its eccentric roll, I saw a fatally familiar screwdriver. "Found it on the floor at Cal's, where a burglary had taken place," the chief said. "The burglar must have dropped it because it doesn't belong to the lady I mentioned. But what I want to call your attention to, Alan, is the *S* stamped on its handle. That's the Studebaker *S*, and of how many Studebakers can Boon boast? I've only known one in all the time I've been here. Can't say why the brand's not more popular. That's a question for the marketing experts, and I am just a backwoods chief of police. I do know for certain, though, that Boon's solitary Studebaker belongs to your landlady, Mrs. Baskins. So naturally I asked her if she recognized this little tool, which she certainly did. She told me she had only very recently gone looking for it. She said it failed to show up, and she wanted to know how I had found it and who had ruined it by thinning out its end. Good questions, aren't they Alan."

I didn't allow myself to flinch. I told him, "Good as any," and I looked him in the eye.

"Exactly what *I* thought," Standard boomed. "I asked myself over and over who had thinned-up the screwdriver's blade until it had exactly the dimensions of what's called a burglar's friend. And who had accidentally left it on the floor of a burglarized house? Not only a burglarized house but a burglarized freezer as well, for it turns out that something of value disappeared from Cal's freezer, and putting two and two together—what with screw-drivers, Studebakers, access and so forth—the finger of suspicion points at you."

"What disappeared from her freezer, Chief? Not heirloom steaks, I hope. A loss like that would devastate a family."

Chief Gallant smiled. "You are close, Alan. And you are clever, too. Most people, informed of a theft from a freezer, would as-sume the freezer was the hiding place of something more valu-able than steaks. The idea of jewelry might occur to them. Diamond rings and pearl necklaces and so forth. Gold coins might be hidden in a freezer. Why not? Frost can't hurt gold. Even cash in paper form probably survives zero temperatures. I don't think any long-term experiments have been done, but in theory at least, though a little freeze-burn might brown the edges, paper money could survive indefinitely."

Alexandra had been listening and interrupted with her own take on the subject. "People put their money into banks. They don't need to keep it in their freezer."

The chief slowly shifted his gaze in her direction. "Quite true, Alexandra. A person has no need to put her money in a freezer unless she doesn't want it known she has it. I'm speaking in purely hypothetical terms here, Alan. What I'm positing is the possibility that someone, not saying anybody in particular, might hope to keep some of her assets hidden from, say, the IRS, and so instead of depositing her money in a bank like a sensible person, she hides it in her freezer. Something like that might tempt a burglar, mightn't it? A burglar might think he could steal a stash of questionable money like that and still get a free pass, even if he were caught. Who is going to prosecute for the theft of a treasure that belongs by right to the government and not to the person who hid it? The person who hid it might wind up prosecuted herself. This is all speculation, you understand, because in all my years in law enforcement I have never been able to understand the devious ways a burglar's mind works."

The burly chief paused to let me speak, if I should have a wish to do so. I let silence lend the moment gravitas. Alexandra knew some game must be afoot. She continued to polish glasses, well within earshot.

The chief had finished his beer. He tilted his glass to see if the few suds left would yield another sip. He couldn't convince himself they would and he slid his glass in Alexandra's direction.

"I only mention this, Alan, as a way of explaining why I told you earlier how close you were to guessing what had been stolen from Cal's. You thought it might have been some heirloom steaks. The heirloom part was just a joke, of course. I appreciate the humor, but I ask you to recall that we are not in a beef-raising part of the nation. We are a fishing community, and the logical thing for a person to keep in her freezer might be a fish of one species or another. It might be a species of salmon. Or it might be a valuable flat fish such as a halibut, and as luck would have it, Alan, that is what I am going to tell you disappeared from Cal's freezer. Not a family-heirloom flounder, of course, but a package of valuable halibut steaks, and since the evidence gathered at the scene so far seems to tie *you* to the crime, I'm going to have to ask you to come with me for questioning. I hope that's not an inconvenience. I will make sure that Mint's informed."

"What you've got's not evidence." I dropped the damning screwdriver right next to his massive paw.

"Arrest first. Evidence after," he said.

Alexandra barked a harsh laugh at his Alice-in-Wonderland joke. As she did, Chief Gallant gripped my upper arm. He jerked me to my feet. The padded stool fell over as I fought, but all my kicking and squirming did no good. Boon's chief of police hoisted me so high I had to tiptoe at his side as he steered me toward the door. We barged through, and he turned me toward jail. He trotted me, propelled me, hoisted me, then wheeled me around a corner from which I could see the green, Federal building straight ahead, with bars on its sixth-floor windows.

My head rattled. The sinews holding my arm to my shoulder stretched. Yet I padded along at the huge chief's side almost gleefully, for I was thinking, 'SG...CG...SG...CG...Standard Gallant...Chief Gallant . . .

I didn't need to crack a code to know the initials spelled 'Corrupt.'

Boon locked up its miscreants in a jail on the floor above Superior Court, so if I were to be beaten to death by sadistic guards, I could take comfort in knowing my blood would drip through the ceiling and fall on writs and depositions Darlene might be typing in the office right below. She would turn her glance up toward the ceiling. She would ponder the possible sources for the ceiling's stain of red. I would expire while her sympathetic gaze rested on the growing blot, mysteriously rose colored. If I could dedicate my spreading blood stain, I would dedicate it to Darlene. I would think of it as spreading in her honor.

I had been hauled before a black-robed district-court judge, a hawk-faced man who knocked over the American flag when he turned to take my file from his timid clerk. Not that I read anything alarming into his knocking over the flag. A lot of district-court judges all over the country must knock over the flag. They may do it on a daily basis and probably think it's part of the court routine, like the clerk clearing his throat and saying, "All rise."

I entertained that thought all through my brief appearance. The stern and accident-prone judge asked me to verify my name. He read the charge against me—that I did willfully and knowingly enter a locked residence at nighttime with the intention of stealing twelve halibut steaks, frozen. He asked me how I wished to plead. When I said, "Not guilty," he set me a prohibitory bail and had me hauled to the hoosegow upstairs. Before I even hobbled out of his pocket-sized courtroom, he had turned his attention and his histrionic talents to terrifying a public urinator.

The judge's crowded docket meant a crowded jailhouse upstairs. Ordinarily the jail had a drunk tank where fourteen or fifteen inebriates can be comfortably accommodated, but because of the recent national holiday, and the obligation to tipple which patriotism mandates, a drunk tank commodious enough on ordinary occasions could not be made to suffice. The standard district court sentence—thirty days or thirty dollars—stretched the sobering-up process out to an entire month. The stubble-cheeked and bleary-eyed lolled on bunks or groaned on benches. They washed their socks in the communal sink. They groused. They grunted. They scratched and sniffed and blew their noses on handkerchiefs handed down from drunkard father to drunkard son for untold generations. The few of us not groaning and holding our heads were forced to step over the tormented and distressed if we wanted to enjoy a cup of coffee on the rough tables that served as our mess hall.

On my second morning in the lock-up I had found a reasonably sanitary spot at one of those tables and sat nursing a cup of coffee while I pondered how to work my SG CG discovery to my advantage. While I did, another guest, in the throes of delirium tremens, kept shouting *Haywire* and going through the motions of pulling on a cable or rope. The man was drenched in sweat. His labors were all imaginary but his muscles didn't know that. His hair lay plastered to his skull. His underarms were dark with perspiration. So was the back of his shirt—a civilian shirt, not a jail-issued one. The jail, I'm sure, had run short of shirts enough for the overflow, post-holiday crowd. *Haywire*, the man yelled, and then he bent to his imaginary labors again.

"A logger," a man who sat down next to me said. "He thinks he's in the woods. Heh heh heh."

The unfortunate victim of alcoholic illusion had taken a second to wipe his sleeve across his sweaty brow. The dark-haired man who'd joined me shouted, "Haywire!" at the deluded inebriate, and instantly the pantomime of pulling and tugging began again.

"Haywire's the cable you string through the woods when you're moving your block," my seatmate told me. "You have to haul and haul, and the mosquitoes think you're lunch. Plus your boss is yelling to get the damn job done, and the guy who's crawling up the hill with the cable on his shoulder cusses you out, too. Thankless job, no matter how you look at it." He paused to yell, "Haywire," at Mr. Sweat again, and after that, with an oily grin, he extended his hand. "Name's Silky Devine," he said. "And you must be the fellow with the flounder."

"I am an innocent victim unjustly accused," I told him as we shook.

His laugh was very hearty, but not sincere, as if I'd told a joke he'd heard before.

If my visitor had been wearing a moustache, I'd have guessed I'd last seen him tying a virgin to the railroad tracks. He'd shaven himself clean, however, with his hair slicked back and an eye-catching gold tooth prominent whenever he flashed his artificial smile.

"There's so many people unjustly accused these days," he said. "Drunk and disorderly is what they got me on, but do I seem like the drunk and disorderly type?"

He didn't wait for me to answer but leaned closer to talk in greater privacy. "You got friends outside." He drew back and fixed me with a knowing look. If he hoped I'd show interest I managed to restrain myself. It would take an affidavit, sworn to in court and affirmed by half a dozen Baptist clergymen, for me to trust what I heard from a person named Silky Devine.

When I didn't answer, Silky drew close again. "Alexandra?" His eyebrows shot up, as if he believed the name of the Amazon bartender would naturally spark my interest.

What he meant I could surmise. Alexandra had heard Chief Gallant refer to my so-called crime.

"She doesn't know shit," I told Mr. Devine.

He drew back again and studied his fingernails. "She can help you, though."

I would have to listen to his deal. I had not yet broken Chief Gallant's hold on me. Freedom wouldn't come until I could utilize the damning notebook information. Before then, night would arrive, and the jail crowd would perhaps have thinned out so much that the minions of the tainted chief could give me more of their attention.

"Alexandra figures it wasn't a frozen flounder you stuck under your jacket and made off with," Silky was back in his sharing-confidences pose, talking so close to me I could smell the citrus-scented lotion that held his hair in place. "She figures what you got was something more worthwhile. That's why there's cops all over the terminal. They won't let a single passenger leave town without going through their luggage."

He let his eye meet mine. Whatever reading he took encouraged him. "What gets me is how you hope to sneak your frozen fish past all those cops. I'm saying 'frozen fish' as a kind of code word here. If you want to sneak it out, you're going to need help. In fact you're going to have to leave without it and trust friends you've made in Boon to mail it to you later."

"Minus their commission?"

Silky spoke with his ten-carat smile. "You took the words right out of my mouth."

He had made his pitch, and at last he leaned away. His glance wandered in the direction of the mess-hall stove as if he'd only just remembered the reason he had wandered in was to enjoy a cup of coffee.

I knew he was guessing about money, and even if he'd had some confidential information that told him he was right, he wouldn't know how much there was. If I trusted him at all I could lie about the thousands in the frosted paper bag. I could say it was five thousand and if he wanted ten percent, I would pay him off up front. Providing he swore he would mail me the rest.

But where would he mail it? Where was I going? And how good is the oath of someone named Silky Devine?

"You know," I said when I had furrowed up my eyebrows so I looked like someone deep in thought, "my father is the former chief justice on the North Dakota Supreme Court."

"No," Silky said with false astonishment. "I didn't know that. I had no idea." He was having fun with the lie I'd told.

"It's true. I don't mention it often because I'm a disappointment to him, and I hate to bring his name up in conversations such as this." I glanced around our noisy tank to let him know my meaning. "The only reason I'm telling you—and I'm telling you in strictest confidence, of course—is because my father's advice before I left for a new life in Alaska was to never trust a person named Silky."

A sly look came to Silky's narrow face, like he knew now what my game was.

"Never trust someone named Silky is what my father said, especially if that person has a gold tooth and hair that smells like a beverage made by squeezing lemons."

Silky kept the same expression, sly and mean. "I can't contest the word of a chief justice of North Dakota. All I know is what I hear around town. And what I'm hearing most recently is that Chief of Police Standard Gallant is pissed. The chief is saying—this is scuttlebutt, of course—that if some lousy, two-bit, half-assed, dumbbell thief—not mentioning any names here—tries to leave our lovely town with any contraband he's going to be stopped."

"What kind of contraband?"

"Let's call it a flounder. Let's call it a fucking flounder and leave it at that."

He was already pushing himself up from the table. "And there's guys in here who aren't as nice as I am," he said before he strode away.

I watched him join two other men at the coffee pot, and from the glances shot in my direction I knew the words they were exchanging had to do with how much it annoyed them when strangers waltzed into their sodden town and bankrolled themselves with a mean whore's money.

I wished I really did have a chief justice father and he could pluck me from this dangerous jail.

Wishful thinking wouldn't help. I had no doubt of that. And I knew I must resign myself to a night-time beating, but a miracle intervened. The chief jailer shouted, "Sweetcheeks." From the tired ring of watchers, a laugh went up, lascivious and mean; as if my name were a natural punchline, and the jailer was not a jailer but a comic entertaining those killing time in hell.

I stood at attention before him.

"You're bailed out, Sweetcheeks."

Bailed?

I could only think *Darlene*, and even as I collected my belongings and waited for the jail door to open, I was rehearsing words that would convey to her my eternal thanks.

When the Federal Building's elevator brought me down to the first floor, I expected to see Darlene Sandusky. I assumed the woman whom I most admired would have paid my bail. Movies train us to expect surprises of that sort, and even in prison they had shown us movies. Greer Garson. I was thinking Greer Garson when the elevator's doors sighed back into their hollow chambers. My thinking was wrong, I immediately discovered. The person waiting for me was Our Lady of Spun-Sugar Hair. I had been pulled back from the jailhouse pit by puff pastry in a human matron's form.

"Mr. Tinsel told me to help you," Mrs. Tinsel said in a fierce whisper. Then she fastened her talons on my arm and propelled me through the post office lobby and out into a raw assault of rain.

I told her I was grateful.

"Don't talk," she said. She had friends to nod to, and each friend cast an inquiring glance. Mrs. Tinsel knew herself as the wife of Boon's most law-abiding citizen. She must have blushed to be seen clinging to the arm of a known parader in his underpants down the island's roads. Her grim smile warded off the questions her friends might have asked, and she had steered me a block and a half down the street before she finally slowed her breakneck pace. We had reached the double doors of what would have been a chapel in any city of a decent size, but which, in tiny Boon, loomed as large as a cathedral. Gilt letters above the doors told me the denomination, *Episcopalian*, and in what saint's name the church was registered, *Andrew*. Neither the denomination nor the church's mascot rang reverential bells for me. If I have reverential bells, they very rarely ring, and when they do they barely make a tinkle. Still, I owed the gum-drop woman my fresh freedom, and when she pulled the arch-topped church door open I snatched off my hat and followed her inside.

We passed through a vestibule with a scuffed, linoleum floor and a homely wooden table labeled *Lost and Found*. I saw a million mismatched mittens. The sanctuary itself—if the interior of a church is called a sanctuary—had captured all the quiet our weekday world could muster. Here I found shadow and stillness. I smelled extinguished candles so faintly that what I smelled might not have been candles at all but the ghosts of the prayers of the faithful. The vaulted ceiling, the story-telling windows, the patient pews, the exalted altar and Christ on his cross hanging above it forced on me such a feeling of solemnity that when I followed Mrs. Tinsel into a pew, I felt I should turn my collar backwards and sing *Amazing Grace*.

I had no intention of singing *Amazing Grace*, of course. I hope whoever keeps track of snotty behavior gives me credit for taking a pass on that one.

I did not kneel when I stepped into the pew. I did what Mrs. Tinsel did. I sat on the bench's thin cushion. Mrs. Tinsel held her dimpled hands clasped together in her lap. She turned just enough to fix me with her auger eyes.

"I'm sorry Ellery ever brought you here, Mr. Sweetcheeks."

"I could say the same, Mrs. Tinsel."

"You had a chance for a new life."

"Yes. That's what your husband's invitation said."

"You could have shown more gratitude."

I read in Mrs. T's stone features how much she hated me. "You wouldn't have bailed me out yourself, would you, Mrs. Tinsel. Not of your own volition. I can't say I blame you. If I did what I'm accused of—if I broke into somebody's house and stole a frozen fish—you'd be justified leaving me in jail."

I hadn't stolen fish, of course. I had liberated a hundred-thousand dollars. I don't believe Mrs. Tinsel knew of my bonanza. Even as a criminal, I was, to Mrs. Tinsel, far from a success. My skulduggery at night, as far as Mrs. Tinsel knew, brought me a mere piscine reward. I didn't want to brag and share more details with her. She was a Christian lady who had done a Christian deed. I sat now in a Christian church, freed from a dangerous jail because of her husband's Christian conscientiousness. I hadn't answered the kindness she showed me with a display of fawning gratitude. I flunked the fawning course at Stateville U. I could at least say thank you, though. I am a lout but not an ingrate. I told her freeing me from jail was something I appreciated very much.

She nodded acknowledgment. Her nod said she'd heard. It didn't say she accepted my thanks. Her understanding of my character may have prevented that. I went a little further. I praised the church she'd brought me to. "Very peaceful and serene."

"We ladies clean the church." Mrs. Tinsel's gaze touched on the altar and the haloed saints pictured in colored-glass windows. "We sweep and dust each week. We call ourselves the Altar Guild. We vacuum. We open up the doors and let the place air out. And see the altar cloths—how nice they look? Not a week goes by when they're not washed and ironed. All to make the church look beautiful. And it *does* look beautiful. At least that's what we ladies think."

She smiled, not at me but at the ironed altar cloths.

"Saint Andrew would be proud, Mrs. Tinsel."

For about seven seconds, she let my comment stand. In those seven seconds, I recalled I had last seen the cast-iron souffle, who now was seated next to me, on one of Boon's residential hillsides. She'd been tripping toward her home like an old, fat incarnation of spring, with fireweed blossoms abundant in her arms. Except for that brief glimpse, I had rarely ever seen Mrs. Tinsel except as a fury or wraith. Although she had one time turned pale and fled from me.

On what occasion was that?

My remark about St. Andrew feeling proud must have moved the needle on Mrs. Tinsel's wise-guy meter, because after she had primed her guns, she blitzed me. "Your sarcasm's so juvenile, Alan. I'm surprised you keep it up at whatever age you are. Your adolescent friends, I'm sure, appreciate cocky irreverence, but grown-ups aren't as easily amused. They have lives to live that don't allow them to be cheeky. Grown-ups have to form the habit of hard work, plus the habits of thrift and foresight and duty—all serious things, which discourage cheap jokes and easy wise-cracks. To say nothing about raising a family. That's another area where adolescent snottiness is not the crutch you might suppose. I have never thought of this before, but your mouthiness has just now put it in my mind: Mr. Tinsel, to my knowledge, has never in his life cracked a sarcastic joke. I'm sure that doesn't merit your applause. It merits mine. It means to me he sees the world as he should. He sees it as a place for striving. Not striving for glamour, nor for money, nor for social standing. Mr. Tinsel's striving is for decency. It's for respect and kindness and concern. Corny things to you, I'm sure. The ambition of some sort of fuddy-duddy, you would say. Well, a fuddy-duddy, Mr. Sweetcheeks, has just paid your bail. You are free because of fuddy-duddyness. So if you want to say Saint Andrew would be proud, you go ahead and say it. It will make you sound sophisticated, won't it."

Mrs. Tinsel drew in a deep breath, as if she'd sprinted a tough mile and come in first across the line. In a sense that's what she'd done. She'd flayed me with the anger she'd been saving a whole year. She'd honed in wakeful nights the things she'd like to say, and now that she had said them, she felt entitled to exult.

I had experienced a tongue lashing. I probably could have made a little joke about it. I probably could have told Mrs. Tinsel she should enter tongue-lashing competitions. *With a little training*, I could have said, *you could be a champ.* What prevented me from cracking wise should have been gratitude. It had been Mrs. Tinsel who had hiked to the court office and plunked down my bail. She had saved me from a beating. I owed her one biting-of-the-tongue for that. In addition, though, she and I sat side by side in a place of ironed altar cloths. The summit of my belief is probably ironed altar cloths. I can appreciate the quiet of that, the serenity, the application to duty, the fellowship, the bonding, the dignity, the pride. But when I spoke, none of that was in my mind.

"Is Cal your sister, Mrs. T?"

The picture I had shown her of the tadpoles in their cornball bathing caps. The fleeing up the curio-store stairs. The slamming of the door. All of that—in a rush—came together for me as I sat at Mrs. Tinsel's side.

The payer of my bail sat calmly gathering her thoughts. Her hands still lay in the middle of her lap, and the only sign she gave of being stirred was the way she rubbed them together, as if a chill had suddenly seized them and she had to warm her cooling blood.

"You win, Mr. Sweetcheeks. Your guess is correct. Capitalize on that triumph as much as you wish. I'm sure it will give you great pleasure."

She had kept her voice quiet and composed. When she finished speaking, she rose. With slow, weighty dignity, she made her way out of the calm harbor of her church, back to the hurl and blare of the everyday world just outside the door.

I turned my eyes to Mrs. Tinsel's tortured god, hanging in his soiled loincloth on the church's wall. *Redemption* is the word churches use to tell you what Christ's suffering was for. I'm not sure I buy it. A guy and I, when we were kids, raced lobsters on his mother's kitchen floor. His mom had bought two lobsters for some special dinner treat They had been waiting out their doom inside the icebox, shoving each other around as lobsters do. A spirit of mischief made my friend take them out. To encourage them to race across his mom's linoleum, he held out Cheerios. Apparently, lobsters are not enticed by Cheerios. At least, these lobsters weren't tempted by that treat. Eventually, we gave up trying to race them and force-fed them Cheerios instead. Or rather, we tried to force-feed them. Anyone who's tried force-feeding a lobster knows what a difficult job that is.

Upon reflection—reflecting in the church named for the sainted Andrew—it came to me I knew what life was all about. It's making lobsters race across somebody's kitchen floor. It's feeding those crustaceans cereal as a reward. Or trying to. It's the pot you've filled with water boiling on the stove.

I had just made someone feel bad about who might be her sister. I had sneered about her ironing altar cloths. Sneering's not quite on a par with making lobsters race, but it's wanton just the same.

There are alternatives. A person can be nice. Being nice isn't something out of anyone's reach. I could walk out the church door and begin being nice wholesale. I could be nice to mailmen, nice to clerks lounging in the doorways of ten-cent stores or dry-cleaning shops, nice to bartenders, and nice to men repairing the plank streets. I could be nice to a homely sailor on his dogged search for love. I saw the opportunities as endless, but I didn't know, given my flaws and the predilections engrained in me by my early education, if I would ever be the man to seize those opportunities and make myself...

And make myself what? That was my question.

Mr. Taggs, all bandaged up, sat at the kitchen table when I got back to Mrs. Baskins'. I didn't have time to ask him what happened because Mrs. Baskins, who'd heard me come in, hollered from the hall, "See what you've done, Sweetcheeks!" She charged into the kitchen waving a torn pillow case. "This is yours," my furious landlady yelled. Then she hauled me to my room.

I saw destruction. All the drawers had been pulled out. My skimpy belongings lay scattered on the floor. Someone had yanked the mattress off the bed. It stood propped against the wall like a prisoner awaiting the firing squad.

"Your friends the cops," Mrs. B bellowed in my ear. I had to tear my arm from her iron grip before I could rush to Taggs' closed door. Mrs. Baskins, hurrying in my wake, yelled, "He wouldn't let them in. He told them no, and you can see what happened."

I pushed her aside and rushed back to the kitchen. I asked, "Mr. Taggs, are you alright?"

What I meant was had anything disturbing happened in the bedroom he had been forced to guard.

Mr. Taggs waved away my question with the brave kind of gesture that says, "Oh, let's not worry about me." When I said I was sorry, he smiled. "I wouldn't let them in, Mr. Sweetcheeks. I said they had to have a warrant or else they had no right."

He spoke very softly, and with his eyes he appealed to me for approval. He looked like he wished me to pat him on his head. I didn't dare touch his head. It was wrapped in white bandages. Two fingers of his left hand were splinted and bandaged. His right eye was blackened and a couple of stitches seemed to be all that was holding half his lower lip in place.

"You're not staying here another night," I heard from Mrs. Baskins. She stood in her hands-on-the-hips mode, blocking the hall door. "I knew the minute I laid eyes on you that you were a rotten, no-good bum. What kind of place you think I run? You think I want the cops coming here and shitting on my face? I'm lucky I was indisposed. They would have beat me up like him. You get your stuff together and you march right out that door. I don't put up with troublemakers."

She flounced off in a dramatic exit but she couldn't resist a final sally. "And fix up that room just like it was." This time when she left, she left for good. I heard her slam her bedroom door.

I turned to Mr. Taggs. He looked like he was fighting off tears. "I'm an American citizen, Mr. Sweetcheeks. I'm fully aware of my rights, and though they tried to bully me, I stood and blocked the door."

A painful picture filled my mental screen. I saw skinny Mr. Taggs with his silk, paisley bathrobe cinched and his cloth slippers on his claw-like feet telling burly officers he wouldn't let them violate his red-white-and-blue American rights.

I sat down at the table kitty-corner from the sufferer. I took his injured hand and examined the splinting. "Like Django Reinhardt," I told him. My reward was seeing him smile.

"You want your cigarettes?" I asked.

He glanced toward the hall as if he feared our landlady might have heard.

"I'll get them. You just wait here. If she says anything, I'll tell her they're mine."

The brief nod he made gave me permission. I left for his room battling what I call my conscience. I didn't care about his cigarettes or about his Django Reinhardt hand. I meant to make sure the stash I'd hidden in his room had stayed safe.

Inside, I dropped to my knees in front of the familiar stack of Collier's. I lifted the pile and reached underneath. My groping hand came in contact with my package. I resisted a convicted killer's natural instinct to faint. Instead, I rushed the bag to safety underneath my bed. I threw the mattress back on the bedframe, locked my room, and rushed back to lay in front of Taggs his beloved Pall Malls. I lit the cigarette he put to his bruised lips, then I patted his shoulder and rushed back to my room. I thumbed through my greenbacks in their bound stacks just enough to assure myself my money was all there. I fished out the package's bonus, the incriminating, four-inch notebook. Then I flattened the paper bag and wrapped my money in its nondescript brown paper sack, which I'd scissored up so it would lie flat and obediently fold itself around my stolen bills. I borrowed a ball of twine from Mrs. Baskins' household-tools drawer. I secured what burglars call their swag. The bundle ended up not much bigger than two bricks. A secure bundle. An anonymous bundle. A bundle suitable for mailing.

Minus, of course, an address to mail it to.

And minus someone who would mail it for me.

I knew only one person in the entire world I could ask.

"Let me help you, Miss Sandusky."

I had found Darlene standing at the bottom of her stairs, contemplating, in weariness, the long climb to her home. To make it clear what help I meant, I nodded toward a canvas bag in her left hand. It sagged with the weight of whatever she'd have to carry the hundred or so steps to her hilltop house.

She was dressed for an outdoor adventure, and as it turned out she had been on a picnic. In the bag was part of a salmon, which picnic friends had cooked and shared with her. They'd grilled it on a beach just minutes after they had caught it, so it was as fresh as fresh could be.

Darlene didn't answer my offer to carry her bag. The look she turned on me was weary, but it was uncomprehending, too. The Alan Sweetcheeks she'd last seen had had a hooker on his arm. Plus, he was a convicted killer, petty thief, and known parader in his underpants down one of her hometown's major roads. He stood accused of stealing halibut, although gossip in the hallways and backrooms of justice might have let her know what had vanished from Cal's freezer was not a bottom-feeding fish.

She surprised me by speaking of none of my known flaws. "Chip is leaving. Did you know?" she said.

A smile, in a wavery way, tried to establish itself on her pretty face. Her smile needed life-support, and she was too weary to supply it. "He's served his term in the Coast Guard. Off he'll go."

"Where to?"

"Who knows?"

"You'll miss him, Miss Sandusky."

Now her warm smile broke through. "We've just been on an outing to say goodbye and wish him well."

"You and he?"

"Chip has a lot of friends, Mr. Sweetcheeks." As Darlene spoke, she released to me the heavy bag she carried. I had a package of my own I had to transfer to my other hand. It was a brick of stolen money, wrapped up in plain, brown paper and carefully secured with twine. I intended to ask Miss Sandusky if she'd mail it to me, although I did not yet know where, when I escaped from her wet island, I meant to go.

She put her foot on the first riser and paced her ascent to mine. She seemed happy to talk. "I spent the afternoon with two young children, Mr. Sweetcheeks. With their parents, and with many others too. The girl—her name is Karen—is a three-year-old. The boy, named Trey, is four. The perfect ages to enjoy a picnic—the splashing in the water, hiking through the woods on the little island where we went, the perfect age for roasting hot dogs at the fire, and for saying ooh and aah about the salmon the men caught."

"The perfect age for dental hygiene lessons, Miss Sandusky."

She turned to smile at me. "Chip is goofy, isn't he, Mr. Sweetcheeks. He is consistently and reliably goofy. I will miss him very much."

We had paused for just an instant while she turned to smile at me. As she spoke, we once more climbed.

"I wish I was goofy, too," I told her.

Silence followed. She didn't look my way. Her face, from the glimpse of it I caught, looked thoughtful. When she spoke again, she spoke looking straight ahead, her eyes on the climbing stairs. "You are reliably non-conforming, Mr. Sweetcheeks."

"What does non-conforming mean?"

She laughed. "It means always surprising."

"Or always screwing up."

"Well, let me just say, *never boring*."

We had climbed to one of the long stairway's frequent landings. The landing served a hillside home, one of about four on the slope below Darlene's. A tricycle sat near the home's front door, and it was obvious whoever owned that childhood treasure could only ride it on the porch, a planked-over surface about fifteen feet long. The alternative, for the child blessed with the three-wheeler, would be inveigling a parent into lugging the trike to a level surface away from the stairs. There, the tyke could saddle up and pedal here and yon. What patience that required from a loving mom or loving dad. A trike is such a little thing, but this trike spoke to me of something quite enormous.

Darlene sat down, unexpectedly, a few stairs above the landing where the trike was. "Sit, too, Mr. Sweetcheeks. You're wearing me out. And you've got two burdens in your hands. Give me the small one. What's in it? If it isn't heavy, I can carry it from here."

I had dropped down to sit beside her. She held out her hand for my brick. I didn't respond to her gesture. I kept my package in my hand. "There's money in it," I said.

Her glance was swift and searching.

"I'm hoping you'll help me with it, Darlene."

"Help how?"

"I meant to ask you to mail it to me whenever I got to a place willing to put up with me long enough to establish a mailing address."

With beautiful calmness, Darlene waited to hear more.

"I know a request that bold would be an imposition, what with your job in the D.A.'s office and so forth."

She let a trace of a smile begin to work its magic on her lips and cheeks and eyes.

"That's why I've changed my mind about imposing a request on you as unsavory as that. I mean, I guess you could call it unsavory."

"I guess you could." She smiled when she spoke.

"So now I have a new idea, and if you can lend me a pencil, I'll write the address for this package, an address that has just come to my mind."

Darlene grubbed a pencil out of the canvas picnic bag I had been lugging up the stairs. I settled the brick of you-know-what on my lap and printed in block letters: "St. Andrews Church."

When I handed it to Miss Sandusky, I said, "Leave it on the ironed altar cloths."

I did not entirely escape sentencing to jail. I had the farcical matter of the supposedly purloined halibut to deal with. I anticipated the cartoon justice that was delivered to me, though, and I had taken precautions to prevent a jailhouse beating. That little notebook with the pay-outs to S.G. inside? I had put it in an envelope and delivered it to Santos after I had loitered in the neighborhood of the Authentic Curio Shop until I could catch him by himself.

"Put it in Mr. Tinsel's hands and no one else's, Santos."

The stoic factotum nodded.

"And tell him that it comes from Cal's."

Another nod, delivered in silence.

"Explain what SG means. And CG."

Nod.

"Do you know what those initials stand for, Santos?"

At last, a response not in sign language. "Who doesn't?" He had turned to me with a look of surprise, but he spoke with cynical wisdom.

By the time the jail door clanged shut behind me again, the power Police Chief Gallant enjoyed in Boon had been broken. District Attorney Richard Chambers had been armed with incriminating evidence. Police Chief Standard Gallant had absconded. He was gone, and a warrant issued for his arrest guaranteed that if he dared return, he would be thrown in his very own jail, with all the Silky Devines of the world.

Cal denied all knowledge of any money missing from her freezer. Her denials made no difference to D.A. Chambers. Chambers knew about the money on St. Andrew's altar cloths. He launched investigations. As is often the case in legal proceedings, those investigations are still going on. But Cal's reign as Boon's unquestioned vice lord ended. She doesn't strut and swagger with the panache of before. She creeps and cringes.

I could not ask for my job back at Pinkham's Dairy. Richie dipped its ice-cream bars in chocolate now. He needed the work more than ever. His absconded father no longer offered the family support.

When I was in the Pan-Am office buying my ticket south, Warren Arsenault minced out of his lobby close by and said in his prissy voice, "Leaving, Mr. Sweetcheeks?"

I said I was seeking opportunities elsewhere. The lie was so blatant he laughed.

Two days later, I lugged my sorry suitcase into Boon's seaplane terminal. I found Darlene there. I saw that she had suitcases, too."

"Travel, Miss Sandusky?"

She had smiled when she first caught sight of me. And my questions, of course was stupid, because a person does not pack a couple suitcases and stand around an airplane terminal for the love of doing so. She might have told me—politely, of course—how dumb I was to even wonder, but before she could speak Chip rolled in, carrying suitcases of his own.

I know my eyebrows rose. I couldn't help it. "You two eloping?" I asked.

Miss Sandusky and her up-on-the-down-teeth friend looked at each other, as if each expected the other to reply to the probing and personal question I had posed. Chip wore civilian clothes, and he managed to look like he'd outgrown them, like he had more wrist and ankle than his blue suit could accommodate.

Miss Sandusky had not parted with her Eleanor-Roosevelt hat. It perched on her wavy hair, a little to the left side of her head, with its miniature veil—the old-fashioned veil—lending her eyes a smoky mystery.

The look the two exchanged lasted long enough to make me fear I'd asked an awkward question. What right did I have, after all, to intrude on whatever their degree of intimacy might be? I had no right whatsoever. I was fleeing their island with just enough money—pocketed before I'd wrapped St. Andrew's money up for him—to get to Seattle and maybe keep me for a week or so in a flophouse hotel. Beyond the flophouse, I could envision no city or town or state or hamlet that would make room for a very broke, very nice, convicted killer.

Perhaps Darlene and Chip had no vision, either.

"We are on an adventure," Darlene calmly told me.

"You should come, too." Chip spoke with puppy goofiness, and he smiled as he extended his invitation.

When I say that that decided it, it decided absolutely nothing. Not where we'd go. Nor how we'd live. Nor what degree of intimacy might come into being among us.

But Miss Sandusky lightly kissed me.

Then Chip did the same. A kiss not raw, but tender—a token of tenderness elusive for me, elusive for all those who pose as toughs, I imagine.

And the hat? It's called a fascinator. I remembered that just then. I'd seen a friend of my mother's wink at me from behind the veil of one once.

We waited to be called for our puddle-jumper flight, and in the bustle of the terminal I asked myself how intimate a trio of one convicted killer, one fascinator wearer, and one flatulent dental hygienist was going to be. Do they even make, I wondered, beds big enough for three?

They do. I do. We do. Three do. Woo woo. Cuckoo. You hoo. See through. Lulu. Too-too. Moo moo. Hoodoo. Voodoo. You do. Whee! Do! Goo-goo.

ACKNOWLEDGEMENTS

With appreciation to Shanna McNair and Scott Wolven for their consistently excellent advice and support. Also to Dick Matheson and others at Mud Season Review (Burlington Writers Workshop) for a careful reading and valuable advice on early drafts of this novel.

ABOUT THE AUTHOR

Robert Kinerk grew up in Ketchikan, Alaska, where he worked as a logger, a pulp-mill worker, a newspaper reporter, a radio announcer, and a clerk in his father's grocery store. His most recent publication, 'Tales from the Territory: Stories of Southeast Alaska,' includes short stories that have appeared in Narrative and other literary magazines. He has workshopped plays at the O'Neill and Sundance, and fiction at Bread Loaf, the Tom Jenks workshop (New York), and the Writers Hotel. His books for children have won national awards. The first play he wrote, 'The Fish Pirate's Daughter,' has continued in performance in Ketchikan since 1966. Kinerk graduated from Santa Clara University in 1962. He and his wife live in Cambridge, Massachusetts, where he is a Distinguished Member of the Harvard Institute for Learning in Retirement.

Also by Robert Kinerk

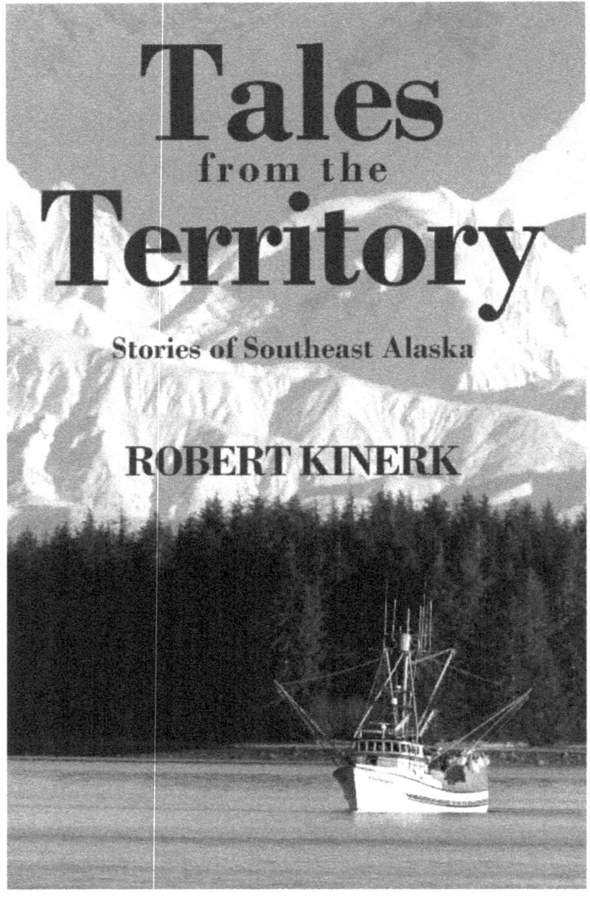

"Gorgeously gut punching, each of these stories is a sly gem and a great pleasure to read. They evoke a world that shifts from moment to moment between the comedic, the ghastly, and the poignant, and feels always deeply true. Like Alice Munro, Kinerk is a master of small town humanity, portraying with great intimacy lives that reverberate in a vast, unforgiving wilderness" –**Anne Emerson,** author of *Letters from Erastus* and *The Missy Box.*

✳ ✳ ✳ ✳ ✳

Tales from the Territory is available at local bookstores and online.